Praise for the novels of Heather Gudenkauf

"*The Weight of Silence* is a tense and profoundly emotional story of a parent's worst nightmare, told with compassion and honesty. Heather Gudenkauf skillfully weaves an explosive tale of suspense and ultimately, the healing power of love."
—#1 *New York Times* bestselling author Susan Wiggs

"Deeply moving and exquisitely lyrical,
this is a powerhouse of a debut novel."
—*New York Times* bestselling author Tess Gerritsen
on *The Weight of Silence*

"Beautifully written, compassionately told,
and relentlessly suspenseful."
—*New York Times* bestselling author Diane Chamberlain
on *The Weight of Silence*

"Gudenkauf's scintillating second suspense novel…
slowly and expertly reveals the truth in a tale so chillingly real,
it could have come from the latest headlines."
—*Publishers Weekly* on *These Things Hidden,* starred review

"*One Breath Away* takes the reader on an electrifying ride that is,
by the end, both terrifying and satisfying. I dare you to forget it."
—*New York Times* bestselling author Elizabeth Flock

"I have burns on my fingers from turning the pages too fast.
Don't miss it. This is her best yet!"
—*New York Times* bestselling author Lesley Kagen
on *One Breath Away*

"Gudenkauf…keep[s] the tension high
and the reader glued to the pages."
—*Publishers Weekly* on *One Breath Away*

Also by Heather Gudenkauf

One Breath Away
These Things Hidden

The WEIGHT of Silence

Heather Gudenkauf

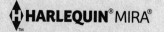

Recycling programs
for this product may
not exist in your area.

ISBN-13: 978-0-7783-1553-7

THE WEIGHT OF SILENCE

Copyright © 2009 by Heather Gudenkauf

For questions and comments about the quality of this book, please contact us at
CustomerService@Harlequin.com.

HARLEQUIN®

www.Harlequin.com

Printed in U.S.A.

For my parents, Milton and Patricia Schmida

There is no one who comes here
that does not know this is a true map of the world,
with you there in the center, making home for us all.
—Brian Andreas

The WEIGHT of Silence

PROLOGUE

Antonia

Louis and I see you nearly at the same time. In the woods, through the bee trees whose heavy, sweet smell will forever remind me of this day, I see flashes of your pink summer nightgown that you wore to bed last night. My chest loosens and I am shaky with relief. I scarcely notice your scratched legs, muddy knees, or the chain in your hand. I reach out to gather you in my arms, to hold you so tight, to lay my cheek on your sweaty head. I will never wish for you to speak, never silently beg you to talk. You are here. But you step past me, not seeing me, you stop at Louis's side, and I think, *You don't even see me, it's Louis's deputy sheriff's uniform, good girl, that's the smart thing to do.* Louis lowers himself toward you, and I am fastened to the look on your face. I see your lips begin to arrange themselves and I know, I know. I see the word form, the syllables hardening and sliding from your mouth with no effort. Your voice, not unsure or hoarse from lack of use but clear and bold. One word, the first in three years. In an instant I have you in my arms and I am crying, tears dropping many emotions, mostly thankfulness and relief, but tears of sorrow mixed in. I see Petra's father crumble. Your chosen word doesn't make sense to me. But it doesn't matter, I don't care. You have finally spoken.

CALLI

Calli stirred in her bed. The heat of a steamy, Iowa August morning lay thick in her room, hanging sodden and heavy about her. She had kicked off the white chenille bedspread and sheets hours earlier, her pink cotton nightgown now bunched up around her waist. No breeze was blowing through her open, screened window. The moon hung low and its milky light lay supine on her floor, a dim, inadequate lantern. She awoke, vaguely aware of movement downstairs below her. Her father preparing to go fishing. Calli heard his solid, certain steps, so different from her mother's quick, light tread, and Ben's hesitant stride. She sat up among the puddle of bed-clothes and stuffed animals, her bladder uncomfortably full, and squeezed her legs together, trying to will the urge to use the bathroom to retreat. Her home had only one bathroom, a pink-tiled room nearly half-filled with the scratched-up white claw-foot bathtub. Calli did not want to creep down the creaky steps, past the kitchen where her father was sure to be drinking his bitter-smelling coffee and putting his tackle box in order. The pressure on her bladder increased and Calli shifted her weight, trying to think of other things. She spotted her stack of supplies for the coming second-grade school year: brightly colored pencils, still long and flat-tipped; slim, crisp-edged folders; smooth rubber-scented pink erasers; a sixty-four-count box of crayons (the supply list called for a twenty-four count box, but Mom knew that this just would not do); and four spiral-bound notebooks, each a different color.

School had always been a mixture of pleasure and pain for Calli. She loved the smell of school, the dusty smell of old books and chalk. She loved the crunch of fall leaves beneath her new shoes as she walked to the bus stop, and she loved her teachers, every single one. But Calli knew that adults would gather in school conference rooms to discuss her: principal, psychologists, speech and language clinicians, special education and regular education teachers, behavior disorder teachers, school counselors, social workers. Why won't Calli speak? Calli knew there were many phrases used to try to describe her—mentally challenged, autistic, on the spectrum, oppositional defiant, a selective mute. She was, in fact, quite bright. She could read and understand books several grade levels above her own.

In kindergarten, Miss Monroe, her energetic, first-year teacher whose straight brown hair and booming bass voice belied her pretty sorority girl looks, thought that Calli was just shy. Calli's name didn't come up to the Solution-Focus Education Team until December of Calli's kindergarten year. And that didn't occur until the school nurse, Mrs. White, after handing Calli a clean pair of socks, underwear and sweatpants for the second time in one week, discovered an unsettling pattern in Calli's visits to the health office.

"Didn't you tell anyone you needed to use the restroom, Calli?" Mrs. White asked in her low, kind voice.

No response, just Calli's usual wide-eyed, flat expression gazing back at her.

"Go on into the restroom and change your clothes, Calli," the nurse instructed. "Make sure to wash yourself the best that you can." Flipping through her meticulous log documenting the date and time of each child's visit to the health office, the ailment noted in her small, tight script—sore throats, bellyaches, scratches, bee stings. Calli's name was notated nine times since August 29, the first day of school. Next to each entry the initials UA—for Urinary Accident. Mrs. White turned to Miss Monroe, who had escorted Calli to the office.

"Michelle, this is Calli's ninth bathroom accident this school year." Mrs. White paused, allowing Miss Monroe to respond. Silence. "Does she go when the other kids do?"

"I don't know," Miss Monroe replied, her voice tumbling under the bathroom door to where Calli was stepping out of her soiled clothing. "I'm not sure. She gets plenty of chances to go…and she can always ask."

"Well, I'm going to call her mom and recommend that she take Calli to the doctor, see if all this isn't just a bladder infection or something else," Mrs. White responded in her cool, efficient manner that few questioned. "Meanwhile, let her use the restroom whenever she wants, send her in anyway, even if she doesn't need to."

"Okay, but she can always ask." Miss Monroe turned and retreated.

Calli silently stepped from the office restroom garbed in a dry pair of pink sweatpants that pooled around her feet and sagged at her rear. In one hand she held a plastic grocery sack that contained her soaked Strawberry Shortcake underwear, jeans, socks and pink-and-white tennis shoes. The index finger of her other hand absently twirled her chestnut-colored hair.

Mrs. White bent down to Calli's eye level. "Do you have gym shoes to put on, Calli?"

Calli looked down at her toes, now clad in dingy, office-issued athletic socks so worn she could see the peachy flesh of her big toe and the Vamp Red nail polish her mother had dabbed on each pearly toenail the night before.

"Calli," Mrs. White repeated, "do you have gym shoes to put on?"

Calli regarded Mrs. White, pursed her thin lips together and nodded her head.

"Okay, Calli," Mrs. White's voice took on a tender tone. "Go put on your shoes and put the bag in your book bag. I'm going to call your mother. Now, you're not in trouble. I see you've had several accidents this year. I just want your mom to be aware, okay?"

Mrs. White carefully searched Calli's winter-kissed face. Calli's attention was then drawn to the vision eye chart and its ever-shrinking letters on the wall of the institutional-white health office.

After the Solution-Focus Team of educators met and tested Calli and reviewed the data, there appeared to be nothing physically wrong with her. Options were discussed and debated, and after several weeks it was decided to teach her the American Sign Language sign for *bathroom* and other key words, have her meet weekly with the school counselor, and patiently wait for Calli to speak. They continued to wait.

Calli climbed out of bed, carefully picked up each of her new school supplies and laid out the items on her small pine desk as she planned to in her new desk in her classroom on the first day of second grade. Big things on the bottom, small things on top, pencils and pens stowed neatly away in her new green pencil case.

The need to urinate became an ache, and she considered relieving herself in her white plastic trash can beside her desk, but knew she would not be able to clean it without her mother or Ben noticing. If her mother found a pool of pee in her wastebasket, Calli knew she would fret endlessly as to what was going on inside her head. Never-ending yes-no questions would follow. *Was someone in the bathroom and you couldn't wait? Were you playing a game with Petra? Are you mad at me, Calli?* She also considered climbing out her second-story window down the trellis, now tangled with white moonflowers as big as her hand. She discounted this idea, as well. She wasn't sure how to remove the screen, and if her mother caught her midclimb she would be of a mind to nail Calli's window shut and Calli loved having her window open at night. On rainy evenings Calli would press her nose to the screen, feel the bounce of raindrops against her cheeks, and smell the dusty sunburned grass as it swallowed the newly fallen rain. Calli did not want her mother to worry more than she did not want to have her father's attention drawn to her as she made her way down the stairs to use the bathroom.

Calli slowly opened her bedroom door and peeked around the door. She stepped cautiously out of her room and into the short hallway where it was darker, the air staler and weightier. Directly across from Calli's room was Ben's room, a twin of her own, whose window faced the backyard and Willow Creek Woods. Ben's door was shut, as was her parents' bedroom door. Calli paused at the top of the steps, straining to hear her father's movements. Silence. Maybe he had left for his fishing trip already. Calli was hopeful. Her father was leaving with his friend Roger to go fishing at the far eastern edge of the county, along the Mississippi River, some eighty miles away. Roger was picking him up that morning and they would be gone for three days. Calli felt a twinge of guilt in wishing her father away, but life was so much more peaceful with just the three of them.

Each morning that he was sitting in the kitchen brought a different man to them. Some days he was happy, and he would set her on his lap and rub his scratchy red whiskers on her cheek to make her smile. He would kiss Mom and hand her a cup of coffee and he would invite Ben to go into town with him. On these days her daddy would talk in endless streams, his voice light and full of something close to tenderness. Some days he would be at the scarred kitchen table with his forehead in his hands, empty beer cans tossed carelessly in the sink and on the brown-speckled laminate countertops. On these days Calli would tiptoe through the kitchen and quietly close the screen door behind her and then dash into the Willow Creek Woods to play along the creek bed or on the limbs of fallen trees. Periodically, Calli would return to the edge of their meadow to see if her father's truck had gone. If it was missing, Calli would return home where the beer cans had been removed and the yeasty, sweaty smell of her father's binge had been scrubbed away. If the truck remained, Calli would retreat to the woods until hunger or the day's heat forced her home.

More silence. Encouraged that he was gone, Calli descended the stairs, carefully stepping over the fourth step that creaked. The bulb from above the kitchen stove cast a ghostly light that spilled onto the bottom of the stairs. She just needed to take two large steps past the kitchen entry and she would be at the bathroom. Calli, at the bottom step, her toes curled over the edge, squeezed the hardwood tightly, pulled her nightgown to above her knees to make possible a bigger step. One step, a furtive glance into the kitchen. No one there. Another step, past the kitchen, her hand on the cool metal doorknob of the bathroom, twisting.

"Calli!" a gruff whisper called out. Callie stilled. "Calli! Come out here!"

Calli's hand dropped from the doorknob and she turned to follow the low sound of her father's voice. The kitchen was empty, but the screen door was open, and she saw the outline of his wide shoulders in the dim early morning. He was sitting on the low concrete step outside, a fog of cigarette smoke and hot coffee intermingling and rising above his head.

"Come out here, Calli-girl. What'cha doing up so early?" he asked, not unkindly. Calli pushed open the screen door, careful not to run the door into his back; she squeezed through the opening and stood next to her father.

"Why ya up, Calli, bad dream?" Griff looked up at her from where he was sitting, a look of genuine concern on his face.

She shook her head no and made the sign for bathroom, the need for which had momentarily fled.

"What's that? Can't hear ya." He laughed. "Speak a little louder. Oh, yeah, you don't talk." And at that moment his face shifted into a sneer. "You gotta use the sign language." He abruptly stood and twisted his hands and arms in a grotesque mockery of Calli. "Can't talk like a normal kid, got be all dumb like some kind of retard!" Griff's voice was rising.

Calli's eyes slid to the ground where a dozen or so crushed beer cans littered the ground and the need to pee returned full force. She glanced up to her mother's bedroom window; the curtains still, no comforting face looked down on her.

"Can't talk, huh? Bullshit! You talked before. You used to say, 'Daddy, Daddy,' 'specially when you wanted something. Now I got a stupid retard for a daughter. Probably you're not even mine. You got that deputy sheriff's eyes." He bent down, his gray-green eyes peered into hers and she squeezed them tightly shut.

In the distance she heard tires on gravel, the sharp crunch and pop of someone approaching. *Roger.* Calli opened her eyes as Roger's four-wheel-drive truck came down the lane and pulled up next to them.

"Hey, there. Mornin', you two. How are you doing, Miss Calli?" Roger tipped his chin to Calli, not really looking at her, not expecting a response. "Ready to go fishing, Griff?"

Roger Hogan was Griff's best friend from high school. He was short and wide, his great stomach spilling over his pants. A foreman at the local meat packing plant, he begged Griff every time he came home from the pipeline to stay home for good. He could get Griff in at the factory, too. "It'd be just like old times," he'd add.

"Morning, Rog," Griff remarked, his voice cheerful, his

eyes mean slits. "I'm goin' to have you drive on ahead without me, Roger. Calli had a bad dream. I'm just going to sit here with her awhile until she feels better, make sure she gets off to sleep again."

"Aw, Griff," whined Roger. "Can't her mother do that? We've been planning this for months."

"No, no. A girl needs her *daddy*, don't she, Calli? A *daddy* she can rely on to help her through those tough times. Her *daddy* should be there for her, don't you think, Rog? So Calli's gonna spend some time with her good ol' *daddy*, whether she wants to or not. But you want to, don't you, Calli?"

Calli's stomach wrenched tighter with each of her father's utterances of the word *daddy*. She longed to run into the house and wake up her mother, but while Griff spewed hate from his mouth toward Calli when he'd been drinking, he'd never actually really hurt her. Ben, yes. Mom, yes. Not Calli.

"I'll just throw my stuff in your truck, Rog, and meet up with you at the cabin this afternoon. There'll be plenty of good fishing tonight, and I'll pick up some more beer for us on the way." Griff picked up his green duffel and tossed it into the back of the truck. More carefully he laid his fishing gear, poles and tackle into the bed of the truck. "I'll see ya soon, Roger."

"Okay, I'll see you later then. You sure you can find the way?"

"Yeah, yeah, don't worry. I'll be there. You can get a head start on catching those fish. You're gonna need it, 'cause I'm going to whip your butt!"

"We'll just see about that!" Roger guffawed and squealed away.

Griff made his way back to where Calli was standing, her arms wrapped around herself despite the heat.

"Now how about a little bit of *daddy* time, Calli? The deputy sheriff don't live too far from here, now, does he? Just through the woods there, huh?" Her father grabbed her by the arm and her bladder released, sending a steady stream of urine down her leg as he pulled her toward the woods.

PETRA

I can't sleep, again. It's too hot, my necklace is sticking to my neck. I'm sitting on the floor in front of the electric fan, and the cool air feels good against my face. Very quiet I am talking into the fan so I can hear the buzzy, low voice it blows back at me. "I am Petra, Princess of the World," I say. I hear something outside my window and for a minute I am scared and want to go wake up Mom and Dad. I crawl across my carpet on my hands, the rug rubbing against my knees all rough. I peek out the window and in the dark I think I see someone looking up at me, big and scary. Then I see something smaller at his side. Oh, I'm not scared anymore. I know them. I think, "Wait, I'm coming, too!" For a second I think I shouldn't go. But there is a grown-up out there, too. Mom and Dad can't get mad at me if there's a grown-up. I pull on my tennis shoes and sneak out of my room. I'll just go say hi, and come right back in.

CALLI

Calli and her father had been walking for a while now, but Calli knew exactly where they were and where they were not within the sprawling woods. They were near Beggar's Bluff Trail, where pink-tipped turtleheads grew in among the ferns and rushes and where Calli would often see sleek, beautiful horses carrying their owners gracefully through the forest. Calli wished that a cinnamon-colored mare or a black-splotched Appaloosa would crash from the trees, startling her father back to his senses. But it was Thursday and Calli rarely encountered another person on the trails near her home during the week. There was a slight chance that they would run into a park ranger, but the rangers had over thirty miles of trails to monitor and maintain. Calli knew she was on her own and resigned herself to being dragged through the forest with her father. They were nowhere near Deputy Sheriff Louis's home. Calli could not decide whether this was a good thing or not. Bad because her father showed no indication of giving up his search and Calli's bare feet were scratched from being pulled across rocky, uneven paths. Good because if they ever did get to Deputy Louis's home her father would say unforgivable things and then Louis would, in his calm low voice, try to quiet him and then call Calli's mother. His wife would be standing in the doorway behind him, her arms crossed, eyes darting furtively around to see who was watching the spectacle.

Her father did not look well. His face was white, the color of bloodroot, the delicate early spring flower that her mother showed to her on their walks in the woods, his coppery hair the color of the red sap from its broken roots. Periodically stumbling over an exposed root, he continued to clutch Calli's arm, all the time muttering under his breath. Calli was biding her time, waiting for the perfect moment to bolt, to run back home to her mother.

They were approaching a clearing named Willow Wallow. Arranged in a perfect half-moon adjacent to the creek was an arc of seven weeping willows. It was said that the seven willows were brought to the area by a French settler, a friend of Napoleon Bonaparte, the willows a gift from the great general, the wispy trees being his favorite.

Calli's mother was the kind of mother who would climb trees with her children and sit among the branches, telling them stories about her great-great-grandparents who immigrated to the United States from Czechoslovakia in the 1800s. She would pack the three of them a lunch of peanut butter fluff sandwiches and apples and they would walk down to Willow Creek. They would hop across the slick, moss-covered rocks that dotted the width of the creek. Antonia would lay an old blanket under the long, lacy branches of a willow tree and they would crawl into its shade, ropy tendrils surrounding them like a cloak. There the willows would become huts on a deserted island; Ben, back when he had time for them, was the brave sailor; Calli, his dependable first mate; Antonia, the pirate chasing them, calling out with a bad cockney accent. "Ya landlubbers, surrender an' ya won' haf to walk da plank!"

"Never!" Ben yelled back. "You'll have to feed us to the sharks before we surrender to the likes of you, Barnacle Bart!"

"So be it! Prepare ta swim wid da fishes!" Antonia bellowed, flourishing a stick.

"Run, Calli!" Ben screeched and Calli would. Her long pale legs shadowed with bruises from climbing trees and skirting fences, Calli would run until Antonia would double over, hands on her knees.

"Truce, truce!" Antonia would beg. The three of them would retreat to their willow hut and rest, sipping soda as the sweat cooled on their necks. Antonia's laugh bubbled up from low in her chest, unfettered and joyous. She would toss her head back and close eyes that were just beginning to show the creases of age and disappointment. When Antonia laughed, those around her did, too, except for Calli. Calli hadn't laughed for a long time. She smiled her sweet, close-lipped grin, but an actual giggle, which once was emitted freely and sounded of chimes, never came, though she knew her mother waited expectantly.

Antonia was the kind of mother who let you eat sugar cereal for Sunday supper and pizza for breakfast. She was the kind of mom who, on rainy nights, would declare it Spa

Night and in a French accent welcome you to Toni's House of Beauty. She would fill the old claw-foot bathtub full of warm, lilac-scented bubbles and then, after rubbing you dry with an oversize white towel, would paint your toenails Wicked Red, or mousse and gel your hair until it stood at attention in three-inch spikes.

Griff, on the other hand, was the kind of father who drank Bud Light for breakfast and dragged his seven-year-old daughter through the forest in a drunken search for his version of the truth. The sun beginning to rise, Griff sat the two of them down beneath one of the willow trees to rest.

MARTIN

I can feel Fielda's face against my back, her arm wrapped around my ever-growing middle. It's too hot to lie in this manner, but I don't nudge her away from me. Even if I was in Dante's Inferno, I could not push Fielda away from me. We have only been apart two instances since our marriage fourteen years ago and both times seemed too much for me to bear. The second time that Fielda and I were apart I do not speak about. The first separation was nine months after our wedding and I went to a conference on economics at the University of Chicago. I remember lying in the hotel on my lumpy bed with its stiff, scratchy comforter, wishing for Fielda. I felt weightless without her there, that without her arm thrown carelessly over me in sleep, I could just float away like milkweed on a random wind. After that lonely night I forewent the rest of my seminars and came home.

Fielda laughed at me for being homesick, but I know she was secretly pleased. She came to me late in my life, a young, brassy girl of eighteen. I was forty-two and wed to my job as a professor of economics at St. Gilianus College, a private college with an enrollment of twelve hundred students in Willow Creek. No, she was not a student; many have asked this question with a light, accusatory tone. I met Fielda Mourning when she was a waitress at her family's café, Mourning Glory. On my way to the college each day I would stop in at the Mourning Glory for a cup of coffee and a muffin and to read my newspaper in a sun-drenched corner of the café. I remember Fielda, in those days, as being very solicitous and gracious to me, the coffee, piping hot, and the muffin sliced in half with sweet butter on the side. I must admit, I took this considerate service for granted, believing that Fielda treated all her patrons in this manner. It was not until one wintry morning, about a year after I started coming to the Mourning Glory, that Fielda stomped up to me, one hand on her ample hip, the other hand holding my cup of coffee.

"What," Fielda shrilly aimed at me, "does a girl have to do in order to get your attention?" She banged the cup down in front of me, my glasses leaping on my nose in surprise, coffee sloshing all over the table.

Before I could splutter a response, she had retreated and then reappeared, this time with my muffin that she promptly tossed at me. It bounced off my chest, flaky crumbs of orange poppy seed clinging to my tie. Fielda ran from the café and her mother, a softer, more care-worn version of Fielda, sauntered up to me. Rolling her eyes heavenward, she sighed. "Go on out there and talk to her, Mr. Gregory. She's been pining over you for months. Either put her out of her misery or ask her to marry you. I need to get some sleep at night."

I did go out after Fielda and we were married a month later.

Lying there in our bed, the August morning already sweeping my skin with its prickly heat, I twist around, find Fielda's slack cheek in the darkness and kiss it. I slide out of bed and out of the room. I stop at Petra's door. It is slightly open and I can hear the whir of her fan. I gently push the door forward and step into her room, a place so full of little girl whimsy that it never fails to make me pause. The carefully arranged collections of pinecones, acorns, leaves, feathers and rocks all expertly excavated from our backyard at the edge of Willow Creek Woods. The baby dolls, stuffed dogs and bears all tucked lovingly under blankets fashioned from washcloths and arranged around her sleeping form. The little girl perfume, a combination of lavender-scented shampoo, green grass and perspiration that holds only the enzymes of the innocent, overwhelms me every time I cross this threshold. My eyes begin to adjust to the dark and I see that Petra is not in her bed. I am not alarmed; Petra often has bouts of insomnia and skulks downstairs to the living room to watch television.

I, too, go downstairs, but very quickly I know that Petra is not watching television. The house is quiet, no droning voices or canned laughter. I walk briskly through each room, switching on lights, the living room—no Petra. The dining room, the kitchen, the bathroom, my office—no Petra. Back through the kitchen down to the basement—no Petra. Rushing up the stairs to Fielda, I shake her awake.

"Petra's not in her bed," I gasp.

Fielda leaps from the bed and retraces the path I just followed, no Petra. I hurry out the back door and circle the house once, twice, three times. No Petra. Fielda and I meet back in the kitchen, and we look at one another helplessly. Fielda stifles a moan and dials the police.

We quickly pulled on clothes in order to make ourselves presentable to receive Deputy Sheriff Louis. Fielda continues to wander through each of the rooms, checking for Petra, looking through closets and under the stairs. "Maybe she went over to Calli's house," she says.

"At this time of the morning?" I ask. "What would possess her to do that? Maybe she was too hot and went outside to cool off and she lost track of time," I add. "Sit down, you're making me nervous. She is not in this house!" I say, louder than I should have. Fielda's face crumples and I go to her. "I'm sorry," I whisper, though her constant movement is making me nervous. "We'll go make coffee for when he arrives."

"Coffee? Coffee?" Fielda's voice is shrill and she is looking at me incredulously. "Let's just brew up some coffee so we can sit down and discuss how our daughter has disappeared. Disappeared right from her bedroom in the middle of the night! Would you like me to make him breakfast, too? Eggs over easy? Or maybe waffles. Martin, our child is missing. Missing!" Her tirade ends in whimpers and I pat her on the back. I am no consolation to her, I know.

There is a rap at the front door and we both look to see Deputy Sheriff Louis, tall and rangy, his blond hair falling into his serious blue eyes. We invite him into our home, this man almost half my age, closer to Fielda's own, and sit him on our sofa.

"When did you see Petra last?" he asks us. I reach for Fielda's hand and tell him all that we know.

ANTONIA

I am being lifted from my sleep by the low rumble of what I think at first is thunder and I smile, my eyes still closed. A rainstorm, cool, plump drops. I think that maybe I should wake Calli and Ben. They both would love to go stomp around in the rain, to rinse away this dry, hot summer, if just for a few moments. I reach my hand over to Griff's side of the bed, empty and cooler than mine. It's Thursday, the fishing trip. Griff went fishing with Roger, no thunder, a truck? I roll over to Griff's side, absorb the brief coolness of the sheets and try to sleep, but continuous pounding, a solid banging on the front door, is sending vibrations through the floorboards. I swing my legs out of bed, irritated. It's only six o'clock, for Christ's sake. I pull on the shorts that I had dropped on the floor the night before and run my fingers through my bed-mussed hair. As I make my way through the hallway I see that Ben's door is tightly shut, as it normally is. Ben's room is his private fortress; I don't even try to go in there anymore. The only people he invites in are his school friends and his sister, Calli. This is surprising to me. I grew up in a family of four brothers and they let me enter their domain only when I forced my way in.

My whole life has been circled by males; my brothers, my father, Louis and of course, Griff. Most of my friends in school were boys. My mother died when I was seventeen and even before that she hovered on the edge of our ring. I wish I had paid more attention to the way she did things. I have misty-edged memories of the way she sat, always in skirts, one leg crossed over the other, her brown hair pulled back in an elegant chignon. My mother could not get me into a dress, interested in makeup or sitting like a lady, but she insisted that I keep my hair long. I rebelled by putting my hair back in a ponytail and cramming a baseball hat on top of my head. I wish I had watched closely to the way she would carefully paint lipstick on her lips and spray just the right amount of perfume on her wrists. I remember her leaning in close to my father and whispering in his ear, making him smile, the way she could calm him with just a manicured hand on his arm. My own silent little girl is even more of a mystery to me, the way she likes her hair combed smooth after a bath, the joy she has in inspecting her nails after I have inexpertly painted them. Having a little girl has been like following an old treasure map with the important paths torn away. These days I sit and watch her carefully, studying her each movement and gesture. At least when she was speaking she could tell me what she wanted or needed; now I guess and falter and hope for the best. I go on as if there is nothing wrong with my Calli, as if she is a typical seven-year-old, that strangers do not discuss her in school offices, that neighbors don't whisper behind their hands about the odd Clark girl.

The door to Calli's room is open slightly, but the banging on the door is more insistent so I hurry down the steps, the warped wood creaking under my bare feet. I unlock the heavy oak front door to find Louis and Martin Gregory, Petra's father, standing before me. The last time Louis was in my home was three years earlier, though I remember little of it, as I was lying nearly unconscious on my sofa after falling down the flight of stairs.

"Hi," I say uncertainly, "what's going on?"

"Toni," begins Louis, "is Petra here?"

"No," I reply and look at Martin. His face falls for a moment and then he raises his chin.

"May we speak with Calli? Petra seems to be…" Martin hesitates. "We can't find Petra right now and thought that Calli could tell us where she might be."

"Oh, my goodness, of course. Please come in." I show them into our living room, now conscious of the scattering of beer cans on the coffee table. I quickly gather them and scurry to the kitchen to throw them away.

"I'll just go and wake Calli up." I take the stairs two at a time, my stomach sick for Martin and Fielda. I am calling, "Calli. Calli, get up, honey, I need to talk to you!" When I reach the hall, Ben opens his door. He is shirtless and I notice that his red hair needs trimming.

"Morning, Benny, they can't find Petra." I continue past him to Calli's door and I push it open. Her bed is rumpled and her sock monkey lies on the floor, its smiling face turned toward me. I stop, puzzled, and then turn. "Ben, where's Calli?"

He shrugs and retreats to his room. I quickly check the guestroom, my bedroom, Ben's room. I rush down the stairs. "She's gone, too!" I run past Louis and Martin, down our rickety basement steps, flipping on the light as I scurry downward, the cool dampness of our concrete basement sweeping over me. Only cobwebs and boxes. Our old, empty deep freeze. My heart skips a beat. You hear about this, children playing hide-and-seek in old refrigerators and freezers, not being able to get out once they are in. I told Griff time and again to get rid of the old thing. But he never did, I never did. Quickly I run over to the freezer and fling open the lid and a stale smell hits me. It's empty. I try to regulate my breathing and I turn back to the steps. I see Martin and Louis waiting for me at the top. I sprint up the steps, past them and out the back door. I scan our wide backyard and run to the edge of the woods, peering into the shadowy trees. Winded, I make my way back to my home. Louis and Martin are waiting for me behind the screen door. "She's not here."

Louis's face is stony, but Martin's falls in disappointment.

"Well, they are most likely together and went off playing somewhere. Can you think of where they may have gone?" Louis inquires.

"The park? The school, maybe. But this early? What is it? Six o'clock?" I ask.

"Petra has been gone since at least four-thirty," Martin says matter-of-factly. "Where would they go at such an early hour?"

"I don't know, it doesn't make sense," I say. Louis asks me if he can have a look around, and I watch, following at his heels as he walks purposefully around my home, peeking in closets and under beds. She is not here.

"I've called in the information about Petra to all the officers. They're already looking around town for her," Louis explains. "It doesn't appear that the girls were…" He pauses. "That the girls met any harm. I suggest you go look around for them in the places they usually go." Martin looks uncertain about this plan, but nods his head and I do, too.

"Toni, Griff's truck is outside. Is he here? Would he be able to tell us where the girls could be?"

Louis, in his kind way, is asking me if Griff is coherent this morning or if he is passed out in our bed from a night of drinking. "Griff's not here. He went fishing with Roger this morning. He was going to leave at about three-thirty or so."

"Could he have taken the girls fishing with him?" Martin asks hopefully.

"No," I laugh. "The last thing Griff would do is take a couple of little girls on his big fishing trip. He's not supposed to be back until Saturday. I'm positive the girls did not go fishing with him."

"I don't know, Toni. Maybe he did decide to take the girls with him. Maybe he left a note."

"No, Louis. I'm sure he wouldn't have done that." I am beginning to become irritated with him.

"Okay, then," Louis says. "We'll talk again in one hour. If the girls aren't found by then, we'll make a different plan."

I hear a rustle of movement and turn to see Ben sitting on the steps. At a quick glance he could be mistaken for Griff, with his broad shoulders and strawberry hair. Except for the eyes. Ben has soft, quiet eyes.

"Ben," I say, "Calli and Petra went off somewhere and we need to find them. Where could they have gone?"

"The woods," he says simply. "I'm going to go do my paper route. Then I'll go look for them."

"I'll call to have some officers check out the woods near the backyard. One hour," Louis says again. "We'll talk in one hour."

BEN

This morning I woke up real fast, my heart slamming against my chest. I was dreaming that stupid dream again. The one when you and me are climbing the old walnut tree in the woods. The one by Lone Tree Bridge. I'm boosting you up like I always do and you're reaching up for a branch, your nail-bitten fingers white from holding on so tight. I'm crabbing at you to hurry up because I don't have all day. You're up and I'm watching from below. The climb is easier for you now; the branches are closer together, fat sturdy ones. You're going higher and higher until I can only see your bony knees, then just your tennis shoes. I'm hollering up at you, "You're too high, Calli, come back down! You're gonna fall!" Then you're gone. I can't see you anymore. And I'm thinking, *I am in so much trouble.* Then I hear a voice calling down to me, "Climb on up, Ben! You gotta see this! Come on, Ben, come on!"

And I know it's you yelling, even though I don't know what you really sound like anymore. You keep yelling and yelling, and I can't climb. I want to, but I can't grab on to the lowest branch, it's too high. I call back, "Wait for me! Wait for me! What do you see, Calli?" Then I woke up, all sweaty. But not the hot kind of sweaty, the cold kind that makes your head hurt and your stomach knot all up. I tried to go back to sleep, but I couldn't.

Now you've gone off somewhere and somehow I feel guilty, like it's my fault. You're okay for a little sister, but a big responsibility. I always have to look after you. Do you remember when I was ten and you were five? Mom had us walk to the bus stop together. She said, "Look after Calli, Ben." And I said okay, but I didn't, not really, not at first.

I was starting fifth grade and I was much too cool to be babysitting a kindergartener. I held your hand to the end of our lane, just to the spot where Mom couldn't see us from the kitchen window anymore. Then I shook my hand free from yours and ran as fast as I could to where the bus would pick us up. I made sure to look back and to check to see if you were still coming. I have to give you credit, your skinny kindergarten legs were running and your brand-new pink backpack was bouncing on your shoulders, but you couldn't keep up. You tripped over that big old crack in the gutter in front of the Olson house, and you went crashing down.

I almost came back for you, I really did. But along came Raymond and I didn't come back to you, I just didn't. When you finally got to the bus stop, the bus was just pulling up and your knee was all bloody and the purple barrette that Mom put in your hair was dangling from one little piece of your hair. You budged right in front of all the kids in line for the bus to stand next to me and I pretended you weren't even there.

When we climbed on the bus, I sat down with Raymond. You just stood in the aisle, waiting for me to scooch over and make room for you, but I turned my back on you to talk to Raymond. The kids behind you started yelling, "hurry up" and "sit down," so you finally slid into the seat across from me and Raymond. You were all nudged up to the window, your legs too short to reach the floor, a little river of blood running down your shin. You wouldn't even look at me for the rest of the night. Even after supper, when I offered to tell you a story, you just shrugged your shoulders at me and left me sitting at the kitchen table all by myself.

I know I was pretty rotten to you that day, but on a guy's first day of fifth grade first impressions are really important. I tried to make it up to you. In case you didn't know, I was the one who put the Tootsie Rolls under your pillow that night. I'm sorry, not watching out for you those first few weeks of school. But you know all about that, being sorry and having no words to say something when you know you should but you just can't.

CALLI

Griff sat with his back propped up against one of the aged willows, his head lolled forward, eyes closed, his powerful fingers still wrapped around Calli's wrist. Calli squirmed uncomfortably on the hard, uneven ground beneath the willow. The stench of urine pricked at her nose and a wave of shame washed over her. She should run now, she thought. She was fast and knew every twist and turn of the woods; she could easily lose her father. She slowly tried to pull her arm from his clawlike clasp, but in his light sleep he grasped her even tighter. Calli's shoulders slumped and she settled back against her side of the tree.

She liked to imagine what it would be like to stay out in the woods with no supplies, what her brother called "roughin' it." Ben knew everything about the Willow Creek Woods. He knew that the woods were over fourteen thousand acres big and extended into two counties. He told her that the forest was made up mostly of limestone and sandstone and was a part of the Paleozoic Plateau, which meant that glaciers had never moved through their part of Iowa. He also showed her where to find the red-shouldered hawk, an endangered bird that not even Ranger Phelps had seen before. She had only been out here a few hours and it was enough for her. Normally the woods were her favorite place to go, a quiet spot where she could think, wander and explore. She and Ben often pretended to set up camp here in Willow Wallow. Ben would lug a thermos of water and Calli would carry the snacks, bags of salty chips and thick ropes of licorice for them to munch on. Ben would arrange sticks and brushwood into a large circular pile and surround them with stones for their bonfire. They never actually lit a fire, but it was fun to pretend. They would stick marshmallows on the end of green twigs and "roast" them over their fire. Ben used to pull out his pocketknife and try to whittle utensils out of thin branches he would find on the ground. He had carved out two spoons and a fork before the blade had slipped and he sliced his hand, needing six stitches. Their mother had taken the knife away after that, saying he could have it back in a few years. Ben handed it over grudgingly. Lately, instead of carving out the silverware, she and Ben smuggled dishes and tableware from their own kitchen. Under the largest of the willows Ben had constructed a small little cupboard out of old boards and hammered it to the tree. They kept their household goods there. Once, trying to plan ahead, they had placed a box of crackers and a package of cookies on the shelf. When they returned a few days later, they found that something had been there before them, probably a raccoon, but Ben said, in a teasing voice, it also could have been a bear. Calli hadn't really believed that, but it was fun to pretend that a mama bear was out there somewhere, feeding her cubs Chips Ahoy cookies and Wheat Thins.

She wondered if her mother had noticed that she was gone yet, wondered if she was worried about her, looking for her. Calli's stomach rumbled and she hastily placed her free hand over it, willing it to silence. Maybe there was something to eat in the cupboard two trees over. Griff snorted, his eyes fluttered open and he settled his gaze on Calli's face.

"You reek," he said meanly, unaware of his own smell, a combination of liquor, perspiration and onions. "Come on, let's get going. We've got a family reunion to attend. Which way do we go?"

Calli considered this. She could lie, lead him deeper into the forest, and then make a break for it when she had the chance, or she could show him the correct route and get it over with. The second choice prevailed. She was already hungry and tired, and she wanted to go home. She pointed a thin, grubby finger back the way they had come.

"Get up," Griff commanded.

Calli scrambled to her feet, Griff let go of her arm and Calli tried to shake out the numbness that had snaked into her fingers. They walked in a strange sort of tandem, Griff directly behind her, his hand on her shoulder; Calli slumped slightly under the weight of his meaty hand. Calli led the two of them out of Willow Wallow about one hundred yards, to the beginning of a narrow winding trail called Broadleaf. Calli always knew if someone or something had been walking the trails before her. During the night spiders would knit their webs across the trails from limb to limb. When the morning sun was just right, Calli could see the delicate threads, a minute, fragile barrier to the inner workings of the forest. *"Keep out,"* it whispered. She would always skirt the woven curtain, trying not to disturb the netting. If the web dangled in wispy threads Calli knew that something had been there before her, and if closer inspection revealed the footprints of a human, she would retreat and wind her way back to another trail. Calli liked the idea that she could be the only person around for miles. That the white-speckled ground squirrel that sat on an old rotted tree branch, wringing his paws, would be seeing a human for the first time. That this sad-eyed creature before it didn't quite belong, but didn't disturb its world, either. Today she carefully stepped around a red maple, the breeze of her movements causing the web to sway precariously for a moment, and then settle.

A flash of movement to the right surprised them both. A large dog with golden-red fur sniffed its way past them, snuffling at their feet. Calli reached out to stroke its back, but it swiftly moved onward, a long red leash dragging behind it.

"Jesus!" Griff exclaimed, clutching his chest. "'Bout scared me to death. Let's go."

Only one animal had ever frightened Calli in her past explorations of the woods. The soot-colored crow, with its slick, oily feathers, perched in crooked maples, its harassed caw overriding the hushed murmurs of the forest. Calli imagined a coven of crows peering down at her from leafy hiding spots with eyes as bright and cold as ball bearings, watching, considering. The birds would seem to follow her from a distance in noisy, low swoops. Calli looked above her. No crows, but she did spy a lone gray-feathered nuthatch walking down the trunk of a tree in search of insects.

"You sure we're going the right way?" Griff stopped, inspecting his surroundings carefully. His words sounded clearer, less slurred.

Calli nodded. They walked for about ten more minutes, and then Calli led him off Broadleaf Trail, where brambles and sticky walnut husks were thick. Calli examined the ground in front of her for poison ivy, found none and continued forward and upward, wincing with each step. Suddenly the thicket of trees ended and they were on the outskirts of Louis's backyard. The grass was wet with dew and overgrown; a littering of baseball bats, gloves and other toys surrounded a small swing set. A green van sat in the driveway next to the brown-sided ranch-style home. All was still except for the honeybees buzzing around a wilted cluster of Shasta daisies. The home seemed to be slumbering.

Griff looked uncertain as to what to do next. His hands shook slightly on Calli's shoulder; she could feel the slight tattoo of movement through her nightgown.

"Told you I'd take you to see where your daddy was. Just think, you could be living here in this fine home." Griff guffawed and rubbed his hand over his bloodshot eyes. "Do you think we should stop in and say good morning?" Much of his earlier bluster was fading away.

Calli shook her head miserably.

"Let's go now, I got a headache." He roughly yanked at Calli's arm when the slam of a screen door stopped him.

A woman, barefoot, wearing shorts and a T-shirt, stepped out of the house with a cordless phone pressed against her ear. Her voice was high and shrill. "Sure, you go running out when *she* needs you, when her precious little girl goes missing!"

Griff went still, Calli stepped forward to hear more clearly, and Griff pulled her back. Calli recognized the woman as Louis's wife, Christine. "I don't care that there are two girls missing. It's her daughter that is missing and that's all that matters to you!" Christine bitterly spat. "When Antonia calls, you go running and *you* know it!" Again the woman fell silent, listening to the voice on the other end of the phone. "Whatever, Louis. Do what you have to do, but don't expect me to be happy about it!" The woman jerked the phone from her ear and violently pushed a button, ending the call. She cocked her arm as if to throw the phone into the bushes, but paused for a moment. "Dammit," she snapped, then lowered her arm and brought the phone back down to her side. "Dammit!" she repeated before opening the screen door and entering her home again, letting the door bang behind her.

"Huh," Griff snorted. He looked at Calli. "So, you've gone missing? I wonder who took ya." He laughed, "Oooh, I'm a big, bad kidnapper. Christ. Let's go. Your mother is going to hit the roof when we get home."

Calli let herself be led back into the shade of the trees and immediately the air around her cooled. Her mother knew she was missing, but she must not have known that she was with her father. But who was the other little girl who was missing? Calli squeezed back tears, wanting to get to her mother, to shed her pee-covered nightgown, to wash and bandage her bleeding feet, to crawl into her bed and bury herself under the covers.

MARTIN

I have visited all the places that Petra loves: the library, the school, the bakery, Kerstin's house, Ryan's house, Wycliff Pool, and here, East Park. Now I walk among the swings, teeter-totter, jungle gym, slides and the monkey bars, deserted due to the early hour. I even climb up the black train engine that the railroad donated to the city as a piece of play equipment. It amazes me that anyone with any sort of authority could believe such a machine could be considered a safe place for children to play. It was once a working engine, but of course all the dangerous pieces had been removed, the glass replaced with plastic, sharp corners softened. But still it is huge, imposing. Just the thing to offer up to small children who have no fear and who feel that they could fly if given the opportunity. I have seen children climb the many ladders that lead to small nooks and crannies in the engine. The children would play an intricate game they dubbed Train Robbery, for which there were many rules, often unspoken and often developed on the spot as the game progressed. I have seen them leap from the highest point at the top of the train and land on the ground with a thump that to me sounds bone crushing. However, inevitably, the children sprang back up and brushed at the dirt that clung to their behinds, no worse for wear.

I, too, climb to the highest point at the top of the black engine and scan the park for any sign of Petra and Calli. For once I feel the exhilaration that the children must feel. The feeling of being at a pinnacle, where the only place to go now is down; it is a breathtaking sensation and I feel my legs wobble with uncertainty as I look around me. They are nowhere to be seen. I lower myself to a sitting position, my legs straddling the great engine. I look at my hands, dusty with the soot that is so ingrained on the train that it will never be completely washed away, and think of Petra.

The night that Petra was born I stayed in the hospital with Fielda. I did not leave her side. I settled myself in a comfortable chair next to her hospital bed. I was surprised at the luxuriousness of the birthing suite, the muted wallpaper, the lights that dimmed with the twist of a switch, the bathroom with a whirlpool bathtub. I was pleased that Fielda would give birth in such a nice place, tended to by a soothing nurse who would place a capable hand on Fielda's sweating forehead and whisper encouragement to her.

I was born in Missouri, in my home on a hog farm, as were my seven younger brothers and sisters. I was well-accustomed to the sounds of a woman giving birth and when Fielda began emitting the same powerful, frightening sounds, I became light-headed and had to step out of the hospital room for a moment. When I was young, I would watch my pregnant mother perform her regular household duties with the same diligence to which I was accustomed. However, I remember seeing her grasp the kitchen counter as a contraction overtook her. When her proud, stern face began to crumple in pain, I became even more watchful. Eventually she would send me over to my aunt's house to retrieve her sister and mother to help her with the birth. I would run the half mile swiftly, grateful for the reprieve from the anxious atmosphere that had invaded our well-ordered home.

In the summers I would go barefoot, the soles of my feet becoming hard and calloused. Impervious to the clumps of dirt and rocks, I could barely feel the ground beneath me. I preferred to wear shoes, but my mother only allowed me to wear them on Sundays and to school. I hated that people could see my exposed feet, the dirt that wedged itself under my toenails. I had the habit of standing on one leg with the other resting on top of it, my toes curled so that only the top of one dirty foot was visible. My grandmother would laugh at me and call me "stork." My aunt thought this was quite amusing, especially when I came to get them to help my mother deliver her baby. She would discharge a big, bellowing laugh that was delightful to the ears, so much so that even I could not help but smile, even though the laugh was at my expense. We would climb into my grandmother's rusty Ford and drive back to our farm. We would pass by the hog house and my father would wave at us and smile hugely. This was his signal that a new son or daughter would be born soon.

In name, I was a farm boy, but I could not be bothered by the minutiae of the farm. My interest was in books and in numbers. My father, a kind, simple man, would shake his head when I would show no interest in farrowing sows, but still I had my chores to do around the farm. Mucking out the pens and feeding buckets of slop to the hogs were a few of my duties. However, I refused to have any part of butcher time. The thought of killing any living creature made me ill, though I had no qualms about eating pork. On butcher day, I would conveniently disappear. I would retrieve my shoes from the back of my closet and tie them tightly, brushing away any scuffs, and I would walk into town three miles away. When I reached the outskirts, I would spit onto my fingers and bend down to wipe away the dust and grime from my shoes. I would double-check to make sure my library card, wrinkled and limp from frequent use, was still there as I stepped into the library. There I would spend hours reading books on coin collecting and history. The librarian knew me by name and would often set aside books she knew I would enjoy.

"Don't worry about bringing these back in two weeks," she'd say conspiratorially, handing me the books tucked carefully into the canvas bag I had brought with me. She knew it could be difficult for me to make the trip into town every few weeks, but more often than not I would find a way.

I would slink back to the farm, the butchering done for the day, and my father would be waiting on the front porch, rolling his cigarette between his fingers, drinking some iced tea that my mother had brewed. I would marvel at his size as I slowly approached my home, knowing that disappointment was awaiting me. My father was an enormous man, in height and girth, the buttons of his work shirts straining against the curve of his belly. People who did not know my father would shrink away from his vastness, but were quickly drawn into his gentle manner as they got to know him. I cannot recall a time when my father raised his voice to my mother or my brothers and sisters.

One terrible day, when I was twelve, I returned from the library after shirking my farm responsibilities and my father was leaning against the wooden fence at the edge of the hog house, awaiting my return. His normally placid face was set in anger and his arms were crossed across his wide chest. He watched my approach with an unwavering gaze and I had the urge to drop my books and run away. I did not. I continued my walk to the spot where he was standing and looked down at my church shoes, smeared with dust and dirt.

"Martin," he said in a grave voice I did not recognize. "Martin, look at me."

I raised my eyes and I looked up into his and felt the weight of his disappointment in me. I thought I could smell the blood from butchering on him. "Martin, we're a family. And our family business happens to be hog farming. I know you are ashamed of that—"

I shook my head quickly. That was not what I thought, but I didn't know how to make him understand. He continued.

"I know that the filth of what I do shames you, and that I don't have your same schoolin' shames you, too. But this is who I am, a hog farmer. And it's who you are, too. At least for now. I can't read your big fancy books and understand some of those big words you use, but what I do puts food on our table and those shoes on your feet. To do that, I need the help of my family. You're the oldest, you got to help. You find the way that you can help, Martin, and you tell me what that is, but you got to do your share. You can't be runnin' off into town when there's work to be done. Understand?"

I nodded, the heat of my own shame rising off my face.

"You think on it, Martin, tonight. You think on it and tell me in the mornin' what your part is gonna be." Then he walked away from me, his head hanging low, his hands stuffed into the back of his work pants.

I slept little that night, trying to find a way that I could be useful to my family. I did not want to mind my younger brothers and sisters, and I was not very handy with building or fixing things. What was I good at? I wondered that night. I was a good reader and I was good at mathematics. Those were my strengths. I pondered on these the entire night and when my father awoke the next morning I was waiting for him at our kitchen table.

"I think I know how I can help, Daddy," I said shyly, and he rewarded me with his familiar lopsided grin.

"I knew you would, Martin," he replied and sat down next to me.

I laid it all out for him, the financial records of the farm, noting in as kind a way as possible the sloppiness and inaccuracies that they contained. I could help, I told him, by keeping track of the money. I would find ways of saving and ways of making the farm more efficient. He was pleased with my plan, and I was appreciative of his faith in me. We never flourished as a family farm, but our quality of life improved. We were able to update our utilities and install a telephone; we could afford shoes for each of the children all year-round, though I was still the only one who chose to wear them in the summer. One winter day when I was sixteen, soon before my father's

birthday, I took the farm truck into town to the only department store, which sold everything from groceries to appliances.
I spent two and a half hours looking at the two models of television sets they had available, weighing the pros and cons of
each. I finally decided upon the twelve-inch version with
rabbit ear antennae. I settled it carefully in the cab of the truck
next to me wrapped in blankets to cushion any jostling that
would occur on the winding dirt roads, and returned to the
farm.

When my father came in that evening, after taking care of
the hogs, we were gathered in the living room, all nine of us,
blocking the view of my father's birthday present.

"What's going on here?" he asked, as it was rare that we
were all congregated in one place that was not the supper table.

My mother began to sing "Happy Birthday" to my father
and we all joined in. At the end of the song we parted to reveal
the tiny television set that rested upon an old bookshelf.

"What's this?" my father asked in disbelief. "What did you
go and do?"

We were all grinning up at him and my little sister, Lottie,
who was seven, squealed, "Turn it on, Daddy, turn it on!"

My father stepped forward and turned the knob to On and
after a moment the black-and-white image of a variety show
filled the screen. We all laughed in delight and crowded
around the television to listen. My father fiddled with the
volume button until we were satisfied with the noise level and
we all watched in rapt attention. Later, my father pulled me
aside and thanked me. He rested his hand on the back of my
neck and looked into my eyes; we were nearly the same height
now. "My boy," he whispered. Those were just about the

sweetest words I have ever heard—until, that is, Petra uttered "Da Da" for the first time.

Holding Petra for the first time after Fielda's long labor was a miracle to me. I had worked for years, trying to shed my farm boy roots, to rid myself of any twang of an accent, to present myself as a cultured, intelligent man, not the son of an uneducated hog farmer. I was dumbfounded at the perfection that I held in my arms, the long, dark eyelashes, the wild mass of dark hair on top of her cone-shaped head, the soft fold of skin beneath her neck, the earnest sucking motion she made with her tiny lips. To me, all amazing.

On top of the engine, I place my face in my dirty hands. I cannot find her and I cannot bear the disgrace of returning home to Fielda without our daughter. I am shamed again. I have once again shirked my duties, this time as a father, and I imagine, again, the disappointment on my own father's face.

DEPUTY SHERIFF LOUIS

On my way over to the Gregory house, I contact our sheriff, Harold Motts. I need to update Harold as to what is going on. Let him know I have a bad feeling about this, that I don't think this is merely a case of two girls wandering off to play.

"What evidence do you have?" Motts questions me.

I have to admit that I have none. Nothing physical, anyway. There are no signs of a break-in, no sign of a struggle in either of the girls' rooms. Just a bad feeling. But Motts trusts me, we've known each other a long time.

"You thinking FPF, Louis?" he asks me.

FPF means Foul Play Feared in the police world. Just by uttering these three letters, a whole chain of events can unfurl. State police and the Division of Criminal Investigation will show up, the press and complications. I measure my words before I speak them.

"Something's not right here. I'd feel a lot better if you called in one of the state guys, just to check things out. Besides, once we call them in they foot the bill, right? Our department can't handle or afford a full-scale search and investigation on our own."

"I'll call DCI right now," Motts says to my relief. "Do we need a crime scene unit?"

"Not yet. Hopefully not at all, but we just might. I'm heading back over to the houses. Better call the reservists," I say. I am glad that Motts will have to be the one who wakes up our off-duty officers and the reservists, take them away from their families and their jobs. Willow Creek has a population of about eight thousand people, though it grows by about twelve hundred each fall due to the college. Our department is small; we have ten officers in all, three to a shift. Not near enough help when looking for two missing seven-year-olds. We'd need the reservists to help canvas the neighborhoods and question people.

"Louis," Motts says, "do you think this is anything like the McIntire case?"

"It crossed my mind," I admit. We had no leads in last year's abduction and subsequent murder of ten-year-old Jenna McIntire. That little girl haunted my sleep every single night. As much as I want to push aside the idea that something similar may have happened to Petra and Calli, I can't. It's my job to think this way.

PETRA

I can't keep up with them, they are too fast. I know he has seen me, because he turned his head toward me and smiled. Why don't they wait for me? I am calling to them, but they don't stop. I know they are somewhere ahead of me, but I am not sure where. I hear a voice in the distance. I am getting closer.

CALLI

The temperature of the day was steadily rising and the low vibration of cicadas filled their ears. Griff had become uncharacteristically hushed and Calli knew that he was thinking hard about something. Anxiety rose in Calli's chest, and she tried to push it down. She focused her attention on trying to locate all the cicada casings she could find. The brittle shells clung to tree trunks and from limbs, and she had counted twelve already. Ben used to collect the shells in an old jewelry box that once belonged to their grandmother. He would spend hours scanning the gray, hairy bark of shagbark hickory trees for the hollow skins, pluck them carefully from the wood and drop them into the red velvet-lined box. He would call out to Calli to come watch as a fierce-looking, demon-eyed cicada began its escape from its skin. They would intently watch the slow journey, the gradual cracking of the casing, the wet-winged emerging of the white insect, its patient wait for the hardening of its new exoskeleton. Ben would place its discarded shell on her outstretched palm and the tiny legs, pin-pricks of its former life, would tickle her hand.

"Even his wife knows something is going on," Griff muttered.

Calli's heart fluttered. Thirteen, fourteen…she counted.

"Even his wife knows he's too interested in her. Toni runs to him when she's in trouble," Griff's voice shook. "Does she come to me? Off she runs to Louis! And me playing daddy to you all these years!" Griff's fingers were now digging into her shoulder, his face purple with heat and dripping sweat. Mi-nuscule gnats were orbiting his head. Several stuck to his slick face like bits of dust. "Do you know how it makes me look that everyone, *everyone* knows about your mother?" He un-expectedly pushed Calli roughly to the ground and a loud whoosh of air escaped her as her breath was slammed from her.

"So, that gets a little noise outta ya? Is that what it takes to get you talking?"

Calli scrambled backward, crablike, as Griff loomed over her. Her head reeled, silent tears streaked down her face. He was her daddy; she had his small ears, the same sprinkle of freckles across her nose. At Christmas, they would pull out the large, green leather picture album that chronicled Calli's and Ben's milestones. The photo of Calli at six months, sitting on her father's lap, was nearly identical to the photo of Griff sitting on his mother's lap years earlier, the same toothless smile, the same dimpled cheeks looking out at them from the pictures.

Calli opened her mouth, willing the word to come forth. "Daddy," she wanted to cry. She wanted to stand and go to him, throw her arms as far around him as they could reach, and lean against the soft cotton of his T-shirt. Of course he was her daddy, the way they both stood with their hands on their hips and the way they both had to eat all their vegetables first, then the entire main dish, saving their milk for last. Her lips twisted to form the word again. "Daddy," she wished with her entire being to say. But nothing, just a soft gush of air.

Griff stepped closer to her, rage etched in his face. "You listen here. You may be livin' in my house, but I don't gotta like it!" He kicked out at her, the toe of his shoe striking her in the shin. Calli rolled herself into a tight little ball like a woolly bear caterpillar, protecting her head. "When we get home I'm gonna tell your mom that you went out to play and got lost and I came out to find you. Understand?" He struck out at her again, but this time Calli rolled away before he connected. The force of the kick caused him to falter and trip off the trail and into a pile of broken, sharp-tipped branches.

"Dammit!" he cursed, his hands scratched and bloodied. Calli was on her feet before Griff, her legs taut, ready for flight. He reached for her and Calli turned on the ball of her foot, a clumsy pirouette. Griff's ruddy hand grabbed at her arm, briefly catching hold of the smooth, tender skin on the back of her arm. Then she pulled away and was gone.

Antonia

I sit at the kitchen table, waiting. Louis told me not to go into Calli's room, that they may need to go through Calli's things to look for ideas of where she may have gone. I stared disbelievingly at him.

"What? Like a crime scene?" I asked him. Louis didn't look at me as he answered that it probably wouldn't come to that.

I'm not as worried about where she is as Martin is about Petra, and I wonder if I am a horrible mother. Calli has always been a wanderer. At grocery stores I would turn my head for a moment to inspect the label on a jar of peanut butter and she would be gone. I would dash through the aisles, searching. Calli would always be in the meat section, next to the lobster tank, one pudgy finger tapping the aquarium glass. She would turn to look at me, my shoulders limp with relief, a forlorn look on her face and ask, "Mom, does it hurt the crabs to have their hands tied like that?"

I'd rumple her soft, flyaway brown hair, and tell her, "No, it doesn't hurt them."

"Don't they miss the ocean?" she'd persist. "We should buy them all and let them go into the river."

"I think they'd die without ocean water," I'd explain. Then she'd gently tap the glass again and let me lead her away.

Of course this was before, when I didn't have to wonder if the next word would ever come. Before I woke up from dreams where Calli was speaking to me and I would be grasping at the sound of her voice, trying to remember its pitch, its cadence.

I have tried Griff's cell phone dozens of times. Nothing. I consider calling Griff's parents, who live downtown, but decide against it. Griff has never gotten along with his mom and dad. They drink more than he does and Griff hasn't been in the same room with his father for over eight years. I think this is one of the things that drew me to Griff in the beginning. The fact that we were both very much alone. My mother had died, my father far away in his own grief from her death. And Louis, well, that had ended. Not with great production, but softly, sadly. Griff had only his critical, indifferent parents. His only sister had moved far away, trying to remove herself from the stress and drama of living with two alcoholic parents. When Griff and I found each other, it was such a relief. We could breathe easily, at least for a while. Then things changed, like they always do. Like now, when once again, I can't find him when I need him.

I nervously fold and refold the dish towels from the kitchen drawer and I think I should give my brothers a call, tell them what's happening. But the thought of putting the fact that

Calli is lost or worse into words is too frightening. I look out
the kitchen window and see Martin and Louis step out of
Louis's car, Martin's shirt already soaked with the day's heat.
The girls are not with them. Ben will find them. They are of
one mind, and he will find them.

DEPUTY SHERIFF LOUIS

Martin Gregory and I approach Toni's front door. Martin has had no luck in locating his daughter or Toni's, and I am hopeful that the girls will be sitting at the kitchen table eating Toni's pancakes, or that they have shown up at the Gregorys' where Fielda waits for them. I am still distracted by my quarrel on the phone with Christine and I try to dismiss her harsh words from my mind.

Toni's door opens even before I can knock and she is there before me, still so beautiful, dressed in her typical summer outfit—a sleeveless T-shirt, denim shorts, and bare feet. She is brown from the sun, her many hours in her garden or from being outside with her children, I suppose.

"You didn't find them," Antonia states. It is not a question.

"No," I say, shaking my head, and we both step over the threshold into her home. She leads us inside, not to the living room as before but to the kitchen, where a pitcher of iced tea sits on the counter, along with three ice-filled glasses.

"It's too hot for coffee," she explains and begins to pour the tea. "Please sit," she invites, and we do.

"Have you any idea where else they could be?" Martin asks pleadingly.

"Ben's still out looking in the woods. He knows where Calli would go," Toni says. There is a curious lack of concern in her tone. Incredibly, she doesn't appear to think anything is actually amiss.

"Does Calli explore the woods often, Toni?" I ask her, carefully choosing my words.

"It's like a second home to her. Just like it was for us, Lou," she says, our eyes locking and a lifetime of memories pass between us. "She never goes far and she always comes back. Safe and sound," she adds, I think, for Martin's benefit.

"We don't allow Petra in the woods without an adult. It's too dangerous. She wouldn't know her way around," Martin says, not quite accusing.

I'm still thinking of the way Toni has called me "Lou," something she hasn't done for years. She resumed calling me *Louis* the day she became engaged to Griff. It was as if the more formal use of my name acted like a buffer, as if I hadn't already known the most intimate parts of her.

"Ben will be here soon, Martin," Antonia says soothingly. "If the girls are out there—" she indicates the forest with her thin, strong arms "—Ben will bring them home. I cannot imagine where else they may have gone."

"Maybe we should go out and look there, too," suggests Martin. "A search party. I mean, how far could two little girls have gone? We could get a group together, we would cover more ground. If more people were looking, we would have a better chance of finding them."

"Martin," I say, "we have no evidence that that is where the girls went. I would hate to focus all of our resources in one area and possibly miss another avenue to investigate. The woods cover over fourteen thousand acres and most of it isn't maintained. Hopefully, if they're out there, they have stayed on the trails. We've got a deputy out there now." I indicate the other police car that is now parked on the Clarks' lane. "I do think, however, we need to let the public know we have two misplaced little girls."

"Misplaced!" Martin bellows, his face darkening with anger. "I did not misplace my daughter. We put her to bed at eight-thirty last night and when I awoke this morning she was not in her bed. She was in her pajamas, for God's sake. When are you going to acknowledge the fact that someone may have taken her from her bedroom? When are you—"

"Martin, Martin, I didn't mean to suggest that you or Toni did anything wrong here," I say, trying to calm him. "There is no reason to believe they were taken, no signs of forced entry. Her tennis shoes are gone, Martin. Do you think an intruder would stop to make Petra put on her shoes before they left? That doesn't make sense."

Martin sighs. "I'm sorry. I just cannot imagine where they could have gone. If they have not been…been abducted and they are not at their usual playing spots, the forest just seems to be the logical place for them to go, especially if Calli is so comfortable there."

Antonia nods. "I bet Ben will be here shortly with the

two of them, their tails between their legs at the worry they have caused."

A thought occurs to me. "Toni, is there a pair of Calli's shoes missing?"

"I don't know." Toni sits up a little straighter, her glass of tea perspiring in her hand. "I'll go check."

Toni rises and climbs the stairs to Calli's room. Martin sips his tea, sets his glass down, then, unsure of what to do with his hands, picks up the glass again.

Martin and I sit in an uncomfortable silence for a moment and then he speaks.

"I have never understood how Petra and Calli became such good friends. They have nothing in common, really. The girl does not even talk. What in the world could two seven-year-olds do for fun if only one of them speaks?" He looks at me with exasperation. "Petra would say, 'Could Calli and I have a sandwich? Just peanut butter for Calli, she doesn't like jelly.' I mean, how would she know that when Calli did not speak? I just do not understand it," he says, shaking his head.

"Kindred spirits," a soft voice comes from the stairwell. Toni steps into the kitchen carrying a pair of tattered tennis shoes in one hand and an equally worn pair of flip-flops in the other. "They are kindred spirits," she repeats to our questioning looks. "They know what the other needs. Petra can read Calli like a book, what game she wants to play, if her feelings are hurt, anything. And Calli is the same. She knows that Petra is afraid of thunderstorms and will take her to her bedroom and play the music so loud that it covers the sound of the thunder. Or if Petra is feeling blue, Calli can get her giggling. Calli makes the best faces—she can get all of us laughing. They are best friends. I don't know how to explain how it works, but it does for them. And I'm glad of it. Petra doesn't care that Calli can't talk and Calli doesn't care that Petra is afraid of thunder and still sucks her thumb sometimes." Toni pauses and holds up the shoes. "Her shoes are still here. We're going shopping for school shoes next week. Her cowboy boots are still in the garage, I saw them earlier. Calli doesn't have her shoes on. She wouldn't go into the woods without her shoes."

Toni's chin begins to wobble and for the first time since her girl has gone missing, she looks scared. I put my hand on her arm, and she does not pull away.

BEN

I have been to all the places where we play. First Willow Wallow, where we would swing from the branches of the weeping willows, pretending to be monkeys. I looked underneath each of the seven willows, thinking that I would find you and Petra there, hiding. I went down to Lone Tree Bridge, one skinny fallen tree over Willow Creek. We would take turns walking across, to see who could cross the quickest. I always won. You weren't there, either. I walked up and down Spring Peeper Pond Trail, sure that I'd find you two looking for tree frogs. But I was wrong on that count, too. I don't want to come home without you.

I begin to think that maybe Dad did take you with him fishing. That would be just like him, to all of a sudden want to do the dad thing and spend time with you. He could ignore us for weeks, then look at us all interested-like and take us to do something real fun. One time he decided to take me fishing down at the creek. We went in the evening, just him and me. We didn't have any night crawlers so we swiped some Velveeta cheese from the fridge and used that. We sat for hours on the shore, just where the creek is widest. We didn't even talk much, just slapped at mosquitoes and pulled in bullheads and sunfish, laughing because they were so small. We had a bet on who could catch the smallest fish, five bucks, and I won. I caught a sunfish the size of a guppy. We ate peanuts, threw the shells into the water and drank soda. When the sun started to go down we could hear the crickets chirping and Dad said that we could figure out just how warm it was out by the number of chirps that a cricket made. I said, "No way!" and he said, "Yes way!" And he told me how. That was the best day. So I'm thinking he thought you and him should do some bonding and took you fishing with Roger, but didn't think to tell anyone. But then again, I don't think he would take two little girls fishing with him. Who knows, he's tough to figure out sometimes.

You've always been a good sport, Calli, I'll give you that. You're no girly-girl. I remember the time when you were one and just starting to walk—all wobbly and unsure. I was six and Mom told us to go outside and play. You followed me around, trying to do everything I did. I picked up the bruised apples from the ground under our apple tree and threw them at the side of the garage and you'd do the same. I didn't much like having a baby following me, but I loved how you'd say, "Beh, Beh!" for Ben. Whenever you'd see me, it was like you were all surprised that I was there, like you were all lucky because I stepped in the room, even if you'd seen me, like, ten minutes earlier.

Mom would laugh and say, "See, Ben, Calli loves her big brother, don'tcha, Calli?" And you would stamp your fat little feet and squeal, "brudder, brudder!" Then you'd come over and grab my leg and squeeze.

Later that same year, when I turned seven, I got the coolest pair of cowboy boots for my birthday. They were black and had red stitching. I wore those things everywhere, all the time. And if a baby could be jealous of boots, you sure were. You'd catch me wearing my boots and admiring myself in the mirror and you'd just go right after those boots and try to pull them off of my feet. It was actually kinda funny; Mom would sit on the bedroom floor and laugh her head off. I don't know if you thought I loved those cowboy boots more than you, or if you just enjoyed seeing me all riled up, but that got to be your favorite pastime for a while. You always ended up getting at least one boot off of me, because you were so much littler than me and I couldn't just kick you away from me. I'd get in a ton of trouble if I did that. Lots of times you'd just sneak up on me while I was watching TV and you'd latch on until that boot just slid right off my foot, then you'd run. Most of the time you'd just throw the boot down the steps or out in the yard, but one time you threw it in the toilet. Man, was I mad. I refused to wear them after that. Mom washed it out and set it out in the sun to dry, but still I wouldn't wear those boots. But you sure did. They were yours after that, even though they were way too big for you. You'd wear them with every outfit you had, shorts, dresses, even your pajamas. More than once Mom had to pull them off your feet after you fell asleep in bed. You still wear them once in a while. In fact, I wouldn't be surprised if you weren't out in the woods in them right now, stomping around.

When you stopped talking isn't real clear to me, but I know

you were four and I was nine. One day you're wearing my boots, telling me the dumbest knock-knock jokes and giggling like mad, and I'd roll my eyes. Then one day nothing, no words. It just got so quiet around here. Like when you step outside after the first real big snowstorm of the year and everything's all smothered in white and no one has shoveled yet and no cars are on the road. Everything is still, and it's nice. For a while. Then it gets kind of creepy, a quiet so big you yell just to hear your own voice, and the buried outdoors gives nothing back.

CALLI

Calli ran down Broadleaf Trail until it intersected with River Bottom, where the trail traveled downward at a steep angle, winding its way down to the creek. Each dip or rise in the forest had its own smell, sweet with spiral flower, pungent with wild onion, fetid with rotting leaves. Each hollow and turn had its own climate, warm and moist, cool and arid. As Calli ran down toward the river and deeper into the woods, the temperature dropped, the trees grew closer together, the vegetation gathered in tight around her ankles.

Calli could hear Griff's large body pounding the trail above her. Her chest burned with each breath, but still she ran, spindly tree trunks and craggy bluffs blurred in the corners of her eyes. Patches of sun briefly shone brilliantly on the ground before her. A stitch in her side caused her to slow and then stop. She listened carefully to the woods. The narrow creek gurgled, a cardinal called and insects droned. Calli searched for a place to hide. Off the trail, she spotted the remains of several fallen trees arranged in a crisscross pattern, behind which she could rest for perhaps a few moments, unseen. She climbed over the gnarled pile and dropped carefully to the side away from the trail. Once seated, Calli pulled stray twigs and branches around her to camouflage her pink nightgown. She tried to steady her breathing. She did not want Griff to hear her huffing and find her trapped within the middle of the branches with no quick escape.

Minutes passed with no Griff, only the comforting knock of a woodpecker somewhere above that rang out over the usual forest sounds. Calli shook in spite of the heat, and rubbed the goose bumps on her arms. The rage that radiated off Griff needled at Calli's memories and she tried to close her eyes to them. *That day.*

On that day in December, it was cold. She was four, and Ben was off sledding with some of his friends. Her mother, belly heavy with pregnancy, was making hot cocoa, plopping white cushiony marshmallows into the steamy chocolate, then adding an ice cube to Calli's mug to cool it. Calli was at the kitchen table, drawing paper in front of her and an arrangement of markers around her.

"What should we name the baby, Cal?" her mother asked as she set the hot chocolate before her. "Don't burn your mouth now."

Calli set aside her drawing, a picture of Christmas trees, reindeer and a roly-poly Santa. "Popsicle, I think," she replied, pressing a spoon against a melting marshmallow.

"Popsicle?" her mother asked, laughing. "That's an unusual name. What else?"

"Cupcake," Calli giggled.

"Cupcake? Is that her middle name?"

Calli nodded, her smile filled with sticky white marshmallows. "Birthday Cake," she added. "Popsicle Cupcake Birthday Cake, that's her name."

"I like it," her mother said, grinning, "but every time I say her name, I think I'll get hungry. How about Lily or Evelyn? Evelyn was my mother's name."

Calli made a face and tentatively took a sip of her cocoa. She felt the burn of the liquid traveling down her throat and she waved a hand in front of her mouth as if to fan away the warmth.

The back door opened, bringing with it a swirl of frozen air that made Calli squeal. "Daddy!" she cried out, "Daddy's home!" She stood on her chair and reached her arms out, snagging onto his neck as he passed by her. The cold that hung on his parka seeped through her sweatshirt and he tried to set Calli down.

"Not now, Calli, I need to talk to your mom." Calli did not release his neck as he clumsily approached her mother and he shifted her so that she rested on his hip.

The smell of beer bit at her nose. "Stinky." She grimaced.

"I thought you were getting here hours ago," Antonia said in a measured tone. "Did you just roll into town?"

"I've been gone three weeks, what're a few hours more?" Griff's words were innocent, but had a bite to them. "I stopped at O'Leary's for a drink with Roger."

Antonia scanned him up and down. "From the smell of things and the way you're lurching around, you had more than a few. You've been gone for a month. I figured once you got back to town, you'd want to see your family."

Calli heard the tension in their voices and squirmed to get out of Griff's arms. He held her tightly.

"I do wanna see my family, but I wanna see my friends, too." Griff opened the refrigerator and searched for a beer, but found none. He slammed the door, causing the glass bottles to rattle against each other.

"I don't want to fight." Antonia went to Griff and hugged him awkwardly, her belly an obstacle. Calli reached her arms out toward her mother, but Griff whisked her away and sat down at the kitchen table, Calli on his lap.

"I had an interesting chat at O'Leary's," Griff said conversationally. Antonia waited, poised for what she knew was to come. "Some guys were saying that Loras Louis has been hanging around here lately."

Antonia turned to a cupboard and began pulling dinner plates down. "Oh, he shoveled the drive one day for me last week. He was over checking on Mrs. Norland. The mail carrier said she wasn't getting her mail out of her mailbox. She was fine. Anyway, he saw me out shoveling and asked if he could help," she explained, turning to see Griff's reaction. "Ben was sick, throwing up. He couldn't shovel, so I went out to do it. He stopped by, no big deal. He didn't come in the house."

Griff continued to stare at Antonia, his face implacable.

"What? You think I would…we would… I'm seven months pregnant!" Antonia laughed humorlessly. "Forget it, think what you want. I'm going to go lie down." Antonia charged out of the kitchen. Calli could hear her weighted, clumsy steps on the stairs.

Griff shot from his chair, raising Calli up with him. The

force caused her to bite down on her tongue and she cried out in pain, the tinny taste of blood filling her mouth.

"I'm talking to you!" he shouted after her. "Don't you want to hear what everyone is saying?" He moved quickly to the bottom of the stairs. "Come back here!" Calli could see a purple vein pulse at his temple, could see the tendons of his neck strain against his skin. She began to cry loudly and struggled against Griff.

"Put her down!" Antonia called down to him. "You're scaring her!"

"Shut up! Shut up!" Griff bellowed at Calli, climbing the steps two at a time, her neck jerking violently with each step.

"Put her down, Griff. You're hurting her!" Antonia was crying now, her arms outstretched to Calli, reaching for her.

"Dirty whore! Taking up with him again. How does that make me look? I'm away slaving to make money for this family, and you're sitting here, taking up with your old boyfriend."

Spittle flew from his lips, mingling with Calli's tears and she arched her back violently, trying to escape his grip.

Antonia screeched, "Oh my God, Griff! Stop it. Stop it, please!"

Griff had reached the top of the steps, stood next to Antonia and yanked her arm. *Slut.* Calli's hysterical wails nearly drowned Griff's ranting.

"Mommy! Mommy!"

"Shut up! Shut up!" Griff tossed Calli to the floor at the top of the stairs. Her head bounced sickeningly off the hardwood floor and she was silent for a moment, her desperate eyes on her mother, who was shoving Griff away from her to get to Calli. Griff held tightly to her mother's arm and she snapped back like a rubber band. For an instant, before Toni tumbled backward down the steps, Griff nearly steadied her. Calli and Griff both watched in horror as Antonia's back slammed into the steps and she fell to the ground below.

"Mommy!" Calli yelped as Griff skidded down the steps to Antonia. He knelt before her where she was crumpled. She was conscious, her face twisted in pain, her arms cradled around her belly, moaning silently.

"Can you sit up? Shut up, Calli!" he barked. Calli continued to sob as Griff settled Antonia into a sitting position.

"The baby, the baby," she cried.

"It will be all right, it will be all right," Griff said pleadingly. "I'm sorry, I'm sorry! Calli, shut the hell up. Can you walk? Here, let's get you to the couch." Griff gently raised Antonia to her feet and led her to the sofa, where he laid her down and placed an afghan over her. "Just rest, just rest. It will be okay."

Calli continued to scream in the background, her weeping getting closer as she made her way down the stairs and moved to her mother's side. Antonia, eyes half-closed, put one arm toward Calli.

"Get away!" Griff hollered. "Jesus, stay out of the way, and *shut up!*" Griff's hands were shaking as he snatched Calli up and took her into the kitchen. "Sit here and shut up!" Griff paced around the kitchen, pulled at his hair, and wiped his mouth with one trembling hand.

Griff bent down to Calli, her tearful screams dropping to grief-stricken hiccups, and whispered into her ear for one full minute. During those interminable sixty seconds Calli's eyes blinked rapidly at Griff's words. His breath hissed across the delicate crevices of her ear and mingled with her mother's soft cries. Then he stood and rushed out the back door with a gust of wintry, bitter wind, taking away more than he arrived with.

That evening, after Ben came home, Calli and Ben sat vigil around their mother as she lay on the couch. Her desperate, mournful moans filled the room until Ben finally called Officer Louis and the ambulance arrived, just in time to deliver a perfect, silent, birdlike baby girl, whose skin was the same bluish color as her mother's lips. The paramedics swiftly whisked the breathless infant away, but not before Calli gently patted her strawberry-colored hair.

Years later, Calli sat among the fallen tree limbs, alert and tense, remembering her father's whispers that still hummed in her ear. She heard a rustle from somewhere behind her. It couldn't be her father. Ranger Phelps? Hope rose in her chest. Did she dare to come out from her hiding place? She weighed her options. If she emerged, Ranger Phelps would surely help her get home, but what if they came across her father? He would hand her over to her father and she wouldn't be able to tell the ranger what had happened. No. She needed to stay put. She knew her way home, she just needed to be patient and wait Griff out. He would give up soon, he'd want to get to fishing with Roger, he'd want a drink. The olive-green pants of Ranger Phelps's uniform flashed past her and Calli resisted the urge to leap from the twiggy den she had created and grab hold of the man. Just as quickly as he'd appeared, he was gone, fading into the lacy ferns, his footfalls silent upon the spongy earth. Calli sat back, tucked her knees beneath her chin and covered her head with her arms. If Calli couldn't see her father, she figured, he certainly wouldn't be able to see her.

MARTIN

I stop by my home to find Fielda standing at the front door, her kinky black hair pulled back from her face, her glasses sitting crookedly on her nose. She looks at me expectantly, I shake my head no and her face falls.

"What do we do?" she asks pitifully.

"The deputy sheriff says to call anyone we can think of to keep an eye out for them. He says to find a picture of her to put on fliers. I am going to take the photos of the girls to the police station. They're going to make the fliers for us, and then I'm going to find some people to help me pass them out."

Fielda reaches for me and circles her arms around me. "What are we going to do?" she cries softly.

"We are going to find her, Fielda. We are going to find Petra and bring her home. I promise." We stand there for a moment, letting the weight of my promise soak into both of our skins until finally Fielda steps away from me.

"You go get those fliers," she tells me firmly. "I am going

to call people. I'll start with the *A*'s and work my way through the alphabet." She kisses me goodbye and I squeeze her hand before I shut the door.

As I drive down the streets of my town, my eyes scan every inch of sidewalk, searching for Petra. I try to see in windows and crane my neck to look into backyards and several times I nearly veer off the road. When I pull in front of the police station my legs are shaking, and it's with weak knees that I trudge through the door. I introduce myself to a man at a desk. When his eyes meet mine I search them to see if I can discern what he thinks of me. Does he suspect me? Does he feel sorry for me? I cannot tell.

"I'll get those fliers for you right away, Mr. Gregory," he says and leaves me.

Now in the sanctuary of my office at St. Gilianus, each excruciating moment of the day stabs at my mind. I cannot concentrate. Sitting in my office on campus with a pile of papers, my beautiful daughter's face gazing out at me from them, I can almost feel Petra's presence in the room. Petra loves to sit beneath my large walnut desk. There she plays with her dolls, which she carries in a large canvas bag with her name painted on the front of it. As I do paperwork, I can hear the intricate conversations that her dolls hold with one another, and I smile at the thought. Petra enjoys learning all about the mysterious history of the college. She walks with me through the buildings, sunlight shining through the jewel-colored stained-glass windows depicting the saints and martyrs of the Catholic Church. She often makes me pause in front of the window showing St. Gilianus, the namesake of the college. In brilliant hues of saffron, lapis, copper and jade, the artist tells the story of Gilianus's life, an old man dressed in brown robes, holding a scroll, flanked by a large bear and a flock of blackbirds. I repeatedly tell her about St. Gilianus, also known as St. Gall or St. Callo, a man born in Ireland sometime in the sixth century. Legend had it that Gilianus, a hermit, ordered a bear in the woods where he lived to bring his reclusive clan wood for their fire, and the bear obeyed. I describe to her the tale of how King Sigebert of Austrasia, now northeastern France and western Germany, implored Gilianus to free his promised wife of demons. Gilianus obliged, and at his command freed the tortured woman of demons who left her in the form of a flock of blackbirds. Petra always shivers with delight at this story and rubs the musical note charm on her necklace nervously.

My colleagues make special stops to my office when they know Petra is visiting. They ask her about school and friends, and she draws pictures for them to hang in their offices. My students are equally enchanted with Petra; she remembers the names of everyone who happens to meet with me while she is present. One distressed junior made an impromptu visit to my office this past winter while Petra played happily under my desk. The young man, normally confident and charming, was near tears, worried about graduating on time. He could not concentrate on his studies, and needed to get another part-time job to help pay his tuition and rent.

"Lucky," I said to the student, "you have too much on your plate right now. It is natural for you to feel stress." I hastened to lure Petra from under the desk and introduce her to the young man before he became too emotional in front of her.

"This is my daughter, Petra. She often comes to my office on weekends to help me. Petra, this is Lucky Thompson, one of my students."

Petra looked critically at Lucky, taking in his shaggy hair, baggy jeans and sweatshirt. "Is Lucky your real name?" she asked boldly.

"No, my real name's Lynton, but everyone just calls me Lucky," he explained.

"Good move," Petra said, nodding her head. "So are you lucky?"

"Most of the time, I guess."

"Do you have a pet?" she quizzed him.

"I do, a dog," he responded, amused.

"Because, you know, they say that having a pet helps relieve stress. What's your dog's name?"

"Sergeant. He's a golden retriever."

"Cool. Dad, doesn't Grandma need help at the café? Maybe Lucky could work there," Petra suggested. With a phone call to my mother-in-law, I confirmed that this was true and arranged for her to meet with Lucky.

"You're a cool kid, Petra," Lucky said, smiling, chucking her under the chin and rubbing the top of her head.

So in her effortless, magical way, Petra once again made everything all better, and the young man left with his spirits buoyed and a lead on a part-time job at Mourning Glory.

I stand now, my joints creaking with the effort. I am very much feeling my age today. I pick up the stack of fliers and a roll of Scotch tape, lock the door to my office, and begin the unfathomable task of tacking my child's face to windows and telephone poles around town.

ANTONIA

My ear aches from all the phone calls I have been making, trying to find Calli and Petra. I've called everyone that I could think of, neighbors, classmates and teachers even. No one has seen them. I can hear, in the pause on the other side of the phone, a silent judgment. I've lost my child, the most precious gift, somehow I let her get away from me. I know what they're thinking, that first I let my daughter's voice be snatched away, now her whole being is gone. "What kind of mother is she?" is what they are not saying. Instead, they wish me luck and prayers and say that they will go out looking and tell everyone they know to look out for the girls also. They are very kind.

I am thinking that I should have put up posters the day Calli lost her voice. *MISSING,* they would say, *Calli Clark's beautiful voice. Four years old, but sounds much older, has a very advanced vocabulary, last heard on December 19th, right after her mother fell down the stairs; please call with any information regarding its whereabouts, REWARD.* Silly, I know, especially when

I've done so little to try and actually help Calli find her voice again. Oh, I've done the basics. Took her to a doctor, to a family counselor even. But nothing has changed. Not one word has been spoken. I have worked so hard trying to forget the day I lost the baby, but little snippets come to me at the oddest times. I could be weeding in my garden and would remember how I named her Poppy; I couldn't actually name her Popsicle Cupcake Birthday Cake, but Poppy seemed appropriate. She had the prettiest red hair; she looked like a little, wilted red-petaled flower when they brought her to me to say goodbye. They had tried so hard to save her, they said, but she never even took one breath in this world.

I could be standing at the kitchen sink washing out a pan when I would recall that day after Griff helped me to the couch, seeing him guide Calli to the kitchen and whispering something to her. I remember thinking, "Oh, he is trying to reassure her, to calm her with comforting words." But after that she said nothing, ever. I never asked Griff what he had said to Calli, and even worse, I never asked Calli.

I step outside and the high temperature instantly assaults me. I see the heat rising from the road, making the air wavery and thick-looking, and the saw of the cicadas is nearly deafening. Ben is walking slowly out of the forest. His shoulders are hunched and his hands are stuffed in his front pockets, he is slick with sweat. To me he looks like a little boy again, always so sweet and unsure, wanting to be one of the guys but not certain of just how to do that. He has always been large for his age. His classmates look up at him, impressed with his bulk, but are always a little puzzled at his gentleness. "Sorry," he'd always say if he knocked down an opponent during a basketball game, and he'd stop in his play to make sure he got up okay.

"Sorry, Mom," Ben whispers as he brushes past me into the house.

I follow him in and find him leaning against the kitchen counter. I reach up into a cupboard and pull down a glass, fill it with ice and lemonade and hand it to him.

"Thank you for trying, Ben. I know you did your best. There isn't anyone who knows the woods better than you do. If they were in there, I know you would have found them."

He takes a long swallow of the lemonade and makes a pinched face at its sourness. "I'm going back out. I'm gonna call the guys and we'll go out looking again. We need to go in deeper. She may have gone farther in, she likes to explore."

"That's a good idea. I'll go, too. I'll call Mrs. Norland to come over and wait, in case they come back. I'll pack some water, you go call the boys."

Ben has his hand on the phone when it rings; he pulls back as if shocked, lets it ring again, and then picks it up.

"Hello?" It is a question. "Just a moment, please." He hands the receiver to me and whispers, "Louis."

"Lou?" I say, and I find myself getting teary. "Any word?"

"No, nothing yet. I've contacted the state police and they're sending a guy over. He'll be here in an hour or so. He'll be wanting to talk to you and Ben and Mr. and Mrs. Gregory, too." He pauses for a moment. "We've tried to contact Griff and Roger Hogan, but can't get a hold of them. Roger's wife said his plan was to pick up Griff about four this morning and to drive over to Julien. I called over to the Julien police station.

An officer is going to drive to the cabin and let them know what's going on."

I try to imagine Griff's reaction to finding out that the girls are gone. Would he be worried, would he come back right away, or stay there and let me deal with this whole ordeal? How I had loved Griff, and still do, I guess, in my way. He was exciting and at one time, before the alcohol overtook my place in Griff's heart, he needed me. "Should Ben and I come into the station?" I ask, returning my attention to the man I had grown up with, the man I should have married. But if I had done that, there would be no Ben, no Calli.

"How 'bout I call you, and we'll drive on over to you. That way if Calli comes home, you'll be there. Toni...I need to tell you, this guy from the state, he does this sort of thing for a living, looking into missing kids. He's seen everything, and he doesn't know you. He'll ask some...some questions you won't like."

"What do you mean?" I ask, and instantly realization dawns on me. "You mean that he might think that we may have had something to do with this? Oh my God." All of a sudden, I feel dirty and guilty.

"I'll be there with you, Toni. These big shots tend to take over, but he's good. He'll help us find Calli and Petra."

"All right, Lou, we'll be here," I say faintly. A silence as heavy as this summer's heat hangs between us.

"Toni, I've reported Calli and Petra missing to the NCIC," Louis says, as an afterthought, as if he wants me to think it's really no big deal. But I know otherwise.

"What exactly is that?" I ask.

"It stands for the National Crime Information Center.

They have a centralized Missing Person file. This way other law enforcement centers will be aware that we're looking for the girls. And I've put a Be On the Lookout bulletin for the entire county. Everyone will be looking for Petra and Calli."

"Oh, that's a good idea," I say, my mind spinning. "What about an AMBER Alert? Can you issue one of those?"

"AMBER Alerts are only issued when it is confirmed that a child has been abducted. We don't know that for certain." We are silent for a moment. "Toni, it will be okay, I promise," Louis finally says with resolve.

I hang up the phone. Ben is watching me, waiting for me to tell him what to do. "Go on and take a shower, Ben. Someone from the state police is coming over—"

"What about looking more?" he interrupts with annoyance.

"Louis says we need to do this, so we will. Go on and take a shower." I sit down once again to wait.

CALLI

Calli's muscles went rigid at hearing a rustling in the brush, then a loud pop of a branch breaking. She was instantly watchful, her heart pounding a dull thud that she could feel in her temple. She sat frozen, waiting for the next sound, half expecting Griff to peek over the mound of tree limbs. A faint crunch of sticks, too light-footed to be Griff, and a whitetail deer stepped into her line of vision, the reddish-brown coat lightly speckled with the white spots of a fawn. It stood still as it sensed Calli's presence. The deer's ears were long and slender, reminding Calli of a jackrabbit, its eyes black and gleaming, the color of the mica minerals Ben kept on his dresser at home. The two regarded one another for a while, and then the curious fawn stepped closer to Calli, so near that if Calli dared she would be able to stroke its polished black nose. Holding her breath, Calli shifted her weight so that she was on her knees. The deer startled and took several steps backward and then stopped. Again they observed one another, both long-limbed and knobby-kneed, alone. Stepping tentatively toward Calli, the deer sniffed the air around her experimentally. Calli dared to pull herself out of the fallen boughs and the deer stutter-stepped back in hesitation. Yet again they stood placidly, each scrutinizing the other, until the fawn took two bold steps to Calli. Surprised, Calli stepped backward, bumping into a birch tree, its white, paperlike bark peeling in her hands as she tried to steady herself. Once recovered, Calli moved toward the deer, one grubby hand outstretched. And on it went. A soundless, tender waltz, under a dome of shimmering shades of green, a carpet of soil under them, lost for a moment, together, each in their own quiet room, saying nothing, but whispering to each other in their odd little dance.

Deputy Sheriff Louis

At my desk, cluttered with the horrible reminder of two missing girls, I wait for the agent from the state. I have just asked Meg, our dispatcher, to send one of our reservists, David Glass, a pharmacist, to be our point man at the homes. He will park our oldest, dented squad car at a point between the two homes. All the information gathered during the investigation will be relayed to David.

The picture of Calli that has been passed out to all police officers stares up at me. She looks so like her mother, the same chestnut hair and brown eyes, the same messy ponytail that Toni had when she was young.

Toni and I met when we were seven, in the winter of our first-grade year. My mother, my sister, brother and I had just moved to tiny Willow Creek from Chicago. My father had died unexpectedly the year before of a heart attack and through a friend, my mom got a job at the college. The quiet and vastness of land made me lonely for the sound of traffic and the familiar sound of neighbors laughing and arguing. I remember lying in my new bed, in my very own room, missing the sound of my little brother's soft snores and not being able to sleep for the calm of the country. Our neighbors were acres away. The only sounds were that of a dog barking or the wind blowing. After so many sleepless nights, my mother finally bought me a small radio to place beside my bed to fill the silence that kept me awake.

I started my first day at Willow Creek Elementary School reluctantly and pretended to be sick; my mother sat on the edge of my bed and looked me in the eye. "Loras Michael Louis," she began gravely, "I, of all people, know that it is not easy to leave what you know and begin something new. Your father is not around to help now. You are the oldest and everyone is looking to see what you do. If you lie in bed moping, so will they. If you get up cheerful and ready to tackle the world, so will they."

"Mom, Katie is three months old, she ain't tackling anybody," I sassed.

"Well, you're the oldest male figure she has to go by now. How you act is what she will grow up thinking what a man should be like. Put that in your pipe and smoke it, mister! Get up."

"Sheesh, Mom, okay."

I crawled out of bed, got dressed and prayed that someone in this godforsaken town would know how to play a good game of stick ball come spring.

On that first day of school my mother drove us. The sky was robin's egg–blue and the ground was covered in snow so brilliantly white it hurt my eyes to look at it. It was very cold and we could see our breath even though my mother had the heat turned to high in the rusty blue Plymouth Arrow she drove. The school was a large, aged, red-bricked, two-story set on the edge of town. It was actually bigger than my old school in Chicago, which was a small private elementary school, but they looked much alike, and that was comforting to me. The next thing I noticed was that students of all ages were running to the back of the school, clutching red plastic sleds and wooden toboggans.

"Come on, Dave," I said to my brother, who was entering kindergarten. "Let's go!" I grabbed my book bag, said a quick goodbye to my mother and we tumbled out of the car.

"Hey!" she yelled. "Don't you want me to walk you in?"

"No, thanks." I threw my bag over my shoulder and we followed the snow-crusted footprints to the back of the school. It was a breathtaking sight to my seven-year-old eyes. Hidden behind the school was an enormous hill that ran the length of the school and then some. The hill was steep in some areas and more level in others and ended in an immense meadow perhaps two football fields long. Kids formed lines at the top of the hill to take their turn down the various sledding paths; there was a definite pecking order to the arrangement. The older kids, probably seventh and eighth graders, were organized near a portion of the hill that descended at a sharp angle and had a number of man-made mounds, carefully rounded and patted to send sleds airborne. The smaller children gathered around the shorter hills with less of an incline. I watched as children whooped with glee on their way down the slopes and viewed their determined journey back up the hill, dragging their sleds behind them.

One small figure caught my eye. The child—a boy, I figured, my age or younger—was decked out in black snow pants, an oversize black winter coat, and black rubber boots. Two mismatched mittens, one red, one green, were on his hands, and a black stocking cap was pulled low over his eyes. I watched as he confidently carried a silver dish-shaped sled to the edge of the big kids' hill and got in line behind three other towering boys. The boys turned, laughed and unceremoniously shoved him out of the line. Not intimidated, he squeezed back into his spot and rooted himself soundly, ignoring the taunts flung at him. When it was his turn, he situated himself onto the disk and a boy behind him shoved the sled with the toe of his big hiking boot. The sledder went careening down the hill, spinning and bouncing off the icy bumps, going airborne for a moment only to strike another frozen ramp. I held my breath for this poor soul who was sure to be killed with all of us as witnesses.

"Holy crap," Dave whispered beside me and I nodded in agreement.

It seemed like forever, him going down that hill, his head jerking around on his neck, but he held on, dangerously tipping only once. Finally, his sled hit the final speed bump so violently that his stocking cap went flying and a brown rope of hair soared behind him in a loose ponytail. He was a *she,* I realized with shock, and as she slid the final two hundred feet to a stop, I had fallen completely and utterly in love. I still have to smile at the memory and am still astounded at how quickly Toni had cornered off a spot in my heart. I am even more amazed that she still has claim to it.

I look up from my desk. I know who my visitor is; I stand and go to greet Agent Fitzgerald from the state police.

BEN

From the window of my bedroom, I see the deputy sheriff pull into the Gregorys' driveway and I crane my neck to see who is with him, hoping it's you, Calli. It isn't. A small man, dressed in brown pants, white shirt and a red tie gets out. I watch as he looks the Gregory house up and down and then walks with Deputy Sheriff Louis to the front door. The policeman Mom was talking about, I figure. Calli, you sure are causing one mighty fuss, and how you do that without saying a word amazes me.

I was supposed to go spend the night at Raymond's house tonight, but I guess that's out, at least until we find you. You never did like it when I spent a night away from home. You'd sit on my bed as I'd pack my backpack, looking at me so sadlike, I'd have to keep saying over and over, "I'll be back tomorrow, Cal, it's no big deal." But you'd still look so disappointed that I'd let you play with my chess set, the one Dad got me for Christmas that one year, and you'd feel a little better.

Mom was about as bad as you. Oh, she'd put on this brave

face and say, "Of course you have to go to your overnight, Ben. We young ladies will be just fine here, won't we, Calli? We have Daddy here now to keep us company."

Truth is, I'd only go on overnights when Dad was home from traveling. I could never stand the thought of you and Mom home completely alone, and sometimes it was just better for me to be out of the way when Dad came home.

Do you remember the night of the "talking lessons"? Last fall, when you were in first grade, and Mom was out, went to some meeting with your teachers, I think, and we were left home with Dad. He thought it was ridiculous, all this to-do at school because of you not talking. He started out all excited, saying, "Calli, you wanna do something nice for your mom?"

Of course you nodded, all happy. Dad had you come over to him where he was sitting in his favorite green chair and sat you on his lap. You looked at him, just waiting for him to tell you what great surprise he had for Mom. Dad looked so glad that I came over and asked if I could help surprise her, too.

Dad smiled. "That's nice, Ben, but this is something that only Calli can do for Mom." Then he looked to you. "Calli, wouldn't it be wonderful if you could tell Mom you love her? That would make her so happy, and me, too."

All of a sudden, your face got all sad, because you knew Dad just asked you to do the impossible. Dad said, "Ah, come on, Calli, you can do it! Just make your mouth say *Mom*."

You started shaking your head and squinching your eyes up tight. "Come on, Calli, say it. *Mom*." He stretched his lips out wide while he said the word, like someone trying to get a baby to talk.

You kept your eyes shut and your lips squeezed together.

"You can do it, Calli. Don'tcha want to make your mom happy? Mmm-ahhh-mmm."

You were having none of it and tried to hop off Dad's lap. "Oh, no, you don't. Come on, Calli, say it. Say it!" he shouted. He held you on him with one arm and grabbed your face with the other, trying to force your mouth into a shape to say the word.

"Stop it," I said, real soft. But he kept right on going, even though you were crying, but not making any noise. "Stop it!" I said louder and this got Dad's attention.

"Go on outta here, Ben. Me and Calli are just having a talking lesson. Go on now," he said.

"Stop it!" I yelled. "Leave her alone! She can't say it, she can't do it! If she could, she would've already! Leave her alone!" I know. I couldn't believe it myself. You stopped crying and both you and Dad looked at me like Martians had landed or something.

"Stay out of it, Ben. Go on to your room," he said in a quiet voice, but I knew he meant business.

"No. Leave her alone, she can't do it!"

Dad stood up real quick and dumped you on your butt to the floor. And I yelled, "Run, Calli!" But you didn't. You just sat there on the floor and looked up at us.

"Fabulous," Dad said all huffy. "I got a retarded mute little girl and a smart-ass know-it-all boy. Fabulous. Maybe there's another way to get her to talk. Stand up, Calli."

You did, quick.

"Ben here thinks he has all the answers. Thinks that you can't talk. Well, I know different, because I remember when you could talk. You yapped just fine. Maybe you just need a little incentive to get that mouth of yours going." Then Dad swung out at me and hit me in the back of my head, about knocked my block off. You covered up your eyes again, but Dad pried your fingers down to make you watch. Then he belted me a few more times, in the stomach, on my back.

He kept looking at you, shouting, "If you talk, Calli, I'll stop." Then he'd punch me again. "Tell me to stop, and I will. Come on, Calli, won't you even say something to help your big brother out?"

I knew you felt so terrible. Between the smacks I could see you trying to say the words, but you just couldn't. I knew you would've if you could. Finally Dad got tired and said, "Hell! You both are hopeless."

Then he sat back down in his green chair and watched TV until Mom got home. I never did tell her what happened and I wore long sleeves for the next month. I figured Dad was only home for a few more days and then he was going back to the pipeline again. You ran upstairs to your room and wouldn't even look at me for the next ten days. But I knew you were sorry. I kept finding Tootsie Rolls under my pillow every day for the next two weeks.

Martin

Fielda is hanging on, but just barely. She is pale, her voice is shaky and high. Her fingers keep plucking at the loose threads on the arm of the couch. She is trying so hard to concentrate on the words that Agent Fitzgerald, sitting with Deputy Sheriff Louis on the couch opposite us, is saying, but is struggling to focus.

"I'm sorry?" she says contritely.

"What time did you see Petra last?" he repeats.

Agent Fitzgerald is not what I expected. I thought he would be much older. Instead, he looks to be forty. He is very short in stature, with a bulldog chin and small feminine hands. His appearance does not fill me with confidence, and I am rather irritated with Deputy Sheriff Louis, as he had said this Agent Fitzgerald was well regarded in law enforcement and a force to be reckoned with.

"Last night," Fielda responds. "Eight-thirty, I'd say. No, nine. It was nine because she came downstairs once to ask me what a word meant in her book that she was reading."

"What word?" Fitzgerald asks kindly.

"What word? Umm, it was *inedible*. She wanted to know what it meant and I told her," Fielda explains.

I begin to shift uneasily next to her. "What does that have to do with Petra being gone? We have answered all these questions for Deputy Sheriff Louis. I do not understand why we need to answer them again. We should be out looking for the girls. Our time would be better spent," I tell him politely but firmly.

"Mr. Gregory, I understand your concern," Fitzgerald says. "It's good for me to ask the questions also and hear your answers, too. You may think of something that you didn't tell Deputy Sheriff Louis. Please be patient. We are all working very hard right now to find your daughter."

"All I know right now is that my little girl is missing, as is her best friend. She is out there somewhere in her pajamas and all I am doing right now is sitting here!" My voice is getting dangerously loud. "Why aren't we out there finding her?" Fielda grabs my arm and begins to cry, rocking back and forth.

"Shh, shh, Fielda," I soothe her. "I'm sorry," I whisper to her.

Fitzgerald leans forward. "If we focus on all the facts that we have, if we look at each little piece, no matter how inconsequential, then we are more likely to find out where Petra and Calli are. So I do understand how repetitive this is for you, but it is very important."

I nod. "I apologize. Please continue."

"Can you give me a list of people who have visited your home in the last month or so?" he asks.

Fielda sniffs and wipes her eyes with the heel of her hand. "Calli, of course, was over. Calli's brother, Ben, he delivers the paper. My friend Martha—"

"Last names also, please," Fitzgerald instructs.

"Martha Franklin. The two men from the furniture store, Bandleworths. I don't know their names, though. They delivered the bookshelf."

"We had a dinner party about two weeks ago, with some of my colleagues from the college. Walt and Jeanne Powers and Mary and Sam Garfield," I add.

"We often have students from the college come and do odd jobs for us," Fielda says. Fitzgerald looks expectantly at her. "Mariah Burton babysat for us on a number of occasions the last two years, Chad Wagner has done some lawn work this summer—he's in one of Martin's economics classes—and Lucky Thompson. Lucky stops by once in a while. I can't think of anyone else, can you, Martin?"

"We have several hikers wander down this way, since we are right next to the woods. Many people from town come out this way to walk the trails, usually on weekends. Just about everyone we know has come near here at one time or another," I explain.

"When we leave, I'd like for you to make a list of everyone that has had contact with Petra, as far back as a year. Some names may be repeats that we've already spoken about. That's fine. We'll run all the names through our system and see if anything unusual comes up.

"Has anyone paid any extra attention to Petra while they were here? Talked to her or looked at her in a way that made you uncomfortable?" Fitzgerald asks, his blue eyes staring unnervingly at us.

"Everyone loves Petra," Fielda answers. "She just lights up a room, she can talk to just about anybody about anything."

"I look forward to meeting her, too." Fitzgerald smiles.

"But think back, did anyone you know maybe go out of their way to give her a hug or speak to her in a way that made you pause, even just for a second?"

Fielda blinks at him several times and I can actually hear the connections clicking together in her mind. But she remains silent.

"I know these are uncomfortable questions for you, Mr. and Mrs. Gregory, but the sooner we look at all the possible scenarios, the sooner we get the girls home. We're sending officers door-to-door and checking on any known sex offenders in the area."

"You don't think Petra and Calli went off on their own, do you? You think someone took them." Fielda looks desperately at Fitzgerald, and when he remains silent, she turns to Deputy Sheriff Louis.

"There are some slight similarities to the disappearances of Petra and Calli to the little McIntire girl," Louis says. "Nothing concrete, but...but like Agent Fitzgerald says, we need to look at everything, no matter how hard."

"Oh my God. Oh my God!" Fielda slowly slides off the slippery chintz sofa to her knees and then curls into a tight ball. "Oh my God!" she wails.

I drop to the floor next to her and glare at Louis and Fitzgerald. "Get out," I say enraged, surprising even myself. Then more calmly add, "Please leave us for a moment, and then we will talk more. Please go." I watch the two men as they stand and unhurriedly walk out the front door into the scorching heat. As the front screen closes and latches with a soft click, I lie down next to Fielda, molding myself to her, pressing my chest to her back, tucking my knees into the soft groove behind hers, sliding my arms around her middle and hiding my face in her hair. She smells sweetly of perfume and talcum powder, which to me will forever on be the odor of deep, deep grief. Her cries do not soften, but become more fraught and my own body rises and falls with each of her shudders.

DEPUTY SHERIFF LOUIS

Fitzgerald and I step out into the Gregorys' front yard, the sun nearly directly above us, hidden slightly behind an enormous maple tree—a perfect climbing tree, Toni would say.

"Jesus," Fitzgerald says in an exasperated voice, and I steel myself for criticism of the way I just handled the last three minutes in the Gregory home.

"How can you stand this sound?" Fitzgerald says disgustedly.

"What sound?"

"Those bugs. It sounds like millions of insects chewing on something. It makes my skin crawl." Fitzgerald pulls out a pack of cigarettes and taps one out, holding it between his slender fingers.

"They're cicadas," I explain. "It's vibrations. The noise they make. It's their skin pulled tight over their bodies."

"It's annoying. How can you stand it?"

"I suppose the same way that you get used to the noises in a big city. It's just there—you don't really notice it after a while."

Fitzgerald nods and lights his cigarette. "Do you mind?" he asks after the fact.

"Naw, go ahead," I reply and we both stand there, listening to the cicadas' anxious song.

"You feel bad," Fitzgerald observes.

"Yeah, I do," I respond blandly.

"It needed to be said, the thing about the McIntire girl. They need to know it's a possibility. Give them a few minutes to let it settle in their minds and they'll be ready to go forward. There's no way they will accept that their little girl could have been lured from her home, raped and murdered, but the possibility will be there, and they will be out here in a moment ready to fight like hell to find her, to prove that's not what happened."

"We need to bring in search dogs, organize a formal search," I tell him, knowing this is already on his mind.

"I agree. We can get a trained hound and handler from Madison or even Des Moines down here by late this afternoon," Fitzgerald responds, taking a deep pull on his cigarette.

"The families are not going to want to hear about a search dog. Sounds too much like we'll be looking for bodies," I say, not relishing the thought of being the one to relay the information to the Gregorys and Toni.

"What's your gut feeling on this one, Louis?" Fitzgerald asks me, leaning against an old oak tree.

I shrug. "Not sure, but between you and me, I would look at Toni's husband a little more closely. He's a shady character, a drinker. Rumor has it he can be violent."

"Violent in what way?"

"Like I said, just rumor. Toni doesn't talk about it, there's never been a domestic call. Several drunk and disorderlies on

Griff, and one DUI. Just something to keep in mind as this all unfolds," I say wearily.

"Good to know," Fitzgerald says looking off toward Toni's house.

"Days like this, I wished I smoked," I say, eyeing his cigarette.

"Days like this, I wished I didn't," Fitzgerald replies, as Martin Gregory steps outside his home.

"I'm sorry," Martin apologizes. "We are ready to go on, tell us what you need to know. Please…come in."

CALLI

Calli had traveled deeper into the forest, beyond any spot she had been before. She was lost, the fawn had long since left to join its mother. Calli wandered around, trying to get her bearings. The trees here were thick and shielded the sun's rays from her, though the air around remained steamy, heavy with moisture. The trail in front of her led upward, a winding, rocky path that disappeared into a stand of hemlocks. Another trail led downward, she thought to the creek. Her tongue felt oversize and dry; she was so thirsty. She considered going back the way she had come, but dismissed the idea, knowing that Griff was still there somewhere. The muscles in her legs were shaky and tired from running and a dull hunger had settled in her stomach. Calli scanned the forest around her; she saw the plump red-and-yellow berries that the cardinals flocked around, but knew she should not eat them. She tried to remember what her mother and Ben had told her about the berries of the forest, what she could eat and what was poisonous. She knew about mulberries, the fat purplish-red berries filled with sweet juice that hung heavily on branches. She could eat those, but she knew not to eat the reddish-brown berries of the toothache tree, because they would cause your mouth to go numb. She trudged upward, eyes inspecting every bush and vine.

Her eyes settled upon a thorny tangled thicket holding blackish berries hanging from a white stem. Black raspberries. Calli hungrily plucked them from the twig, their juice bursting out of their skin with her touch, staining her fingers. The sweetness filled her mouth and she continued picking, fanning mosquitoes away from her find. Her mother had taught her where to find the wild black raspberries and she and Ben would collect as many as they could in old ice cream buckets, trying not to eat too many. When their buckets were full, they would carry them home to their mother, who would carefully wash them and bake them into pies that she served with homemade ice cream. Calli loved homemade ice cream and everything that went into making the concoction. She would tromp down the basement stairs where they stored the old hand-crank ice cream maker. It awed her how just adding the eggs, vanilla, milk and rock salt would create something so delicious. She didn't even mind the ache in her arm from turning the crank, and Ben would take over when she couldn't turn it anymore. The first thing she would do, she decided, when she got home was to haul that old ice cream maker up the steps so they could make a batch.

When she finished eating all the raspberries she could reach, she wiped her blackened fingers on her nightgown and rubbed the back of her hand across her mouth, the imprint of her lips left behind like lipstick. Her hunger sated for the moment, Calli decided to continue her climb upward, to the highest point on the bluff. From there, perhaps she could see exactly where she was at and which direction would lead her home. But it was so hot and she was so sleepy. Just to lie down for a few moments, just to rest. She found a shady cluster of evergreens, well off the trail, cleared away the sharp branches that lay at its base, and, using her arms as a pillow, shut her eyes and slept.

BEN

We've been waiting for eons for Deputy Sheriff Louis and the other guy to get here. Mom made me put on a nice pair of shorts and a shirt with a collar for when they come over to talk to us. I'm starving, but feel weird making a sandwich or something when you're out all by yourself with maybe nothing to eat. I grab a box of crackers and take 'em upstairs to eat in my room. When I walk by the door to your room, there's this little stretch of crime scene tape stretched across the door frame. Stupid, I think, people rifling through your stuff in your room when we should all be out looking for you in the woods.

I see Mom sitting on the floor of her bedroom, pulling things out of your treasure box. It's really an old hat box filled with junk. I got one, too. Mom calls it our treasure box because she wants us to put all the important stuff from our life in it. Then when we're old and gray, as she says, we can dig through all the things that at one time were so valuable to us. Actually, I'm already on my second treasure box because my first one got all filled up. She doesn't notice me standing there so I just watch all quiet. She's surrounded by a bunch of your school papers and art projects and she's touching each one, gentlelike, as if one wrong move will cause them all to turn to dust. She reaches into the box again and brings out something that I can't quite figure what it is. Neither can she, because she just stares at it for a long time, turning it around in her fingers; it's whitish-gray and about three inches long. Mom hears me behind her, turns and holds it out to me.

"What do you think it is?" she asks me as I take it.

I shrug and pick at some of the gray bits that look like fur sticking out of it. "I think it's an owl pellet," I say. "Look, you can see little bits of bone sticking out."

Mom looks and takes it back from me. I love that about her. Most mothers would freak out at the sight of something like owl throw-up, but she doesn't.

"Yeah, I think you're right. Why would Calli have this in her treasure box?" she asks.

I shrug again. "I guess for the same reason that I have a box of periodical cicada shells in my room." This causes her to laugh and I'm glad, she hasn't laughed much lately. She carefully sets the pellet back in the box and pulls out a pile of something that looks like cotton.

"I know what this is!" Mom exclaims, smiling. "It's dandelion fluff all bunched together!"

"Okay," I say, "I can kinda understand the owl pellet, but I don't get the dandelion fluff."

"Don't you remember?" she asks me. "'When fairies dance upon the air, reach out gently and catch one, fair. Make a wish and hold it tight, then softly toss your pixie back to summer's night.'"

"I wonder what she wished for," I say.

"I wonder why she didn't let them go," Mom adds.

"Maybe she was saving the wishes up for something real big, then she was going to let them all go at once."

It's Mom's turn to shrug and she lays the fluff back into your treasure box on top of all the other stuff, puts the lid back on and slides it under her bed.

"Come on, Ben," she says. "Let me make you a sandwich. Louis will be here soon."

I have an idea of what you might have wished for, because they're the same wishes as mine. Number one—for you to talk again. Number two—get a dog. Number three—that Dad would just go on back to Alaska and not come back. God knows you'd never admit it and neither would I, but those would be your wishes. I know.

ANTONIA

As I make Ben and me a ham sandwich and slice an apple in half, I think of Calli's treasure box. The dandelion fluff reminds me of Louis, of when we were kids.

The summer after Louis moved here, we'd go out to the meadow behind my house, the very house I live in now. Our field would be filled with happy yellow dandelions, and my mom would pay us a penny a weed to dig them out by the roots. No easy feat. We'd get old spoons to dig down as deep as we could, under the roots, and then toss them into an old plastic bucket. We could wrench out about one hundred in a day. My mother would give us a dollar, one shiny quarter for each of our grimy hands, and we'd hop on our bikes, ride downtown to the Mourning Glory Café and pool our earnings. I'd buy us a cherry Coke, not the kind that comes in a can like today, but the kind straight out of a soda fountain, with the cherry juice squirted in.

Mrs. Mourning would always put in two straws and two cherries, one for Louis and one for me. Louis would buy us a basket of French fries, piping hot and salty. He would write my name out on top of the fries in ketchup from the squirt bottle and then script his own directly below it. The fries with my name on them were mine, the fries with his name, his to eat. Some days, we'd each buy a candy bar. I always picked Marathon bars, and he would choose a Baby Ruth. Petra's mother, Fielda, was often at the café helping her mother. Friendly and sweet, Fielda would stand behind the counter watching us carefully, refilling our sodas. Looking back, I can see that Fielda wanted to be my friend, but I had Louis, and, well, he was all I needed, all I wanted. Years later, when we became neighbors and were eventually pregnant with our girls at the same time, Fielda tried again, invited me over for coffee, for walks, but once again, I was aloof, this time for completely different reasons. I was afraid she'd get an inkling of my sad marriage, catch my husband and me in a bad moment, see the bruises. Eventually she gave up and left me alone, just as she had eventually done when we were young.

Our dandelion weeding would last approximately ten days. By then we were bored with the job and had our fill of cherry Cokes and fries. We hadn't even made a dent in removing all the dandelions. They were beginning to seed and white puffs were whirling in the air above us, undoing all that we'd accomplished.

"You know," Louis told me, "these really are fairies."

"Yeah, right," I said, unconvinced.

"They are. My dad told me. He said that dandelion fluffs are magical fairies. If you grab one before it hits the ground, the fairy will be so grateful she will give you a wish once you set her free."

I sat up, setting down my dirt-crusted spoon. This interested me. Louis never spoke of his father, ever. "I didn't know they had flowers in Chicago."

"Yeah, they have flowers and weeds and grass in Chicago," he said indignantly. "Just not so much of it.

"My dad would say, 'When fairies dance upon the air, reach out gently and catch one, fair. Make a wish and hold it tight, then softly toss your pixie back to summer's night.' My dad said his granny from Ireland told him that and that the wishes really come true. Every summer when we'd see dandelion fluff we tried to catch one, make a wish, and then blow it back into the air."

"What'd you wish for?" I asked.

"Stuff." Louis, all of a sudden bashful, dropped his spoon and ran toward the woods, grasping at fluff as he went.

"What kind of stuff?" I called as I chased him.

"For the Cubs to win the pennant, things like that." He wasn't looking at me.

"What about your dad? Do you ever wish for your dad?" I asked softly. His shoulders sagged and I thought he would take off running again.

"Naw, dead is dead. It doesn't work for stuff like that. You gotta wish for money or to be a movie star or something." He handed me a soft white wish. "What are you going to wish for?"

I thought for a moment, and then blew it gently from my hand, the cottony wisp floating away.

"What did you wish for?" he asked again.

"For the Cubs to win the pennant, of course," I responded. He laughed and we ran off to play in the creek.

That wasn't my wish though. I wished for him to have his dad back, just in case.

Eight years later, when we were sixteen, we were back at the creek. We had just made love for the first time and I was tearful. I couldn't put into words what I was feeling. I knew I loved him, I knew that what we had done wasn't a mistake, but still I wept. Louis was trying to make me smile, tickling me and pulling funny faces, but tears just kept rolling down my face no matter what he tried. Finally, in an act of desperation, I suppose, he ran from the creek. I sat there, devastated, pulling my clothes on, mucus dropping from my nose. I had lost Louis, my best friend. He came back moments later, though. He held his two hands in front of him clenched tightly.

"Pick a hand," he said, and I chose his left. He opened his palm and inside were three frail white tufts of a dandelion. "Three wishes," he said and then opened his other fist to reveal three more dandelion fairies, "for each of us."

"You first," I said through my tears, finally, a smile on my face.

"That the Cubs win the pennant." He grinned and I laughed. "That I become a policeman." Then his young man's face became serious. "And that you will love me forever. Your turn," he said quickly.

I thought for a moment. "To live in a yellow house." I looked carefully at Louis's face to see if he was laughing at me. He wasn't. "To visit the ocean," I continued. "And…" the tears resumed, great sloppy tears "…that you'll love me forever."

Three years later, Louis had gone away to college and I married Griff. Damn fairies, I thought to myself now. I don't live in a yellow house, I've never been to the ocean, and Louis didn't love me forever. And my Calli, my dear heart, is missing. All that I touch gets damaged or lost.

DEPUTY SHERIFF LOUIS

Once again I am sitting at Toni's kitchen table, a sweating glass of iced tea in front of me. This time Agent Fitzgerald is sitting next to me instead of Martin. I worry, when this is over, Martin will never speak to me again. And I fear that Toni won't, either. I can tell Toni doesn't know what to make of Fitzgerald, his precise, unemotional questions. She wonders if he is judging her and her mothering. I see her turning over each of his questions, searching for any hidden meaning, any tricks, I suppose because she is so used to Griff's manipulative ways.

Finding Toni curled up on her couch, delivering a dead baby girl four years ago, I'd hoped that she would wise up and get rid of Griff for good. Granted, I don't know exactly what happened that winter night, just that Ben had come home and found his mother covered in a blanket on the sofa with Calli sitting by, patting her shoulder. I couldn't get Calli to talk to me. She just looked up at me with her big, brown eyes and sat there as the ambulance carried her mother away.

I asked Ben where his father was, and he couldn't say for sure, but guessed that he was probably at Behnke's, a bar downtown. I debated just phoning over there and talking to Griff, but decided a face-to-face conversation would be more effective. I asked a neighbor to come over and watch the kids and I went over to Behnke's.

I saw Griff through a smoky haze, sitting at the bar next to a bunch of his old high-school friends. His friends were laughing and talking, reminiscing, I'm sure, about the good old days, about the only thing that group had going for them. Griff was uncharacteristically quiet, slamming back shots, nodding and smiling once in a while at what someone said. I walked over to him, and he glanced up at me. He didn't look surprised to see me. I felt the eyes of all the patrons of Behnke's on me, watching what would happen next. My history with Toni was no secret in Willow Creek. I waited for Griff's usual sarcastic greeting. "Deputy Sheriff," he'd say in a pompous wise-ass voice that made it sound like he was addressing a king or head of state. But he just looked expectantly up at me and a hush fell over his cronies next to him.

"Go outside for a minute, Griff?" I asked politely.

"Gotta warrant, Deputy Sheriff?" Roger, his idiot side-kick, asked, laughing hysterically.

"You can talk to me here, Louis," Griff said mildly and then downed another shot. "Can I buy you a drink?"

"No thanks, I'm on duty," I replied, and for some reason his friends thought that was funny, too, and collapsed in laughter.

I leaned in close to him. "It's about Toni, Griff," I said in a low voice, not wanting these jokers to hear.

Griff stood up. I'm a good four inches taller than Griff, but he's broad and built like a weight lifter. I had no doubt that he could beat the shit out of me, just like he did when I was nineteen and had come from college to try to get Toni to come back to me. I had gone to her house, where she still lived with her dad, who seemed to have aged decades since Toni's mother died. I took one look at Toni's face that night and knew something was irreparably broken between the two of us. We could never go back to the way it was. At the time, I didn't want to stay in Willow Creek and Toni didn't want to leave. My mom had remarried earlier that year and moved back to Chicago with my brother and sister. I loved college, loved Iowa City, and wanted Toni to come back with me. There wasn't really anything left for her in Willow Creek, I thought. But she said no, with regret, I think. Said she was seeing Griff Clark and was doing just fine. That she couldn't leave her father alone, he'd lost too much already. Then she crossed her arms over her chest like she always did when she made a decision and it was final. I leaned in to kiss her goodbye, but she dropped her chin at the last second and my lips landed on her nose.

Griff waited until I had driven away. He waited until I had driven forty miles and stopped for gas. He waited until I was just about ready to get back in my car after paying the clerk and then he came out from the shadows and sucker punched me in the stomach and while I was bent over, he kicked me in the balls. "Stay away from Toni, asshole," he hissed at me. I could smell the alcohol on his breath. "We're getting married," he slurred before one boulderlike fist crunched into my face. Those three words hurt more than the punch. A few months later, I heard through a friend that Toni and

Griff had gotten married. And it wasn't all that many months later when I heard about Ben. It didn't take a genius to do the math. I should have tried harder. I shouldn't have let her go.

"Let's go," Griff said, the yeasty smell of beer that emanated from him bringing me back to Behnke's, and I followed him out of the bar. The cold brisk air of the parking lot was welcoming after the stale nicotine cloud we just left.

"What's up?" he asked innocently. "Is Toni okay?"

"She's at Mercy Hospital," was all I said. Even as much as I hated the guy, I couldn't tell him that his baby had died.

"What happened? What'd she say?" Griff asked.

"Not sure," I replied. "She's not saying much right now. Ben called for help." I left out that Ben had called me at home, knowing that this could cause him grief later.

Griff paused at his truck, keys in hand and turned to me. "Probably not a good idea for me to drive, huh?"

"Probably not," I agreed. We looked at each other for a moment. "Come on," I said finally. "I'll drive you over."

We climbed in and I started the cruiser. The only sound was the heater trying ineffectively to warm the car. After driving for a few moments, Griff cleared his throat.

"What'd Calli say?" he asked, not looking at me.

"What do you think she said?" I asked, knowing full well Calli hadn't uttered a sound, not since I got there, anyway.

He cleared his throat again. "Toni fell, but she was fine. She got right back up. She said she was okay. She settled herself on the couch. She was fine when I left."

"She's not so fine now," I said, pulling into the parking lot of the hospital. When I stopped the car I turned to Griff and said, "Griff, if I find out that you did anything to hurt Toni,

I will come after you. I will come after you, arrest you, throw you in a jail cell, and some night, when no one is looking, I will beat the crap out of you."

Griff laughed as he opened the car door. "No, you won't, *Deputy.*" There was that obnoxious tone. "Naw, you won't. You're a by-the-book kinda guy. But hey, thanks for the ride." He slammed the door and left me, my breath frosty-white, curling around my head.

And damned if he wasn't right.

BEN

When I was seven I started playing in a summer soccer league. Mom thought it would be good for me to get out and get some exercise, make some new friends. I was big, but not exactly the athletic type. My feet always seemed too large and I'd end up tripping over them and making a fool of myself. After squashing about three of the kids on the other team, plus one of my own teammates, the coach put me in as goalie. That, I could do. I was about twice the size of anyone else, so it was more likely that I could stop a ball from flying into the net. I would snatch balls out of the air as they came whizzing toward me, blocking the soccer ball with my body. No one scored on me in four matches. I could see you and Mom hollering on the sidelines, cheering me on. You were two, I guess. Sometimes you'd try to run out onto the field to come and see me and then the referee would have to stop the game and Mom would come over and scoop you up saying, "Sorry, sorry," to everyone.

One time Dad was in town and he came to one of my

games. It had rained earlier and the grass was all slippery. Dad came a little later, after the game had started and I was standing in the goalie box, wearing my blue soccer shirt with the number *four* on it and my black goalie gloves. They were so cool, I thought, those gloves. They looked all professional-like and had these bumpy knobs on them for a better grip to hold on to the ball. You and Mom were sitting on an old blanket, but Dad was pacing up and down the sidelines. I kept watching him, walking, walking, walking, like some caged-up lion. He'd be yelling, "Come on, boys! Get that ball, move it up the field." When the ball came toward me, I'd have to force my eyes off him, trying to concentrate. My hands were out in front of me, my knees were bent and my legs were spread apart, trying to take up as much space as I could, just like the coach told me.

"Come on, Ben," he shouted. "You can do it, get that ball! Grab it, grab it!"

I can still see the ball flying at me, the black and white spots on the ball spinning so fast they looked gray. The ball sped right past me; I didn't even get one fancy-gloved finger on that ball. I expected to hear Dad shouting and yelling at me and Mom trying to shush him. But when I looked to the side-lines, to where he'd been pacing, he wasn't there anymore. I searched and searched the crowd and finally spotted him, walking back to his truck.

We won the game four to one. Mom took you and me out for ice cream to celebrate, but I wasn't very hungry. Dad didn't say anything about the game when we got home, which was worse in its own way.

ANTONIA

I meet Louis and the other officer at my front door. From my living-room window I had seen them drive down our lane. The man with Louis is compact, dressed nicely but casually. He wears expensive-looking shoes and carries a leather portfolio.

I welcome them into my home and we settle at the kitchen table. Louis looks miserable and the man introduces himself as Kent Fitzgerald, federal agent. I hold back a giggle. He says it as if he were a superhero or something.

"Missing and Exploited Children Division," he adds and I sober quickly. I must look puzzled because he explains, "We take missing children, any missing children, very seriously."

"We don't know that they are *missing,* missing," I say lamely. "I mean, of course, they're missing, but what are you thinking? Do you know something?" I look to Louis. He isn't looking at me.

"We know as much as you do, Mrs. Clark," Agent Fitzgerald says. "I'm here to assist Deputy Sheriff Louis and his team in bringing the girls home. What time did you last see Calli?"

"Last night at about ten," I begin. "We watched a movie together and had popcorn. Then I helped her get ready for bed."

"Who else was in the house last night?" he inquires.

"My son, Ben. He's twelve. He didn't watch the entire movie, he went up to his room at about nine, I guess. And my husband, Griff, he came home at about midnight or so."

He nods. "Deputy Louis tells me your husband, Griff… Is that his real name?"

"No, no, it's a nickname. His real name is Griffith, but everyone just calls him Griff."

"Griff, Deputy Louis tells me, went on an early-morning fishing trip."

I bob my head in agreement and wait for his next question, but it doesn't come, so I continue. "I'm not certain what time he left, but when I talked to Roger's wife, she said he left to pick Griff up at around three-thirty this morning. And sometime early I heard a truck in the drive. I assumed it was Roger's."

"Roger's last name again?" Agent Fitzgerald asks.

"Hogan. Roger Hogan," I respond. My hands are beginning to sweat and my head aches.

"Have you been able to contact your husband or Mr. Hogan as of yet?"

"Laura Hogan tried Roger's cell phone, but the call wouldn't go through. Griff isn't answering his phone, it goes right to voice mail. I'm sorry, Mr. Fitzgerald…" I say.

"Agent," he corrects me.

"I'm sorry, Agent Fitzgerald, but why focus on Griff and Roger? I don't understand."

"There is no focus at this point. We're just getting the logistics." He smiles briefly. His teeth are small and white, and he has an underbite that thrusts his chin forward. "We asked the Julien police to head over to the cabin where your husband is staying. The officer said that he found the cabin and Roger Hogan's truck. The cabin's boat dock was empty. It appears the men are out fishing on the river. The officer is going to wait for them to return."

I know it, but don't say so. I know Griff has nothing to do with this.

"What was Calli wearing last night?" Agent Fitzgerald asks me.

"A pink short-sleeve nightgown that went down below her knees."

"Shoes?"

"No, no shoes."

Agent Fitzgerald sits quietly for a moment, his small fingers holding a pen, scratching away in his portfolio.

"Did Calli mention that she was planning to go anywhere today?" he asks, not looking up from his notebook.

I look at Louis. "You didn't tell him?" He shakes his head. He is being very quiet and it irritates me. I look at Agent Fitzgerald again. "Calli doesn't speak," I explain. A neutral expression remains on his face. "She hasn't spoken since she was four."

"Was she ill?" he asks, looking me in the eye.

"No," I gaze levelly back at him. "I don't understand what this has to do with anything," I say as I fold my arms over my chest and uncross my legs.

"Calli witnessed her mother fall down the stairs and lose her baby. It was very traumatic for her," Louis says softly.

I glare at Louis. *Now* he's talking.

Agent Fitzgerald sits up, very attentive now. "How do you communicate with each other?"

"She nods and shakes her head, she points and gestures. She knows some sign language," I say.

"What do her doctors say?"

"That she'll talk when she's ready, not to force it." I stand up and go to the kitchen window.

"Is she seeing anyone?"

"Like a shrink?" I ask, anger in my voice.

"Excuse me, Agent Fitzgerald, may I speak with Mrs. Clark privately for a moment?" Louis speaks up, his voice tight. *Mrs. Clark,* I wonder to myself. He has never addressed me this way before.

"Sure," Agent Fitzgerald replies. He closes his portfolio, tucks his pen behind his ear and stands. Louis and I both watch as he goes out the front door. Louis regards me carefully.

"What?" I finally ask.

"Toni, this is serious."

"Dammit, Louis, I know it is! It's my daughter that is missing!" I shout. "So don't you dare come into my home and tell me to be serious!" I am crying now, and I hate to cry in front of anyone, especially Louis.

He comes over to me. "Toni, I'm sorry," he says quietly. "I'm sorry, I didn't mean...I'm sorry." He grasps my hands in his. "Look at me, Toni," he instructs. I do. "We're going to find Calli, I promise. You need to talk to Agent Fitzgerald. The more thoroughly and quickly you answer his questions, the more quickly we can go out and find her."

"I've made so many mistakes," I whisper. "I cannot bear to lose another child. I could not bear it."

"You won't, I promise," Louis says firmly. "You go get Ben and I'll get Fitzgerald. Let's get this interview over with so we can go out there and find Calli."

He squeezes my hands one more time before dropping them and I climb the stairs to find Ben.

PETRA

I am lost. One minute they are there, and the next they are gone. I hear sounds and things in the bushes and a snake just wriggled over my shoe. I am lost and I don't know what to do, so I just sit on an old log to rest.

Calli would know. Everybody thinks I'm the tough, smart one. But I'm not, not really. I didn't even know Calli when we were in kindergarten. I knew she was my neighbor and everything. But we never played together. I found out from Lena Hill that Calli didn't talk. Not a word. Ever. I didn't believe Lena, but she said that they were in the same class in kindergarten and that Calli never, ever said a word, even when the principal asked her a question. I asked Lena if Calli was in a special class for the kids who don't learn so good. She said no, but that Calli got to go with Mr. Wilson, the new school counselor. I thought that was pretty neat. Mr. Wilson is cool.

At lunch the second week of first grade, I budged Jake Moon so I could sit next to Calli. He didn't mind so much. I wanted to see if she really didn't talk. Lots of kids didn't say much when we were in the classroom, but everyone talked during lunch. But she didn't. She just sat there, eating her sandwich.

"What kind of sandwich do you got?" I asked. She didn't say anything but peeled back the top layer of bread on her sandwich to show me that she had peanut butter and something white and creamy.

"I sure hope that's not mayonnaise. Gross!" I said. Calli wrinkled her nose and stuck out her tongue to tell me she thought that was gross, too. She handed me half of her sandwich and I took a bite.

"Peanut butter fluff!" I said. "Lucky. I never get good sandwiches like that. My mom puts everything on wheat bread." Calli shook her head like she understood.

We walked out to recess together. I saw my group of friends that I always played with. I said, "Come on," to her, and she followed me to where the kids were jumping rope. We got in line.

"I like ice cream, I like tea, I want Petra to jump with me!" Bree called. And I stood just outside the middle of the turning jump rope. I had to plan my jump in just right. Then I jumped and Bree and I were hopping, hopping, hopping, until she jumped out and it was just me jumping.

"I like popcorn, I like the sea, I want Calli to jump with me!" And Calli hopped right in with me. Around and around and around the rope went, swishing against the cement. And we were smiling at each other; we both had the same two front teeth missing. Then I jumped out because that's how the game goes. Calli just kept jumping and jumping, not calling out that she liked coffee or that she liked bees.

Everyone started getting all mad, and yelling at her, "Come on, Calli, call someone!" and "Stop hogging the jump rope!" Then the rope turners just stopped and the rope fell in a heap on the ground. The recess bell rang and then everyone ran to line up.

In line, Nathan stood behind me and started saying, "I don't want to stand next to bushy hair! Someone trade places with me. Someone trade me places!"

And no one would. Even Lena and Kelli, who are my friends, wouldn't stand next to me. My heart felt all pinched right then. And then out of the blue, Calli came up and budged right in front of Nathan and next to me. Best of all, she stared him down. She looked him right in the eyes until he said, "Good, you two weirdos can stand next to each other."

The next day, I sat next to Calli at lunch again; she had bologna and peanut butter that day.

"I'll have to pass, thank you," I said when she held out half to me. When we went out to recess I grabbed her hand and pulled her into line for jumping rope again. She didn't look too happy about it and the other kids didn't, either.

When it was my turn I called out, "I like watermelon, I like to climb a tree, I like Calli to jump with me!" And we jumped and jumped until I hopped out. Then it was just Calli again and before anyone could get all nervous and mad at her, I yelled, "Calli likes bologna, Calli likes me! Calli wants to jump with Lena!" I know it didn't exactly rhyme but it worked. Lena jumped in with Calli, they jumped awhile, and then Calli jumped out.

I wish Calli were here. She'd help me find the way, or at least we could be lost together.

I'm so thirsty.

DEPUTY SHERIFF LOUIS

Ben comes slowly down the steps. I'm struck at how much he looks like his father, and I am jealous. My boy, Tanner, looks just like his mother's side of the family, dark and small with gray-blue eyes. Ben looks nervous, but then he always seems jittery to me, quick to startle, but nice, polite.

"Ben," I say, "this is Agent Fitzgerald. He's here to help find Calli and Petra." Fitzgerald holds out his hand for Ben to shake. We all settle at the kitchen table, Toni right next to Ben. Fitzgerald and I sit across from them. Fitzgerald looks to Toni.

"Mrs. Clark, we like to interview family members separately. It sometimes allows them to speak more freely."

"Oh, well, I think I'd rather stay here with Ben," Toni says firmly.

"Toni, I'll be right here. Don't worry," I reassure her and she reluctantly rises from her chair and leaves the room.

"Ben," begins Fitzgerald, "how old are you?"

"Twelve," he answers softly. Fitzgerald continues to ask Ben easy questions, keeping everything light, I know, to make Ben feel more at ease.

"Tell me about your sister, Ben," Fitzgerald instructs.

"She's good," Ben says. "She never gets into my stuff, she does what I tell her to—"

"What do you tell her to do?" Fitzgerald interrupts.

"Things. Help take out the garbage, help put away the dishes, stuff like that," Ben answers, shrugging his shoulders.

"Did you two ever argue?"

"No, it's hard to argue with someone who doesn't talk back."

Fitzgerald chuckles at this. "She ever say no to you, Ben?"

"Not really. She likes to help out."

"You two pretty close?"

"I guess. We hang out a lot together."

"You're what, twelve? Isn't it unusual for boys your age to hang out with their seven-year-old little sisters?"

Ben lifts his shoulders and then drops them. "Calli doesn't have a lot of friends so I play with her."

"What about Petra Gregory? She's Calli's friend, right?"

"Yeah, but she isn't around all the time," Ben explains.

Fitzgerald seems satisfied with his answers.

Quickly though, Fitzgerald changes his approach with Ben.

"Ben, I've heard some very nice things about you," Fitzgerald says smoothly. "Your teachers, neighbors all think you are a nice boy."

I think I know where this is going. Fitzgerald had asked me about it earlier, when looking through files. I told him it had nothing to do with this and to leave it alone.

"But," Fitzgerald continues, "the parents of Jason Meechum

have had some concerns about you, Ben, and their son. Can you tell me about that?"

"Jason Meechum is a jerk. And a liar," Ben says stiffly.

"Tell me about it, Ben?"

"I don't hafta tell you anything," Ben says petulantly.

"No, you don't," Fitzgerald says mildly, "but you should. You want to help Calli, don't you?"

"Yeah, but sitting around here answering these stupid questions isn't gonna help her." Ben is standing now, shouting. "The only way we're going to find her is if we go looking for her. She's somewhere in the woods!"

"How do you know that, Ben?" Fitzgerald questions softly.

"Because, that's where she goes. When she wants to get away or be alone, that's where she chooses to go!" Ben shouts.

Fitzgerald says, his voice just a low whisper, "What if she didn't have a choice?"

And Ben runs.

ANTONIA

I hear the loud voices in the kitchen and hear the name Jason Meechum spoken. "What in God's name was that all about?" I ask angrily as I come into the room. "What did you say to him? Do you actually believe that Ben has something to do with any of this? He's trying to help, for God's sake!"

I am furious. This stranger ran my son out of his own home and Louis just sat by and watched. He is looking down at his fingers now, something he has done since he was seven and knew he was in trouble. Agent Fitzgerald doesn't look upset in the least. But of course, he wouldn't. He just swoops into a place, creates havoc, and then picks up and leaves. I tell him so.

"I'll go after him," Louis offers, but I shake my head.

"He'll be fine. I know exactly where he is going. I'll go after him, and I'll go look for Calli while I'm at it. Nobody else appears to be doing anything but insulting the family who is missing somebody," I mutter.

"That's not a good idea, Mrs. Clark," Agent Fitzgerald informs me. "It's not in the best interest of the investigation."

"What about Ben?" I ask. "Who is serving his best interest? What's all this nonsense about Jason Meechum? This has nothing to do with Calli, and I don't understand why you're bringing it up." My voice is shrill and I hate the fact that I was losing control of it.

More softly, I continue. "Deputy Sheriff, I am surprised that you found it necessary to share that information with Agent Fitzgerald." To Fitzgerald I say curtly, folding my arms in front of me, "Tell me now what it is that you think I should be doing. Then you tell me what it is you are going to do in order to find my daughter."

Agent Fitzgerald stands and mirrors my own stance. I wonder if that was something that they taught him in agent school to put me more at ease.

"I'm sorry about upsetting your son. However, as I have said many times, we must look at all angles. Have you considered that someone may be upset with someone in your family and be taking it out on Calli? I'm not saying this is so, but we must look at all possibilities. As for Deputy Sheriff Louis, he had no idea I was going to broach the subject of Ben and Jason. Please don't blame him." Fitzgerald looks properly chagrined.

I shake my head in disgust. "What is this? Good cop, bad cop? I'll stay here. You go do what you have to do to find Calli, but if you do not find her by six o'clock this evening, I'm calling everyone I know, forming my own search party and going into those woods. I know she's in there, and I am going in after her."

"I will not support a search after dark," he replies. "But I understand your need to participate in searching for her. We are, at this moment, organizing a search. The key word is *organizing*. We don't just want anybody out there stomping through the woods looking for the girls. We may bring in dogs to aid in the search and do not want the area to be compromised more than is needed. We have officers out looking now. If we need more, we will get the manpower. Everyone is doing all that they possibly can to find your daughter, Mrs. Clark.

"I will also need to speak with your son again. Getting upset and running away will not help Calli."

"Ben would do anything for Calli," I say through clenched teeth.

"I believe that is true, Mrs. Clark. We'll speak soon." Fitzgerald turns to leave.

"Wait," I call after him. "What are you going to do now?"

"We are going to follow up some leads, interview neighbors and other individuals and we are going to search for Calli and Petra."

"What leads? What individuals? Do you know something?" I ask desperately.

"Nothing concrete that I can share with you at this time, Mrs. Clark. Oh, and please be aware that the media will most likely be contacting you shortly. This can be a very good thing. I suggest that you say no more than that your daughter is missing. Get the girls' pictures out there. The more people who see their faces, the more likely that they will be spotted. A crime lab team will also be here shortly to gather evidence from the home. Please stay out of Calli's bedroom. We want to have as much evidence intact as possible. I suggest that you stay at a family or friend's home for the duration of this. Please let the officer know where you will be staying. We'll talk soon, Mrs. Clark. Goodbye."

They are gone before I can argue about not wanting to leave my house. Ben's gone, Calli's gone, and I am in my home all alone, except for the police officer, and I hate that feeling. I walk outside, trying to decide on whom I can impose by showing up on their doorstep. Who wants to be dragged into the middle of this mess? Maybe Mrs. Norland, our elderly neighbor. She is as close to a friend that I have anymore, even though most of our interactions are simple waves from across our yards. My eyes take in my garden, which needs weeding, and I decide to wait a bit for any news before calling Mrs. Norland. I'm not going to let a stranger run me out of my own home. I go to the shed to gather up my gardening gloves, trowel and bucket. I haven't watered in days, but know not to do so now. The blazing sun would evaporate the droplets immediately and the plants would not be able to drink.

In the darkened shed, a knotty, peeling structure that is be-ginning to lean, I grab my gardening tools and notice among the cobwebs four old gallons of paint, a soft, creamy yellow. Years ago, my brothers had moved away and my father joined them soon after. The house was too lonely, he said, without my mother. After Griff and I were married, he handed me the keys to the white, peeling two-story, and wished us much happiness there. I was eighteen.

I still had wanted to live in a yellow house. I had spent hours in the hardware store, staring at paint chips, trying to decide on the perfect shade for our home. I lugged the gallons of paint home the week after the wedding; Griff smiled and said he would get right on it. He never did. I was eighteen then. Now I'm thirty-one and still no yellow house.

I step back out into the blinding sun and scrutinize my flower beds. Where to start? They are all neglected; it has been too hot to venture out into the heat these past weeks. My vegetable garden is brimming over with overripe tomatoes and zucchini. My flower beds are filled with creeping charlie, deer-bitten blossoms and wilted stems. My eye settles on a patch of dirt just beyond my vegetable garden. I had sowed it with grass seed earlier in the summer, but it didn't take. Instead, it appears that the plot has expanded to a stretch of soil about five feet long and three feet wide. I step over an overgrown stalk of rhubarb and examine the patch. Two perfectly shaped child's footprints are imprinted in the dust. The toes are entirely defined. Larger prints of a man's boots are facing the smaller marks, almost toe to toe. Then a few steps farther just the boot prints, somewhat swept over by drag marks. My stomach fills with dread. The footprints could be old, I reason, but I know better. I bend down, lightly touch the dust and rub it between my fingers. I stand quickly and run back to the house to tell an officer and to call Louis.

Martin

Before Fitzgerald and Louis leave they encourage us to go over to a relative's or a friend's house for the remainder of the investigation. They say it will be comforting to have family and friends nearby and that we shouldn't compromise any evidence in the house by having people coming in and out.

"What if Petra comes home?" Fielda argues. "I need to be here for her!" They assure her that someone will be at the house at all times and someone will contact her with all updates.

I drive Fielda and myself over to Fielda's mother's home. Mrs. Mourning greets us tearfully and flutters nervously about Fielda. Fielda looks ill and we both persuade her to go lie down.

Her head is aching and I search through the bathroom medicine cabinet for some Tylenol PM's to help her rest. I suspect she needs something more, but I would never give her something stronger. I bring the tablets and a glass of ice water to the bedroom where Fielda is curled up under the quilt her grandmother had made. She looks so frail there, and old. This surprises me. Fielda, when in motion, is solid and vibrant, a force of nature, young. I am not used to this, taking care of her; she always has looked after me. Odd, I know, because being a bachelor until I was forty-two ensured that I took care of myself quite efficiently until I met Fielda.

I enter the bedroom and close the door behind me. The room is hushed and cool. Fielda obediently lays the pills on her tongue and sips the water that I offer her. I pull the sheet up around the curve of her shoulders as she settles her head on the pillow. "Just for a minute," she says about resting. She doesn't want to, doesn't know how she possibly could rest with our daughter out there somewhere, but I murmur softly into her ear to just close her eyes for a moment. Her curly hair fans out, dark on the crispness of the pillowcase. I long to crawl in next to her, to swallow a handful of pills and let sleep pour over me. I cannot, though; I need to be alert, prepared to aid in the search for Petra. Louis and Fitzgerald assured me that they would contact me when their interviews with Antonia and her son were complete.

When Fitzgerald and Louis had finished questioning Fielda and me, shaken my hand and climbed into the car, a feeling of dirtiness edging toward perverseness crept next to me. Agent Fitzgerald did not accuse me of anything, certainly. However, he did request that Fielda and I stop in at the police station and have our fingerprints taken. Exclusionary purposes, Fitzgerald reassured us. I am not an uninformed man— oblivious at times, I admit, to the world around me—but not unaware that family members are the initial suspects in any missing child situation, and that more often than not, they are the guilty ones. The verity that the police, my community, my colleagues would entertain the notion that I could harm two young children, *my daughter,* makes me angry. I know that Fielda and I had no part in this and the fact that crucial minutes are being squandered in that consideration makes me ill.

I recall feeling the same when Fielda left me, the second of two instances when we have been apart, a panicked, out-of-control sensation that started in my extremities and coursed through my veins toward my center, tossing me off balance. Since the day Fielda and I were married, Fielda spoke of children, a home full of curly-haired, dark-eyed babies who loved books as I did and who loved food as Fielda did. To be honest, I was so astonished to have this wondrous, beautiful woman next to me, the whole of being married seemed unreal to me, magical. I viewed children in the same manner. I could not imagine being a father.

Fielda would spend hours looking through parent magazines and children's clothing catalogs, perusing and planning. I always nodded and made a noncommittal noise when she showed me a particular article about prenatal health care or organic baby food. Months passed, then a year, and no baby. Looking back, I should have seen the change in Fielda—the gradual slump of her shoulders, the slight pull of the corners of her mouth downward, the way she would stare at new mothers in grocery stores and at church—but I did not notice.

For two years, three, then four, Fielda continued to pore over parenting books. All she could talk about was babies. How to become pregnant with one, having one, raising one. I'm ashamed to say that I lost patience with her. I'm not a handy individual, but once in a while I've been known to try and tighten a pipe or replace a fuse. I went down to our basement where I keep my toolbox, nearly pristine from lack of use. I was going to attempt to change the showerhead in our bathroom. I don't know why the box caught my eye, but it did. It was a large, plain, clear plastic container with a blue lid and it appeared to be filled with clothing. Maybe it was the bright pink fabrics that were such a contrast to the gray dark basement that made me take notice. I don't know. But I pulled the box down from the shelf and opened it, almost fearfully, as if I was doing something wrong. Inside were dozens of tiny baby outfits in pinks and blues and yellows with the price tags still hanging from them. There were dresses for a girl and overalls for a boy, there were socks that would barely cover my thumb. There were bibs in bright colors that said Daddy's Little Girl or Got Milk? It wasn't the money, though the amount of clothing in that box must have cost a small fortune, that bothered me. It seemed to me so sad in some way. Pathetic, really. Looking back, I can see that it was simply hope. That for Fielda, purchasing the clothing meant that she was going to conceive and have a child. She had to, she already had the outfits. I didn't look at it that way, though. I grabbed a fistful of the clothing, dropping impossibly small T-shirts and booties behind me as I stomped up the steps.

"Fielda!" I bellowed, startling her so that she dropped the pot of spaghetti she was carrying to the sink to drain. She hopped back to avoid the scalding water, and limp strings of pasta slid across the floor.

"Martin!" she snapped back impatiently. "What's the matter?"

"This is the matter!" I said, holding out the baby clothing. "Are you crazy?" I asked. Words I immediately regretted because, by the look on her face, I think she may have wondered the exact same thing of herself. Still I ranted on. "Fielda, there is no baby. There may never be a baby. Maybe it's time you faced it."

"I'm going to have a baby, Martin," she told me, her voice low and dangerous. "I can't *not* have a baby. I've got to have a baby," she went on, and I saw a light go from her eyes. A sense of dread wheedled through me but I pushed it away.

"Oh, don't be so dramatic," I said cruelly. "I'm not going to sit by and watch you waste money on a baby that doesn't exist." I might as well have slapped her. The hurt on her face still takes my breath away and the fact that I caused it to be there still makes my face burn with shame.

She stalked out of the room, nearly slipping on the spaghetti as she left. She didn't talk to me for nearly a week. And even after she did begin to talk to me, she didn't allow me to touch her. She spent endless minutes in the bathroom and she would emerge with red, swollen eyes, but she never cried in front of me. One day I found the sleeping pills in the medicine cabinet. Good, I told myself. Maybe she would begin to sleep through the night again instead of the endless pacing, pacing. If I had thought about it, I would have known. I should have known. I should have thrown that bottle away the minute I saw it.

Then one day it was as if nothing had ever happened and she appeared to be the same old Fielda. I thought she had come to her senses, decided to let nature take its course. But I was wrong. Her mission to become a mother was as strong as ever, and I found out about the doctor's appointment when the receptionist from the office called to confirm the appointment. "We have the test results in," the receptionist explained. "He'd like for Fielda to come in to discuss them."

I gave her the message, trying to conceal my wounded feelings at being left out of this part of Fielda's life. Though I must say, I couldn't really blame her. I had told her to stop, which is something Fielda never did, give up, I mean. She thanked me for the message, staring at me levelly as if daring me to call her on it. I didn't.

Instead I canceled and rescheduled my classes that drizzly October afternoon to accompany her. In the office I tried to hold her hand, which she shook impatiently away. I tried reading aloud bits from outdated magazines but she ignored me. Instead, she paced around the waiting room, looking at walls tacked with Polaroid snapshots of weary mothers holding tiny babies in their arms, sometimes a shell-shocked husband or boyfriend standing nearby. When the nurse called her name, Fielda marched back to the examining room without a backward glance toward me. Moments later, however, the nurse returned to the waiting area and called my name.

"Mr. Gregory, would you please come on back? Dr. Berg would like for you to join us," she said, smiling.

I followed her, heartened at her smile. Good news, I thought. Fielda will return to her former self, her shoulders would straighten and laughter would return to her eyes. When I entered the room Fielda sat, fully dressed, on the examining table, crossing and uncrossing her ankles nervously. The doctor was a dark-skinned man with a serious face. His hair was black and slicked back from his forehead, and he had caring eyes.

"Mr. Gregory, I am Dr. Berg, Mrs. Gregory's gynecologist. Please, take a seat." He indicated a plastic chair across the small room.

"No, thank you," I replied and continued to stand next to Fielda.

"We asked you both to come in today to share with you the results of some initial tests that we have done in order to find out why Mrs. Gregory has not conceived."

I nodded and reached for Fielda's hand. This time she did not pull away.

"The good news is, we cannot find anything conclusively wrong that is preventing conception with Mrs. Gregory. There is, of course, further testing that we can do, but I would recommend that you try some other avenues."

"For example…" I began.

"For example, I would suggest that you, Mr. Gregory, have a sperm sample taken. This could address any concerns with sperm viability."

"Oh," I laughed uneasily. "I don't think that will be necessary. I believe that these things come in due time. Perhaps parenthood is not for us."

I felt Fielda pull her hand from mine. It was not a violent pull, more like an easing away. It did not alarm me. Fielda's next act, however, did. She slid off the examination table and breezed out of the room without a backward glance or an acknowledgment to the physician, which surprised me, as Fielda is normally unfailingly polite. I thanked the doctor for the both of us and quickly made my exit. When I stepped out into the wet parking lot I could see Fielda speeding away in our car.

I walked the nearly two miles home, ruining my dress shoes, the chill of autumn pouring into them as I sloshed through puddles. When I arrived at our house Fielda was not at home. I decided to give her some time to think, to be on her own, but the minutes stretched into hours and evening arrived. I finally called the Mourning Glory and asked Mrs. Mourning, albeit awkwardly, if she had seen Fielda. She had not.

"Did you all have your first fight?" Mrs. Mourning teased good-naturedly. "'Bout time, you've only been married four years!"

I laughed feebly and asked her to tell Fielda to call me if she happened to hear from her.

It had stopped raining, but darkness was gathering, pressing in on the house so that I nearly choked on its emptiness. Finally, I abandoned the notion that Fielda needed some time to herself and climbed into our other car, "the regular folk" car Mrs. Mourning would say, a Chevette that was a shade of bronze that fortunately covered the rust stains eating away at its edges. I spent the next hour driving up and down side streets, looking for Fielda; I drove past the library, the fabric store, the candy shop, searching to no avail. I even paused briefly in front of the Mourning Glory and glanced into its gleaming storefront, lit warmly, but did not see Fielda or our Camry. I decided to drive into the Willow Creek Camping Grounds, a dismal, junky spot, I thought, to which people who had nothing better to do with their time would pull cumbersome campers in order to sit around a fire and drink beer all day and all night. I could not imagine that Fielda would be there, but I had run out of ideas. As I pulled into the paved entrance area lined with gigantic maples, their bright red plumage shadowed in the dusk, I saw the car almost immediately and pressed my foot to the pedal, sending my car lurching forward. I pulled in next to Fielda and could see at once that something was not right, that something very, very bad had happened here. Slowly—I do not know why I did not rush—I opened my car door, stepped out and firmly shut it again. I could hear my shoes slapping against the wet pavement as I approached the still car. No movement inside. I went first to the driver's side of the car and pressed my forehead against the glass, framing my face with my hands to get a better look. My Fielda was seated, if I can call it that, in the driver's seat, but sprawled in such a way that her head lay on the passenger's side, her arms tucked up around her face as if she was sleeping. But she was not. I attempted to open the car door, but Fielda had locked it. I fumbled for what seemed an eternity with my key chain, found the correct key and tried to insert it into the lock. I had to stop myself to take a breath and steady my hands. Finally, I yanked the door open and pulled Fielda toward me. I could smell it first, the vomit, an acrid odor, and then I saw the mess on the car floor and car seat. Fielda had been lying in it. I do not know if I spoke, I do not recall that I did, but I remember thinking, *Please don't take her away from me!* I held her close to me, I know, rocking her back and forth for a moment, until I pulled myself together. I pushed her away as gently as possible, but knowing the urgency that was upon me, not as gently as I would have liked.

I climbed into the Camry and breaking every traffic law, drove to Mercy Hospital, where the hospital personnel took Fielda away from me. I was not allowed to see her. They pumped her stomach. I handed the emergency room nurse the empty bottle of pills Fielda had ingested, and she informed me with a scathing look that it was a miracle that she had

survived and would be recuperating on Four West, a place described by my students as "Four West, Nut Nest." I knew I
deserved these looks, I knew I had failed my wife, and I was
punished. She was taken from me. For two weeks, even when
they allowed her to have visitors, she refused to see me. I did
not teach and I did not go to my office; I went to the hospital
and sat in the waiting area, begging the nurses to let me see
her for just one moment, no more. I sent flowers, candy,
orange poppy seed muffins, but still she refused. At last, at the
insistence of Mrs. Mourning, I am sure, Fielda sent for me.

Alone, I entered her room, not dark and sad, as I thought
it would be, but sunny and cheerful, smelling of roses, my
flowers surrounded her bedside along with cards and well
wishes from family and friends. The nurse left us, telling
Fielda to call for her if she needed anything. Fielda would not
meet my eyes. She looked thinner, smaller to me, and tired,
very, very tired. But still I went to her, still I removed my
jacket and shoes, and still I crawled into her small hospital bed,
molding myself to her. Together there we cried, the two of
us, begging each other for forgiveness and quietly, tearfully
we both forgave and allowed ourselves to be forgiven.

Now ten years later, in the swelter of summer, our daughter
missing, Fielda has pulled the bedcovers up around her head,
and I can hear her breath in sleep, heavy and even. I touch
Fielda's shoulder before treading softly from the room and
closing the door behind me. I hesitate in the hallway; I don't
quite know what to do with myself. I know I cannot stay here
at my mother-in-law's home, too far away from what is going
on. I need to be near the officers, I need to be there at a
moment's notice. I had already let my daughter down once

by letting her be taken from our home, hadn't I? I would know, would I not? Someone entering my home, in the dead of night, slinking up the stairs, past my bedroom, down the hallway, to my daughter's door, standing on its threshold, listening to the whir of the box fan, watching the rise and fall of Petra's chest.

Here is where I must stop. I cannot imagine what could have happened beyond this point. I would know, wouldn't I? Someone in my home, I would know.

BEN

I run until my chest is ready to explode. My face is hot with tears. I stumble over a fallen log and tear my dress shirt on a thorny branch, but still I run, down to the creek. I could tell by the way that cop looked at me, the way he talked to me, that he thought I might have hurt you, Calli. At least, he thought I knew who hurt you.

Jason Meechum, bastard. Figures he would be brought up. I could have killed him. I could have. But not really. But I was so mad, furious. It started in math class last spring. I was doing some god-awful division problem with fractions on the board and I couldn't think. The numbers just blurred together and I couldn't think. If I had a pencil and a piece of paper and was sitting at the kitchen table, with you swinging your feet in the chair next to me, drawing butterflies, I would have been fine. Instead, I was standing at the blackboard in front of twenty-seven other kids with a fat piece of crumbly chalk in my hand, and I couldn't think. Jason Meechum started it all. I could hear his whiny, weasely voice.

"Retard!" he coughed, concealing his mouth behind his hand.

The other kids giggled, but said nothing. The teacher didn't hear him, of course, and told me to keep on trying. More laughter, I could feel dozens of eyes on me, burning into my back. I glanced back over my shoulder and could see Meechum making faces and whispering, "Retard," to me. I remember trying to swallow, but my mouth was dry. I can't believe I did it, I really can't. But Meechum had bothered me before, making cracks about my wino father and my stupid sister. This just topped it all off, and I snapped. I spun around, the thick chalk in my fist, and I flung it at him, as hard as I could; I'm a big kid and have a strong arm. The minute it flew from my fingers I was reaching to get it back, but it was too late. I had visions of the chalk hitting a classmate or worse yet, the teacher. But it didn't, it hit Meechum dead center between the eyes. I heard the weird thunk as the chalk hit and saw his hands cover his face. The classroom went completely quiet and Miss Henwood sat at her desk with her mouth wide-open; I'm usually not the guy who causes problems in the classroom. Then I walked right out of the classroom and went home, like, three miles.

My mom was expecting me when I got home. She wasn't mad or nothing. She just looked sad, and of course, that made me start bawling. She just set me on her lap like I was three, I'm sure I about crushed her, and I cried and she told me everything was going to be all right.

It wasn't, though; we had to have a big meeting with the

principal. I had to say sorry to Meechum, and I did, even though I still believe he deserved it. Meechum's parents went on for a while, saying that I should've been suspended or something, but I wasn't. Wish I was.

That next week Meechum and his buddies cornered me after school and pushed me around a bit, called Mom a whore, said she was screwing the deputy sheriff. I walked away that day, but later, when Meechum was alone I snuck up on him and wrenched his arm behind his back and told him I was gonna kill him if he ever said anything about my family again. Meechum blubbered to his mother and she called the school and the police. Another meeting was called, but I denied everything, and he couldn't prove anything. Mrs. Meechum said something about me being just like my no-good father, and boy, did Mom hit the roof with that one. But the damage was done. Everyone looked at me a little different after that. I wasn't the quiet one anymore.

Calli, I'd never hurt anyone. I'm not like Dad, I'm not. I'd never hurt you. I'll find you, even if it takes all night. I'll bring you home and then they'll know.

CALLI

Calli slept fitfully. The ground was hard and unforgiving. Mosquitoes hovered around her exposed parts, though she had tried to tuck her legs underneath her nightgown, and they bit at her ankles and forearms.

She dreamed intermittently of flying among the branches of the trees. She felt cool air on her forehead, and the pleasant swoop in her stomach that came with flight, like the Tilt-A-Whirl at the county fair. Below her she could see the creek, cool and beckoning; she tried to will her body to fly down to the water so she could dive into it. But she could not. She continued to soar, following the crooked path of the creek. She caught a glimpse of her father's fiery hair and her stomach lurched in fear. He was looking up at her, anger etched on his face. She quickly passed over him and saw the rabbit-eared fawn drinking at the water's edge. Its soft eyes calmly summoned her and Calli winged down and hovered just a few feet above the deer. She reached out her hand to stroke its hide, but it darted out of her reach and into the woods. Calli tried to follow, the puff of its white tail raised in warning, her beacon. In and out of firs and buckeyes it twisted and turned. Calli concentrated to keep up. A hand snatched at her from behind and tried to grab at Calli, but only caught the hem of her nightgown. Looking over her shoulder, she could see that it was Petra who waved happily after her. Another hand clamped briefly on her arm and her mother smiled up at her. Calli's flight slowed, but did not stop, and she momentarily spied her mother's hurt, confused look as she flew onward. Then the wood was filled with people who were familiar to her, grabbing at her in a friendly way, like children chasing bubbles. There was Mrs. White, the school nurse, and her kindergarten teacher, and Mrs. Vega, her first-grade teacher whom she loved dearly. Mr. Wilson, the school counselor, held her opened journal, pointing at something in it, but she couldn't see what it was. What was he pointing at? She so badly wanted to know. She tried to will her body to fly down toward Mr. Wilson and look at that journal, but she could not, she kept soaring onward. There was Mrs. Norland, Deputy Sheriff Louis, Mr. and Mrs. Gregory, Jake Moon, Lena Hill, the librarian, all there reaching out for her. She peered through the throng of people searching for Ben, but she could not find him. Now there were people grasping at her that she did not know and this was frightening to Calli. She tried to kick her feet and swim upward with her arms through the air, onward she flew, following her doe. Soon she came to a beautiful clearing. Trees circled the small green meadow. A small pond was nestled in the center and the fawn stopped for a drink. She was so thirsty, but could not pull herself down to the bank. Suddenly Ben was there. Big, strong, kind Ben. He called to her. She tried to tell him that she was thirsty, so thirsty, but no words came. He seemed to know, though, Ben always seemed to know, and he dipped his hands into the water and pulled them out, cupped full of water. Still Calli could not bring her body down to him, but he tossed the water up at her and she caught a drop on her tongue. It was cold and sweet. Calli reached out for her brother, but it was as if she was filled with helium and she kept rising, higher and higher, above the treetops. Ben quickly began disappearing, his red hair a small flag below her. She continued to travel upward. The temperature rose as she rose, until she crashed into the sun.

Calli awakened with a start, momentarily disoriented. She sat up and tried to wet her cracked lips, but her tongue was thick and heavy and held no moisture. Her dream had fled from her mind as she blinked herself awake, but was left with the comforting feeling that Ben was nearby. She stood slowly, her muscles tight, her feet sore. Downward, she decided, toward the water, and she began her slow descent down the bluff toward where she thought the creek might lay. As she walked gingerly along the path, avoiding broken twigs and jagged rocks, Calli recalled snatches of her dream and the image of the school counselor, Mr. Wilson, holding her journal, pointing at something inside of it.

At their first meeting, Mr. Wilson, a tall, thin man with bone-white hair and a long nose, invited her to sit next to him at the circular table in the guidance office. In front of them lay a black journal made with a rough raspy paper with little natural fibers poking out. The book was held together with white silky ribbon. Calli thought it was a beautiful book and longed to flip through the pages to see what was inside. Next to the journal lay a brand-new box of colored chalk, not the thick variety that came in only four colors and was used for drawing on the sidewalk, but a real artist's set with wonderful bright, rich colors. Her fingers itched to open the package.

"Did you know, Calli," began Mr. Wilson, "that some of the best conversations people have are not with the spoken word?" He waited, as if expecting Calli to answer.

Immediately Calli became guarded. Last year's counselor, Mrs. Hereau, a mousy woman who only wore baggy clothes in shades of gray and tan, would wait for Calli to answer, as well. She never did, though.

"Calli, I'm not going to get you to try and talk," Mr. Wilson said, as if reading her mind. He rubbed his long nose with one extended fingertip and looked at her straight in the eye. Mrs. Hereau never even seemed to look at Calli's face, always talked to her while jotting notes down in a notebook. Mr. Wilson's straightforward manner unsettled Calli a bit.

"I do want to get to know you, though," he continued. "That's my job, to try and get to know the students, and help them if I can.

"Oh, don't look so suspicious, Calli," Mr. Wilson chuckled. "Talking is overrated. Blah, blah, blah. I listen to people talking all day! Then I go home and listen to my wife talking, and my kids talking, and my dog talking…" He slid his eyes toward Calli, who wrinkled her nose and smiled at the image of Mr. Wilson listening to a black Lab or German shepherd sitting at the kitchen table, talking about its day.

"Okay, so my dog doesn't *talk,* talk, but everyone else does.

So this quiet will be good for me. I thought," he said, stretching his lean legs under the table, "that we could have this journal here and write to each other. Kind of like pen pals, but without envelopes or stamps. Our conversations could be right in here." He tapped the journal with one finger.

"What do you think, Calli? Don't answer that. Think about it, decorate the cover, whatever. I'm just going to sit over here at my desk and work and enjoy the quiet." Mr. Wilson smiled encouragingly, stood and went to his old oak desk in the corner of the office. He settled his long frame into a chair and tucked his legs underneath the steel-framed chair, bent his slender neck over the contents of a file folder and began to read.

Calli regarded the book in front of her. She loved to draw pictures and write stories. She could write lots of words, even though she was only in the first grade. She wrote stories about horses and fairies and cities under the ocean. She never had a pen pal, never even wrote to her father while he was away—that had never occurred to her. She couldn't imagine that anyone would be interested in what she wrote. Everyone wanted to hear what she had to *say,* as if the words she said would somehow drip jewels.

She flipped open the journal. Its creamy, unlined pages were oddly welcoming. The pages contained the same flecks of fibers that were in the cover, each page uniquely flawed. She softly closed the book and her attention shifted to the chalk in front of her. Selecting a purple that held the same shimmer as the dragonflies down at Willow Creek, she held it in her fingers, admiring it. In the lower right-hand corner she slowly printed her name with great care: *Calli.* She glanced up at Mr. Wilson, who was still engrossed in his paperwork. Calli carefully replaced the purple chalk back into the box and wiped the excess dust from her fingers onto her jeans, leaving iridescent streaks. She pushed her chair back from the table, stood, picked up the journal and carried it over to Mr. Wilson. She held it out to him.

"Just set it over there, Calli," he said, indicating the round table. "We'll meet again on Thursday. Have a good day."

Calli paused. Was that all? No *"You need to speak now, Calli. You're worrying your mother needlessly. Stop this nonsense. There is nothing wrong with you!"* Just *"Have a good day"*?

Calli turned away from Mr. Wilson and gently laid the book on the table, gave a small breath of relief and walked out the door.

Calli spent two half-hour sessions a week with Mr. Wilson, writing and drawing pictures in her journal. Often, he would draw a picture or write back to her, only if she asked him to in writing. Her favorite pictures and writings were about his dog, named Bart. He told tales of Bart being able to open doors with his paws and the time when he was begging at the dining-room table and actually said the word *hamburger* in his little dog voice. Sometimes Calli would have to point at a word for Mr. Wilson to read to her, but most often she could read what he wrote on her own. She looked forward to the beginning of second grade and her meetings with Mr. Wilson. She felt safe in his quiet little room with her chalk, a sharpened pencil and her journal. Mr. Wilson had said he would keep the journal over the summer and that it would be waiting for her when school began again. She had written to him, during their second to last meeting of her first-grade year, asking him what they were going to do when the journal was filled up. He'd replied, "Get a new one, of course!" She had smiled at that.

Calli wondered what Mr. Wilson had been pointing at in her dream. Which page in the journal was he trying to show to her? She didn't know. They had written so much in it, none of it particularly important, not to an adult anyway, except Mr. Wilson had a way of making you feel as if everything you wrote and did was important.

A ground squirrel skittered by and startled Calli. She listened for the gurgle of the creek, but heard nothing but the cicadas' steady thrumming.

Downward, she told herself, downward is where the creek will be, with cold water and silver fish. Maybe she'd see a frog and shimmering purple dragonflies that sparkled as they skimmed the water. Downward.

DEPUTY SHERIFF LOUIS

Fitzgerald and I have gone our separate ways for the moment. Fitzgerald is focusing on getting a search dog over here, and on trying to trace the whereabouts of Griff from the GPS in his cell phone. I will be meeting with the other deputies to give and receive updates on our progress in finding Calli and Petra.

Our sheriff, Harold Motts, is getting on in years, and has taken a mostly hands-off approach to his job in the past year. He's passed as many of his duties that he could over to me. There has even been talk that I should run for sheriff in the next election. Most of the staff have been accepting, though grudgingly, of my leadership role, but one. Deputy Logan Roper has tried to make my job as a deputy sheriff hell. I figure it had more to do with Roper being a close pal of Griff Clark more than any genuine dislike that he has for me, but who knows? We've come to a mutual understanding. We show professional respect toward one another and communicate when we need to, but that's all. It's too bad, actually, but as long as our tension doesn't interfere with the job, I can live with it.

Griff and Logan were five years ahead of Toni and me in high school. I never really knew much about them, just that they were wild and could be mean. I'm not sure how Griff and Toni were first introduced, but I suspect it was through her job as a clerk at the Gas & Go, a convenience store on Highway Ten. Toni worked there on weekends and after school. I told her I didn't like her working in a gas station so late at night and so close to the highway; anyone could take off with her and would be well on his way without anyone knowing. Toni would just laugh and call me "cop boy." I hated that.

By April of our senior year of high school, Toni wasn't talking to me and was dating Griff, apparently hopelessly in love with him. I thought she was trying to make me jealous and it worked, but I wouldn't give her the satisfaction of letting her know that. I didn't think, however, that a year later she would be married to him.

November of our senior year was when Toni and I really started talking about our future together and what we wanted. We had spent a chilly early winter morning walking through the woods. She wore an old brown barn coat that belonged to one of her brothers and a multicolored hat knit by her mother, who had died earlier that fall. She had cropped her hair short and it made her face seem even younger than her seventeen years; she had lost weight since her mother passed and she looked breakable. I was excited. She knew I wanted to go to college. Toni said she was supportive of that, but I could tell she wasn't really. I couldn't afford the tuition at St.

Gilianus so a state college was my only option. The problem was that the University of Iowa was over a hundred miles away from Willow Creek. I had already filled out my application and had been accepted; I would leave the following August.

As I told Toni, she wouldn't even look at me. She sat on the edge of the fallen tree we called Lone Tree Bridge because it fell across a portion of Willow Creek. Her normally un-guarded face went stony as I described to her that the college wasn't really all that far away and that I'd come to see her on holidays and on weekends. I went on to say that there was nothing stopping her from coming with me. She could enroll in classes or get a job. We could still be together.

"Everybody leaves me," she whispered, tucking her arms into the pockets of her coat.

She meant her mother dying and her brothers moving away. It was just her and her dad in their house, and accord-ing to Toni, her dad was thinking of moving to Phoenix to be with Tim, his oldest son.

"I'm not leaving, not for good," I told her. But she shook her head.

"You won't come back. You'll go to college with all these important people and important ideas. You'll outgrow this place," she said matter-of-factly.

"No," I insisted. "I will never outgrow you."

"All I've ever wanted was to live in a yellow house," she said softly before she walked away, leaving me standing alone among the naked trees. I could hear crispy leaves crunching under her feet long after I couldn't see her anymore. We tried to carry on as we always had for the next month or so, but something had changed. She would shrink from my touch, as if the feel of my hands on her hurt her somehow. She would become uncharacteristically quiet when I talked about college and a shadow came across her face whenever I tried to make love to her. I hadn't even left yet, but she was already gone.

She broke up with me at the beginning of December and from then on, it was as if I didn't exist. She didn't take my phone calls, didn't answer the door when I came over, walked right past me in the hallways at school. I finally cornered her in Willow Creek Woods. She was walking slowly, her head down, her eyes on the trail before her. It was snowing, the flakes impossibly big. I briefly considered scooping up a snowball and pelting her in the back with it. I was pretty pissed at her. But I didn't. There was something about her walking there alone that made her seem as naked and vulnerable as the giant, leafless trees. "Toni," I called softly to her, trying not to startle her. She whipped around, clutching her chest. On seeing me, she dropped her hands, fists tight, as if preparing for a fight. "Hey," I said. She didn't respond. "Can we talk?" I asked.

"There's really nothing to talk about," she said, her voice as cold as the air around us.

"Do you really want to do this?" I asked.

"Do what?" she asked as if she didn't know what I was talking about.

"This!" My voice echoed through the trees. She took one step toward me and then stopped, as if coming any closer to me might make her change her mind.

"Lou," she said firmly. "For months I watched my mother die…"

"I know," I said. "I was there, remember?"

"No, you weren't there. Not really. For months I watched my mother dying. There was nothing, nothing, that I could do to make her better, to make her live. Now I'm losing my dad. In a completely different way, but the minute I graduate he's out of here. Out of Willow Creek forever. He can't stand the thought of living here without my mother. I do not want to end up like that. Ever!" She looked at me fiercely.

"It's not the same," I pleaded with her.

"It's exactly the same," she shot back. "You're going to leave, and that's fine, whatever. But I'm not going to spend the rest of my life waiting for you. I spent way too much time on you as it is."

"What's that supposed to mean?" I asked angrily. "That I was just a waste of time?"

"It just means that I'm not going to invest one more minute in someone who isn't going to stick around, who doesn't love me enough to stay. Just leave me alone!" She turned away from me and moved noiselessly through the woods. I shouldn't have done it, but I did. At that moment, I hated her. I bent down and scraped up a handful of the wet snow, forming a perfect white ball. I didn't throw it hard, but at the last second she turned to say something else to me, and the snowball pelted her right in the face. She stood stone still for a fraction of a second and then turned and ran. I tried to follow her, to apologize, but she knew the woods better than anyone, plus she was faster than I was. I never caught up to her, never said I was sorry. Never found out what she was going to say to me before the snowball hit.

In the end, she outgrew me, or maybe I outgrew her, I guess. I knew I was starting to look like a fool. Everyone knew

I loved Antonia and that she wanted nothing to do with me anymore. She married Griff that next year, while I was away at school, and had Ben soon after. I learned about Toni the way strangers learned about her, through newspaper clippings and idle gossip. We had become strangers, she and I.

I met Christine four years later and we married. She reminded me nothing of Toni, and I didn't mean to hold that against her, but I guess I did. I'm surprised, actually, that Christine was this patient with me, especially after I brought her here to Willow Creek to live and raise a family. She never quite settled in, always felt out of place, unwelcome. It's not her fault that the people of Willow Creek are intertwined by a common history and by blood. Maybe she doesn't fit in because she doesn't want to, or maybe because I don't want her to. I don't know. But I don't have time to waste on this; I have to focus on the matters at hand.

As soon as I walk into the station, Officer Tucci is there, waiting for me.

"We got some info on some of the names you wanted run," he tells me. "There's not much. Mariah Burton, the babysitter, is completely clean. Chad Wagner, one of the students, was arrested when he was in high school for underage drinking. Got a hold of him and he's home visiting his mom and dad in Winner. Nothing's come up on this Lucky Thompson, but we can't contact him. He isn't at home or he isn't answering his phone. The men from the furniture store are accounted for and are being interviewed. We're also checking on all the teachers at the girls' school. Calli spent a lot of time with the school counselor, a Charles Wilson. We haven't been able to contact him, either. Only other red flag was on Sam Garfield. He teaches at St. Gilianus. Been here for about three years. Before that he was at another college in Ohio. Left under a cloud. Had an affair with a student.

"Oh, and Antonia Clark called about twenty minutes ago," Tucci says. "She says she's found footprints that look like Calli's, and a man's footprints, too. She was very upset, crying and carrying on. Couldn't make much sense of her after that."

"What did you tell her?" I ask.

"Told her I would let you know as soon as I could. She said she wanted to talk to you. Had to talk to you. I tried to explain to her that you weren't available at a second's notice." Tucci sounds irritated. "That you're a busy man."

"Who's over there now?" I ask, already heading back out the door.

"Logan Roper," he says.

"Great," I mutter under my breath.

"Well, he was there and available," Tucci blusters, sounding confused. "Shouldn't he be the one?"

"That's fine," I say regretfully. "I just want to be made aware of any developments in this case. Call me no matter what from here on out."

"Do you think it's like that McIntire girl?" he asks.

"I don't know. But that outcome is the one we want to avoid." I pause at the double doors. "Is there anything else I need to know before I head on back to the Clark place?"

"Actually, yes. Channel Four's been calling all morning asking about the missing girls. They want a statement. And Mrs. McIntire called twice. She wants you to call her back. Wants to know if she can be any help to the families of the missing girls. Says she's driving over this afternoon."

"Dear Lord," I mumble. "Get me Fitzgerald. We need to get an official statement written up for the press. When was the last time you spoke with Mrs. McIntire?"

"About forty minutes ago, I guess. She should be here anytime now."

I retreat to my desk. I'd have to see about Toni later. For now, I had to trust my department, especially Roper, to do what they were trained to do. I quickly jot down a rough copy of a statement that could hopefully satisfy the press, and my phone rings. "Deputy Sheriff Louis speaking," I say.

"Yeah, Louis," Fitzgerald begins, "I just got word about the footprints at the Clark house. The state crime lab should be pulling up there momentarily. Who do you got over there?"

"Officer by the name of Logan Roper. Should be fine, except…" I hesitate.

"Go ahead. Say it. Something's bothering you," Fitzgerald prods.

"He's a decent cop, but he's also great pals with Griff Clark. Conflict of interest, maybe," I say. Like I was one to talk, but I didn't trust Griff and I didn't quite trust his buddies, either.

"I see what you mean," says Fitzgerald. "Pair him up with someone you completely trust. How 'bout you?"

"Well," I begin, "there could be a bit of a problem with that, as well."

Better to get it all out now, Toni and my history together. Shouldn't matter, but it does. I settle in to tell Fitzgerald all about it when I hear a soft clearing of the throat, and at my desk I see the tired, sad face of Mrs. McIntire.

"Hey," I say to Fitzgerald. "Let me call you back."

We disconnect and I face the woman I had hoped not to

see again until we had the man who destroyed her life and lives of her family members, the woman whose battered, abused daughter was found dead in a woody area two miles from her home. The woman who I had to help pick up off the floor of the morgue after she identified the body as her Jenna's, and the woman who cursed me last time she talked to me for having to bury her daughter without knowing who had done this to her.

"I want to help," she says simply.

I offer her a chair and try to figure out the best way to tell her that the last thing the Gregory and Clark families want is any sort of reminder that their daughters could be dead.

MARTIN

I can't sit around and wait. I tell Fielda's mother that I am going to check on the investigation and I drive back toward my home. I park on the shoulder of Timber Ridge Road. Something is going on at the Clark house. A flurry of activity. Several police cars drive past and turn down the Clarks' lane. My heart quickens and for a moment I think that I am having a heart attack, but I do not collapse, though I feel a heart attack would be preferable to what is going through my mind right now.

The sun is bearing down more ferociously now, if that is possible. The car thermometer reads ninety-nine degrees, and that does not even include the heat index. I step from my car and make my way toward the Clark house.

The woods and this quiet, uneventful neighborhood were what brought Fielda and me to our home. We like the fact that, while we have neighbors, there are only four close by. The Olson and Connolly families live to our right and the Clarks and old Mrs. Norland are on the left. One hundred yards separate each of our homes, so we are close enough to call each other neighbor but far away enough for privacy's sake. We never let Petra visit the Clark house when Griff was home from wherever he works, the Alaska pipeline, I believe. We don't tell Petra that Griff is the reason she cannot go over there at times; we simply say that Calli has so little time with her father that we must not disturb their family time. Petra accepts this good-naturedly, and I do not believe she knows of Griff's illness. Calli certainly never speaks of it.

On the other side of Timber Ridge is another line of trees, not the forest that lies behind our homes, but a high bluff that separates us from the rest of Willow Creek. Many miles down Timber Ridge a few other homes are situated in much the same manner, neighbors here and there with backyards fading into the forest. My feet crunch on the grass, burned yellow from the sun and lack of rain. From a distance, I see some officers speaking with Antonia in her front yard. She is pointing and gesturing, but I cannot see her face.

I see a van speed past and turn down the Clarks' drive. It is a television van. I can't quite make out the call letters, and they are obviously in a great hurry. Again my heart flutters and I quicken my step. I decide to cut through the back of our yards to hopefully avoid any reporters or cameras. Antonia, too, sees the media van and hurries into her home while the officers stride toward the vehicle, arms waving, ordering the driver to stop. I run a football field's length to the Clarks' back door and a police officer stops me short. I am covered with sweat and I bend over to try and catch my breath. Why so many police officers, I wonder.

"Sir," the officer addresses me, "you are not supposed to be here. This is a crime scene."

"I'm Martin Gregory," I explain as another police officer steps past me and begins unwinding yellow crime scene tape and attaching one end to a concrete birdbath settled among Antonia's garden. "What's going on?" I ask.

"Martin Gregory?" the officer asks.

"Petra Gregory's father," I say impatiently.

"Uh, yes, sir. I'm sorry. Please step toward the front of the house."

"What's going on?" I repeat. "Did you find something?"

"I think I should let Agent Fitzgerald speak with you," he says over his shoulder as he walks into the house. "Please stay here."

I ignore his direction and follow him into the house. "Antonia," I call out. She is sitting on her couch, her face in her hands. "Antonia, what's going on? Did something happen? Did you find something out?" My voice is trembling.

"Footprints," Antonia says, shaking. "We think we found Calli's footprints and a man's."

"What about Petra? Did you find some footprints that may be hers?" I ask.

Agent Fitzgerald speaks up, I had not even seen him in the corner of the room, speaking with another man who could have been a policeman, but was dressed in everyday clothes. "Mr. Gregory, I'm glad you're here." He reaches out his hand to shake mine, and I wipe my sweaty palm on my slacks before I accept his.

"What is going on?" I ask yet again. No one is really listening to me.

"Please, come sit down," Agent Fitzgerald says as if this is his own living room.

I sit.

"Mr. Gregory, Mrs. Clark has noticed a child's footprints, along with an adult male's shoe prints. They could have been there for quite some time. As you know, it hasn't rained for a few weeks. We're concerned because it appears, from the impressions in the dirt, that there was a struggle between the adult and the child. We are investigating this. We will also be checking more thoroughly around your home, as well. At this point, however, there appears to be only one set of child's footprints." Agent Fitzgerald pauses, letting this information soak into me, then continues. "We've called in a crime scene unit from Des Moines. They'll be here shortly. The crime lab will be doing a thorough search of this yard and of your yard, as well, to see if any other footprints or evidence can be found.

"The media has arrived," Fitzgerald announces. "This is a good thing for you and Mrs. Clark, although it makes things somewhat more difficult for us logistically. We don't want anyone getting in the way of us doing our job."

"I need to go tell Fielda what is going on. What should I say to her?" I ask.

"Tell her the truth. You can't hide anything from her during this. You two need to stick together and be strong. But I have to insist that you stay away from your home." To Antonia he says, "Mrs. Clark, we need you to also stay away from your home. This is now a crime scene. Do you have anyone with whom you can stay?"

Toni looks dazed. "I think…I suppose Mrs. Norland's

house—over there." She motions weakly toward our neighbor's home.

"Good. If the reporters ask you questions, tell them you will be speaking with them in about…" Fitzgerald checks his watch "…one hour. Will that give you enough time to gather your thoughts and speak with Mrs. Gregory?"

I nod, though, in fact, I have no idea if I will be ready or not.

"You and Mrs. Gregory and Mrs. Clark will speak first. Then I will give the press a brief overview of the status of the investigation and answer any questions that may be asked. Okay?"

I nod again and stand. "I'll go and get Fielda," I say resignedly.

All at once there is a commotion outside, a series of shouts, not in anger. The press, perhaps. Agent Fitzgerald moves quickly to the front of the house.

"Mr. Gregory, you better get out here," he instructs. "Damn press," he mutters.

I rush to his side and see what concerned him so. I see Fielda emerging from her mother's car, walking dazedly down the Clarks' lane. A lone reporter and cameraman begin to press in around her, and she looks so confused. Her eyes dart anxiously around for help and I fly out of the house and run to her side.

"Are you related to one of the missing girls?" the reporter asks. "What do you know about the evidence that was found in the backyard?"

Fielda looks at me desperately. Her flowered sundress is wrinkled, her hair is flattened on one side, disheveled, her mascara is smudged beneath her eyes and one cheek bears a slight imprint left behind from the bed linens.

"We have reports that the mother of Jenna McIntire is in town. Have you met with Mary Ellen McIntire? Has she given you any advice on how to handle this?" The reporter, a serious woman in a red suit, thrusts a Channel Four microphone under her chin.

Fielda goes rigid and she gapes up at me. For one horrible moment I think she will faint. Her eyes briefly roll back in her head, but I wrap my arms firmly around her shoulders and hold her close to me. She steadies and I lead her away from Antonia's house. Antonia follows close behind us. Agent Fitzgerald steps forward and introduces himself to the reporter.

Fielda takes several deep breaths. "I'm fine, Martin. Tell me what's going on. I can handle this."

I must look doubtful, because she gives me a steely glare. "Martin, I am fine. I promise. I need to be fine if I am going to be any help to Petra. Tell me what is going on so we can figure out what to do next."

BEN

Calli, remember the time I slept in a tree? The huge climbing tree just past Willow Wallow? I was nine and so you must have been four, not talking anymore. I was just so sick of everyone trying to get you to talk. That's all Mom cared about anymore, getting you to say something, anything.

She'd sit you at the kitchen table and say things like, "Do you want some ice cream, Calli?"

You'd nod your head. I mean, what kid wouldn't want ice cream at nine-thirty on a Tuesday morning?

"Say please, Calli," Mom would tell you, "and you can have some yummy ice cream!" She'd talk in this high, annoying voice, like she was talking to a baby, trying to feed it crappy mashed up sweet potatoes or something.

'Course, you never said anything back to her. But Mom would try forever. The ice cream would get all soupy and warm, and she'd still be sitting at the table, trying to get you to eat it, when all you really wanted to do was go watch *Sesame Street*.

In the end, you wouldn't say anything and Mom would give you a fresh bowl of ice cream to eat in front of the TV anyway. So it wasn't much of an incentive, if you ask me. After one or two times of that, even a four-year-old is smart enough to figure out that if you wait long enough you'll get the ice cream.

One day I just had enough. I was sick of sitting there watching Mom trying to bribe you into talking, when even I knew it wasn't gonna happen. Mom pulled the ice cream out of the fridge and reached up into a cupboard for the sugar cones.

Oooh, I thought, she's pulling out the sugar cones, big-time bribes today. Mom started as she usually did. "Do you want some ice cream, Calli? Hmm, what do we have here? Tin Roof Sundae! Your favorite, Calli!"

"How do you know?" I asked. I couldn't help it.

"What?" Mom asked. She was digging into the ice cream container with the ice cream scoop.

"How do you know her favorite is still Tin Roof Sundae?" I asked, and Mom looked at me kind of confused-like.

"I just know," she answered. "Look, Calli, sugar cones!"

"She doesn't like the peanuts in it anymore. She always eats around them," I said.

"Ben, go play," Mom said, kind of snotty-like, I thought.

"No, this is stupid," I said loudly, surprising myself.

"Ben, go play," Mom said again, like she meant business.

"No. Calli can't talk, she can't do it! No matter how much ice cream you give her, or candy or pop, she isn't gonna say anything. She can't talk!" I shouted.

"You be quiet, Ben," Mom said real soft.

"No!" I said, looking her in the eye, just daring her to make me. "You wanna know why she can't talk, I'd go talk to Dad." I remember looking around me to see if maybe he could hear, even though I knew he was traveling.

"Ben, stop it!" Mom shouted back, her chin trembling.

"No!" I grabbed the ice cream scoop out of her hand and walked to the back door, opened it and flung it out into the yard. I don't know why, it just seemed like the right thing to do at the time.

The whole time, Calli, you just sat there, with your big eyes, all scared. Then, when the yelling started, you put your hands over your ears and closed your eyes.

For a minute, I thought Mom was going to hit me. She had that same look in her eyes that Dad gets.

I yelled, "Go ahead, hit me! You're turning into Dad anyway. A big bully, trying to make people do what you want them to do, no matter what!"

I ran and ran and ran. Kinda like what I did today. Not so brave, huh? I spent the night in that old tree down by Willow Wallow. You and Mom came looking for me and I sat on my branch all quiet, looking down at you two, thinking that you didn't see me. But I caught you looking up at me, you gave me a little wave and I waved back. Mom must have figured out where I was because later on she came back with a paper sack full of sandwiches and some pop.

She set it at the bottom of the tree and said to you, "I'll just set this here for Ben, Calli, so if he gets hungry he'll have a little something to eat."

I spent all day and night in that tree. I came down only to grab the bag of food and to go pee. You and Mom came back to check on me a bunch of times that day, and I was just sure Mom was going to try and make me come down. But she didn't, she just lay an old pillow and blanket down on the ground under the tree.

I slept in that old tree and climbed down the next morning all stiff and sore, but I did it. Mom didn't get mad like I thought she would. She didn't say a word about the whole thing. She stopped trying to bribe you into talking with ice cream, though. She never did that again. Oh, we had ice cream, but it was never Tin Roof Sundae and it never came with a "Say please, Calli."

Calli, if we get you home safe today, I'll buy you the biggest ice cream sundae, without nuts, that I can buy with my paper route money.

Calli

Calli walked slowly down the trail. It opened up to a golden meadow on either side. Dainty Queen Anne's lace waved at her. She had never been this far before, but the open sky made her feel safer. There were fewer shadows and hidden figures behind trees. Orange tiger lilies framed the trail, as did wilting purple coneflowers.

Petra always called them purple daisies and would pick one from a ditch in front of her home and tuck it behind her ear and then gather armfuls of flowers. She'd plan intricate weddings with dolls and stuffed animals. Once when one of her father's students, a man named Lucky, stopped by the house this summer with his dog, Sergeant, Petra and Calli had hurriedly designed invitations for the wedding.

Please join us to celebrate wedded bliss between
Gee Wilikers Gregory
And
Sergeant Thompson
This afternoon in the backyard

Gee Wilikers was Calli's stuffed Yorkshire terrier. Calli slipped black-eyed Susans into Sergeant's red collar and had woven crisp white daisies into chains for Gee Wilikers, Calli, and Petra to wear as crowns. Petra presided over the ceremony and Calli was the flower girl. Lucky, Martin, Fielda and Antonia were all guests and sat in lawn chairs in the backyard. Ben wanted nothing to do with all that business.

Petra hummed the wedding march as Calli walked Sergeant and Gee Wilikers down the makeshift aisle, an old lace table runner. Lucky pretended to cry with happiness, wrapped his arm around Petra, drawing her close to him, declaring the wedding "Just beautiful!" Antonia took pictures and Petra's mother served lemon sherbet ice cream and Kool-Aid.

She remembered playing tag with Lucky and Petra. Remembered trying to climb the oak in Petra's backyard, Lucky boosting her up from below and then climbing up himself. They had tossed acorns down, watching Sergeant chase after them. With Lucky's arm steadying her, she felt no fear of falling. It was such a happy day. Calli remembered throwing her arms around Sergeant, his bushy reddish-brown fur heated by the sun. It came out in shaggy tufts and stuck to Calli's fingers and face, sticky with ice cream.

Now sitting among the wild grasses Calli wove a chain of purple coneflowers into a wreath and set it on her head. Then she began to make another crown for Petra. Petra, she missed Petra. After Petra and Calli had become friends, Petra became her official spokesperson at school. From that day forward, Petra was Calli's voice, her verbal communication with the world around her. Mrs. Vega, their first-grade teacher, was very accepting of this and often regarded the girls as one entity. Once, while on a field trip to Madison to visit the zoo, they stopped the school bus at a fast-food restaurant. Mrs. Vega, asking Calli what she would like to eat, looked at Petra to answer.

Petra answered with little thought. "She wants a hamburger with just mustard, French fries and a Sprite. Calli loves mustard."

Most of the adults that Calli encountered at school were accommodating to her special needs. However, one day when Calli came to school, it was not Mrs. Vega greeting them at the classroom door, but a substitute teacher. She was a large woman, round and doughy, with a great mound of gray, curly hair and a stern, wizened face. Her name was Mrs. Hample and she had none of the good humor or patience that Mrs. Vega had. When Mrs. Hample asked each child his or her name and came to Calli, she did not respond, but just looked shyly down at her desktop.

"Her name is Calli," Petra piped up.

Mrs. Hample looked sharply at Petra. The first hour of school passed uneventfully enough, but after the third time that Petra spoke for Calli, Mrs. Hample erupted.

"Petra, do not answer for Calli again, do you understand? I did not call on you," she ordered in a firm voice.

"But Calli doesn't…" Petra began, but Mrs. Hample interrupted her.

"You're not listening to me. Now, do not speak for Calli again! If she has something that needs to be said, she can tell me herself."

Just before recess Calli timidly approached Mrs. Hample and made the sign for bathroom. Her thumb was pushed up between her first two fingers to form the letter *T* for toilet and then she rotated her wrist side to side.

"What is that supposed to mean? Are you deaf?" Calli shook her head no. "My goodness, if you need to say something to me say it, Calli!" Mrs. Hample said exasperatedly.

"She's shy. She doesn't talk. She has to go..." Petra tried to explain, but Mrs. Hample held her hand up to stop her from speaking further.

"Petra, you may stand against the wall at recess time for not listening to me!" she barked. "And Calli, if you won't tell me what you need, then you can just sit at your desk until you decide to do so. The rest of you, let's line up to go out to recess."

So while Calli sat in her desk, squeezing her legs together, Petra stood last in line while the first graders filed one at a time out the door to recess. Instead of going outdoors with the others, however, Petra snuck up the steps and down the corridor to Mr. Wilson's office. The counselor was sitting at his desk, speaking on the phone, but when he saw the desperate look on Petra's face he quickly hung up.

"Petra, good morning, what's the matter?" he asked.

"It's the substitute teacher," Petra whispered as if afraid that Mrs. Hample would be able to hear her. "She's real mean. I mean *really* mean."

Mr. Wilson chuckled. "I know substitute teachers aren't like your regular teachers, Petra, but you still have to listen to them."

"I am, but it's Calli. She's being really mean to Calli. She won't let her go to the bathroom."

"What do you mean?" Mr. Wilson asked.

"I've been trying to help Calli, like I always do, by sayin' stuff for her, but Mrs. Hample won't let me. Calli tried to tell her she had to go to the bathroom, but Mrs. Hample said, 'If you can't tell me yourself, you can't go!'" Petra said in a remarkable likeness of Mrs. Hample.

"Come on with me, Petra. We'll go figure this out."

"Nuh-uh!" Petra exclaimed. "I'm supposed to be outside, standing by the wall for recess. If she knows I told, I'm gonna be in *big* trouble!"

"You go on outside then and stand by the wall. I'll go check on Calli and visit with Mrs. Hample. And Petra, you're a good friend. Calli is lucky to have you," Mr. Wilson told her and Petra smiled her big, toothless grin at him.

Mr. Wilson went to the classroom, looked through the window in the door and saw Calli, sitting at her desk, her head bent forward and her long hair shielding her face. He entered the room, stood beside Calli's desk, and watched as big, fat tears plopped down, causing a wet stain to slowly spread across the brown-gray handwriting paper that lay in front of her. "Hey, Calli, ready for our appointment?" Mr. Wilson asked her in a cheerful voice. Calli looked up at him in surprise; they never met on Friday, only on Tuesdays and Thursdays, and in the late afternoons, near to the time that school ended.

"I'm sorry I'm late." Mr. Wilson looked concernedly down at his watch. "I was stuck in a meeting. Let's go on up to my office." Calli stood and looked fearfully at Mrs. Hample. "I'll bring her back in about twenty minutes, right before lunch." He addressed his last comments to Mrs. Hample.

"She should be in a special classroom. She doesn't talk, you know," she said as if Calli could not hear her. "Or maybe in a behavior disorder class. She's being obstinate, not talking like that."

"All our students are special here, and Calli is right where she belongs. You won't be needed for the rest of the day, Mrs. Hample. You may sign out at the office. Thank you."

When Calli finished using the restroom, he sent her outside to play with her classmates for recess. She and Petra played hopscotch with some other children. Mrs. Hample left and never returned and Mr. Wilson was their substitute teacher for the rest of the afternoon. When she arrived home from school that day, her backpack held a note for her mother from Mr. Wilson. Calli watched carefully as her mother read the note, her face drooping more and more at each line she read. Finally, she set the letter aside and beckoned Calli to her.

"Petra's a nice girl," her mother whispered to her as she gathered her on her lap. Calli nodded and played with the collar on her mother's shirt. "We have to do something nice for her, don't you think?" Again Calli nodded. "Cookies, you think?" Antonia asked her. Calli slipped off her lap, opened the refrigerator and began pulling eggs and butter from inside.

"You remember what a good friend she's been to you, Calli. Don't ever forget it. Petra will need you to be just as good a friend someday, okay?"

Calli and Antonia delivered the cookies, still warm and soft, later that evening to the Gregory house. Petra's mother and father had smiled proudly at their daughter's kind actions on Calli's behalf. Calli and Petra had run off into the porch to sit and eat the chocolaty cookies.

Now, in the meadow, her stomach growled in remembrance of those chocolate chip cookies as she wove a crown of flowers for her best friend. Calli felt her nose begin to burn from the harsh sun, and she headed back into the woods and its dim calm.

ANTONIA

Martin, Fielda and I huddle together. We sit on Mrs. Norland's sofa, trying to decide what to do next. We need to talk to the press, that much is certain, but don't know where to begin. Don't know quite what to say. I mean, how does a parent get up in front of a camera and say to the whole world, "I've lost my child, please help me get her back." How does one do that?

But it needs to be done. I hold in my hand a collection of pictures of Calli. Calli in her first-grade picture, a hesitant smile on her face, her two front teeth missing, her hair brushed and curled, staring right into the camera. Calli wearing her yellow bathing suit earlier this summer, her skin slightly pink from the sun, her hair in pigtails. Calli and Petra, just last week, sitting at the kitchen table, arms thrown around each other, heads touching.

"Let's go," I say, standing.

Startled, Martin and Fielda look up at me.

"We'll figure it out as we go," I assure them. "Come on."

I hold on to Fielda's hand as we approach the front door, and she holds on to Martin's hand. We make an odd little train as we leave the house. We walk down the long lane to Timber Ridge Road to where the reporter is waiting for us. I shield my eyes from the glare of the sun and the reporter looks expectantly at us. Quiet greets us for a moment and the woman in the red suit addresses us.

"I'm sorry to hear about your daughters. My name is Katie Glass. I'm a reporter for KLRS. Could you answer a few questions for me?"

"My name is Antonia Clark," I begin, "and this is Martin and Fielda Gregory. Our daughters, Calli and Petra, are…missing." I hold up the photo of Calli and Petra together at the kitchen table. My hand is shaking.

Fielda squeezes my hand and says in a quiet voice, "Please help us find our girls. Please help us find our girls," she repeats. "They are seven years old. They are best friends. They are good girls. Please, if anyone knows where they are, please tell someone."

I look over to Martin. His eyes are closed and his chin is tucked into his chest.

"What time did you report the girls missing?" the reporter asks.

Agent Fitzgerald steps forward. "Petra Gregory was reported missing at approximately four-thirty this morning. Calli Clark, soon after. Both girls are seven years old. Petra Gregory was last seen wearing short blue pajamas. Calli Clark was last seen wearing a pink nightgown. The girls were last seen in their own homes, in their own beds."

"Do you have any suspects?"

"We have no suspects, no persons of interest at this time,"

Agent Fitzgerald explains. "However, we are trying to contact Calli's father, Griff Clark, and his friend Roger Hogan. They left early this morning for a fishing trip and we need to let these gentlemen know of this situation. Anyone who knows where these two men are should have them contact the Jefferson County Sheriff's Department."

"Are the two men suspects?" Katie Glass asks.

I gasp and the Gregorys look at me in surprise.

"Griff Clark and Roger Hogan are not suspects in any manner. We just want to let Mr. Clark know that his daughter and Petra Gregory are missing."

"Where did they go fishing?"

"Somewhere along the Mississippi, over near Julien."

"Do you have photos of the two men?"

"We do not. They are not suspects. I repeat, they are not suspects, but they need to return to Willow Creek."

"Is there any relationship between the missing girls and the Jenna McIntire case?" the reporter inquires. My stomach flips with dread. I hadn't heard this connection before.

"We cannot comment on any connection between the two cases at this point," Fitzgerald says crisply.

"Is it true that Mary Ellen McIntire, Jenna McIntire's mother, is here in Willow Creek to give assistance to the families?"

"I am not aware of the arrival of Mrs. McIntire. That is all for now. When we have more information regarding Petra Gregory and Calli Clark, we will pass that information to you. As for now, the Gregory and Clark families, along with the Jefferson County Sheriff's Department, would appreciate anyone with any information regarding the whereabouts of Petra Gregory and Calli Clark to please contact local authorities."

With that, Agent Fitzgerald steps away from the microphones and heads back toward Mrs. Norland's house. We follow behind him. Fielda had dropped my hand at the mention of Griff, though she still holds tightly to Martin's hand.

Once we are in the privacy of the Norland home, Fielda turns on me. "What's this about your husband leaving early this morning? Could he know something about Petra and Calli? Why isn't he here?"

"Hold on," I stop her, holding my hand up. "Griff knows nothing about the girls. He and Roger went fishing early this morning. They've been planning it for weeks." I try to keep the anger from my voice, but fail.

"He had been drinking," Martin says.

"What?" I ask.

"Griff had been drinking. This morning there were beer cans everywhere."

"That doesn't mean anything," I say, shrugging it off. "So he had a few beers. So what?" I notice Agent Fitzgerald out of the corner of my eye. He is watching us carefully.

"I've seen him drunk," Martin says. "He is not exactly nice when he has been drinking."

"That is none of your business," I sputter.

"My daughter is missing!" Fielda yells. "My daughter is missing and you think that your husband's drinking has nothing to do with it? Maybe, maybe not. And while we're talking about it, what about your son? Where is he right now? He sure spent a lot of time with the girls. Kind of odd, if you ask me. A teenager hanging out with a bunch of first graders."

"How dare you?" I shout. "Ben would never hurt the girls. Never! How *dare* you? You come in here, pointing fingers. How do we know that you two didn't have something to do with this?"

"Us?" Fielda screeches. "Us? My God. You're the one with the drunken husband and the daughter who never speaks. And why is that, do you think? Why doesn't Calli talk? Seems to me that something really odd must be going on in your house if a perfectly healthy little girl doesn't talk!"

"Get out," I say softly now. "Just go."

Agent Fitzgerald steps between us. "We need to work together on this. There is no reason that you should be pointing fingers at each other. No reason. Let us do our work here."

"I'm sorry," I turn to Fielda and say weakly after a moment's silence. "I know you would never do anything to hurt the girls. I'm just…worried."

"I'm sorry, too," Fielda says. "And I know Ben would never hurt them. I'm so sorry. We'll talk soon." Fielda pats my arm and they leave.

I notice that she hadn't said that she knew Griff wouldn't have hurt the girls, either.

Griff has not always been the way he is now. Not at first, anyway. He always drank a lot, I knew that back when I was first dating him. I just thought it was his age, just being wild, having fun. It was exciting to be around him. I was thrilled that someone older than me would be interested in seventeen-year-old me. And he was sweet and *wanted* to be with me.

I was so lonely at that time. My mother had died, my brothers had left and my dad was moping around the house, missing my mother, missing my brothers. That winter of my senior year, Griff sauntered into the Gas & Go, the convenience store where I worked. He smiled at me, went back to the beer display, grabbed a case, a bag of Fritos and a Ding Dong, and set them all in front of me on the counter.

"Great supper, huh?" he asked.

"Very nutritious," I observed as I rang up the items. "I'll need to see an ID, for the beer."

"Why? Don't I look twenty-two?" Griff asked, grinning.

"Didn't say that. I just have to check everyone's, even if they look eighty." I grinned back.

"You sayin' I look eighty?"

"That's what a diet of beer, Fritos and Ding Dongs will do to you," I replied, trying not to laugh. God, I was so dumb.

"How old're you? Twelve?" Griff shot back.

"Funny. No, I'm almost eighteen," I said, straightening my shoulders, trying to appear taller, older.

"Huh, I would've thought maybe…" he peered at me closely "…thirteen. Fourteen, maybe, on a good day."

"Ha, ha," I deadpanned. I felt my face redden and hoped that I wasn't sweating too much.

"I'm Griff Clark, by the way," he said as he pulled his driver's license from his wallet and laid it in front of me.

"I'm Antonia Stradensky," I said, using my full name, hoping at least to sound older.

Griff was looking at my name tag. "Then who the hell is Toni?" he asked. "And where'd you put her?"

"I'm Toni," I said, flustered. "I mean, you know that. Toni's short for Antonia." Mortified, I laid his change in his outstretched palm.

"See you later, Antonia!" Griff flashed a huge smile at me. "And let that Toni girl out of the cooler before you go home."

"Yeah," I said. "I'll do that."

Griff stopped by nearly every time I was working after that. When he didn't, I worried, wondered if he wasn't really interested in me. Then he'd walk in, his red hair a beacon, and my stomach would swoop and I would smile for the rest of the night.

One night in April, he finally asked me out, sort of. I was just closing up the store at midnight. It was a beautiful early-spring night and Griff was waiting out in the small parking lot as I locked the doors.

"Young girl like you shouldn't be working out here all alone this late at night. It ain't safe."

"Well, good thing you're here then," I replied.

"Good thing. Hey, wanna go for a drive?"

I hesitated. "I better not. My dad will be waiting up for me." This was not true. I don't think my father had stayed up past nine since my mother died.

"How 'bout a short walk then?"

We walked; it wasn't a short walk, though. We walked for two hours, winding ourselves around the streets of the town at least three times and found ourselves up at St. Gilianus College, among the old gothic-looking buildings.

"What do you do?" I asked.

"I do lots of things," Griff laughed. "I eat, I sleep, I go for walks…"

"I mean for a job, what do you do?"

"Right now I'm workin' over in Lynndale for my uncle, farm stuff. But I'm workin' on getting a job working for the pipeline over in Alaska."

"Oh." A pebble of dread dropped into my stomach. "You're moving away."

"Maybe. Never was much to stay around for before."

"Before what?"

"Before this kid started hangin' around me."

"I'm not a kid."

"Oh, yeah? Prove it."

And I did. There behind the field house.

Afterward, Griff was quiet, the first of his silent rages I would have to endure.

"What?" I asked. "What's wrong?"

"Who was he?"

"What? Who?" I asked, thoroughly confused.

"Who did you *date* before me?" He said *date* as if it was a curse word.

"No one. I mean, someone, but it was nothing."

He wrapped his fingers in my hair and held tightly, but didn't pull. It didn't hurt. "Stay away from him. Don't talk to him no more."

"I won't. I mean, we don't talk anymore."

"Good." He relaxed and smiled at me.

He walked me back to my car, kissed me good-night and sent me on my way.

We saw each other every day after that and were married that next fall.

I don't regret my marriage. I have, after all, two amazing children. I do wonder often, however, what would have happened if I hadn't married Griff. Would I have married someone else, Louis, maybe? Would I still live in Willow Creek or would I live by the ocean in a yellow house? But I don't wish what I have away.

DEPUTY SHERIFF LOUIS

Mary Ellen McIntire is about the saddest woman I've ever seen. Deep grooves are etched into her cheeks and it's hard to meet her puffy, weary eyes. The hurt just bores into you. I welcome her into my little domain. I wish that Fitzgerald was here, but he's not, so I offer Mrs. McIntire a seat.

The whole Jenna McIntire affair was a complete and total tragedy. All around, every which way. Beautiful ten-year-old girl goes missing from her house in the middle of the night. No one knows why. She'd never left before. Jenna loved to play with dolls, had a whole collection of those American Girl dolls. I saw her room. Dolls everywhere, dressed in these little outfits. No sign of a break-in, no struggle. Just a little girl gone. The dad swore that he had locked the back door the night before, but it was found unlocked the next morning.

Always, always, the parents are the first suspects, it seems. Even when every indication is that it's not so. Most missing child cases are perpetrated by a family member or someone known to the child. The most humiliating thing is for parents to know they are persons of interest, when in fact they would die, they would open their wrists, bleed slowly and painfully, do anything to bring their child home safely.

Jenna McIntire was found six days later, in a wooded area two miles from her home. There was plenty of evidence collected. Each horrible, unspeakable act on Jenna was chronicled, but still no resolution. We don't know who did this. Why? Yeah, some sick son of a bitch. Not even sick, *evil* is a better word.

So now, sitting before me is Mary Ellen McIntire, daughterless. If the gossip is accurate, she and her husband are separated. She has an older boy, fourteen, I think. I ask after him.

"Jacob is doing fine, I guess," she says. "You know teenage boys, though. Always somewhere to be, something to do. I'll be happy when school starts. Then at least I'll know where he's at."

I hear voices and the shuffle of many feet near the front door and I crane my neck to see what is going on. I see two reservists escorting a dazed, disheveled-looking man into the building. "Excuse me, Mrs. McIntire," I say, standing. The man being brought in is tall and thin. He towers over the other officers, but looks fragile, like a brittle stick. His hair is white and he looks as if he might cry. Mary Ellen McIntire is staring at me, a look of impatience spreading across her face. She is tired of being put off, tired of having to fight for her dead daughter. I pull my eyes away from the man, sit down and return my attention to Mary Ellen.

"What brings you here to Willow Creek, Mrs. McIntire?"

"I heard," she begins. "I heard about the missing girls. And I thought maybe I could, you know, help."

Carefully weighing my next words, I say, "Do you think that it's a good idea to be a part of this kind of…kind of situation, so soon?"

Mrs. McIntire swallows hard. "I think that this is just where I need to be right now. I know how they feel, the families. I know what they are going through."

"There is really no proof, you know, that Petra's and Calli's disappearance has anything to do with Jenna's."

"I know that," she says shortly. "I'm not here to ask about Jenna's case. I could do that by phone, and do, and will keep on doing. I…I just keep thinking of those poor mothers, not knowing where their daughters are. It's a horrible, horrible feeling."

"The girls could just be off playing," I say, though I feel certain that is not true. "They could come strolling home at any moment. You know that, don't you? We are still very much in the initial stages of this investigation."

"I know," she says tiredly. "Please, please just tell them I'm available, if they would like me to sit with them, pass out fliers, call people. Anything. Please, will you tell them?"

"I will," I promise. "Can I get you something? Coffee?"

She shakes her head no. "I have my cell phone. Do you still have my number?"

"Yes, I'll call you. Either way, Mrs. McIntire."

She stands and holds her hand out to me. This is her first offering to me since the whole bad business with Jenna. I take it and shake it, gratefully, and pray that these two cases are not related in any way.

CALLI

Calli pounded up the narrow, steep trail. The path was covered with jagged rocks, like makeshift stairs, her damaged feet numb with pain. She wanted to go off the trail, but forced herself not to. It would be too easy to get hopelessly lost if she were to veer away. What had caused her to retreat upward again? She wasn't sure. She had been strolling, almost in a carefree manner, down the trail when she heard it. Just a rustle really, just a murmur of movement, but it caused her to pause. Below her, just off the path, she saw the silhouette, an indeterminate figure, too tall for an animal, maybe too tall for a human, or could it just be the lengthening of late-afternoon shadows? A spasm of fear thumped in her chest. She didn't wait to find out, but tore back the way she had come. Up, up, but instead of taking the trail that meandered off to the right, she chose the left, a scrubby, overgrown path. She didn't dare look over her shoulder, frightened of what she might see. She clambered upward, using her hands to pull her up the steep track, dirt and small bits of rock wedged under her ragged nails.

She figured she was almost to the top of the bluff. She pushed away the low-hanging branches that whipped her face, leaving thin, raised welts. Dusk was nearing and the terror of being in the forest at night kept her moving; she could only hear the sound of her breathing, harsh and gasping, and she prayed that he could not hear her, as well. Her steps slowed as the trail leveled out and she doubled over, hands on her knees, trying to gulp in the cooled air, the heat of the day finally beginning to falter. Sweat dripped into her eyes and she pulled her snarled hair from her face. As her breath steadied, the early-evening sounds of the forest swirled about her head—the insects droning, birds calling to each other, the scampering and *chock, chock* of a chipmunk chattering.

She stared in front of her and glimpsed a tiny glint of silver on the ground about ten feet away. Its shiny luster looked out of place here, too garish, just a wink among the mottled brown leaves. Still hunched over, Calli hobbled over to the spot where the shining item lay nestled and inspected it. With her pointing finger she poked at it, brushed aside the moldy-smelling leaves to reveal a delicate silver chain. She pinched the chain between two fingers and slowly began to lift it. When she had raised the length of the chain a small charm slithered off the end and landed noiselessly among the leaves. Calli dug into the pile, and retrieved the charm, a diminutive musical note; she blew away the speckles of dirt clinging to it and carefully threaded the charm back onto the broken chain.

What she saw, what she heard, and what happened next caused Calli's chest to seize in fright. She scuttled backward into the brush and hid. *Petra, Petra, Petra.* She silently moaned as she closed her eyes and covered her ears and rocked back and forth on her haunches. She pictured the deer she had encountered earlier that day, in what seemed ages ago. She focused on its bright eyes and velvety ears and rocked back and forth; she imagined their silent dance until once again she was back in her own quiet room, alone.

MARTIN

Upon leaving Mrs. Norland's home, Fielda and I stand outside our cars. I cannot believe the gall of Mrs. Clark, accusing me of harming our children when it is her husband who is the troubled one.

Fielda complains bitterly to the deputy who has the unfortunate luck of walking us to our cars.

"Why aren't you looking into where Griff Clark is?" she asks the young officer, who must have been in his early twenties.

"Ma'am, I know the department is looking into everyone involved in this case."

"Yes, yes," she says impatiently. "But why haven't you found Griff? How hard can it be to find him if he really is fishing with this Roger person?"

"I really am not able to discuss any details with you, ma'am. I'm sorry," he says uncomfortably.

"You can't discuss the details with me? I'm her mother, for God's sake." I rest my hand on Fielda's shoulder. She brushes my hand away with irritation. "Where is Deputy Louis?" she asks. I wonder the same thing. "He, at least, has tried to keep us informed of what has been going on."

"I think he's meeting with someone at this time." The officer opens the car door for Fielda.

Fielda turns to face me. "Who do you think Louis is meeting with? Do you think maybe they found Griff?"

"I'm not sure," I answer her.

"Maybe he has a suspect. Maybe they've found the girls. Do you think they've found the girls?" Hope radiates on her face for a moment.

"I think we would have heard the moment they found Petra and Calli. I think they would have called us." We both climb into our cars and drive back to my mother-in-law's house. She is standing on her front step and talking to a strange man.

We park the cars and join Mrs. Mourning and the stranger.

"I was so worried about you," Mrs. Mourning scolds. "Fielda, you should have told me you were leaving. This is Mr. Ellerbach. He's a reporter with Channel Twelve."

"Good afternoon, Mrs. Gregory." The man offers her his hand. "Would you have a few moments to visit with me?"

I see Fielda hesitate and I step forward. "We're really not quite prepared to visit with you at this time, but we'll answer what we can."

"Thank you. Have the police found your daughter yet?"

"No, they have not," Fielda says. I am more than a little surprised at the forcefulness of her voice. She sounds strong, capable, determined.

"Are there any more developments in the case? Are there any suspects that you are aware of?"

"Nobody has spoken to us about suspects," Fielda answers.

"Have you or your husband been questioned in the disappearance?"

"Of course we've been questioned. Petra's our daughter."

"Please," I say impatiently, "no more questions. We need to focus on finding our daughter. Please go." The gray-haired reporter thanks us for our time and begins to leave.

"Wait," Fielda calls after. "Wait! Please keep putting her picture on the TV. Please keep talking about her. I'll get more pictures for you," she pleads and I see pity on the reporter's face.

Lawrence Ellerbach quickly steps back toward us and presses something into Fielda's hand. "Please call us if you'd like to talk more. We'll keep the girls' pictures on the air."

"What did he give you?" I ask curiously after he has left.

Fielda hands me the business card. Printed in simple script was the name Lawrence Ellerbach, followed by an e-mail address and telephone number. Centered at the bottom of the card was the Channel Twelve logo. I look at it for a long moment before meeting Fielda's eyes.

"What do you think?" she asks me, biting her lip.

"Maybe we need to talk to Louis or Agent Fitzgerald before we agree to speak with Mr. Ellerbach," I say.

"Maybe," she echoes me. "But maybe we should just do it. I mean, Agent Fitzgerald said to use the media. That they could be helpful. We could get Petra's name out there."

"And Calli's name, too," I remind her.

A shadow passes over Fielda's face. "Of course Calli, too. I still think that Griff Clark has something to do with this. It's just too convenient that he happens to be home from Alaska, and then goes on a fishing trip just when the two girls disappear. It doesn't add up."

"I don't think we should do anything that the police don't approve of, Fielda. What if we go against their wishes and something bad happens because of it?" But I can see that her lips are set in a determined line. Her mind is made up.

"Martin, what if we don't give an interview and someone who knows something could have seen it and could have seen Petra's picture? What if that person didn't know to come forward? I really don't care if it's handy for the police to have us give an interview or not. They haven't brought our daughter home, and this is one way that I can help."

"If you feel so strongly, I think that you should give an interview," I tell her as I drape my arm around her shoulder. My shirt is wet with sweat, but she does not step away. She comes closer to me and kisses my cheek.

"I do feel strongly about this, Martin." She pauses before continuing. "You aren't going to do the interview, are you?"

I shake my head. "I'm going to go look for Petra and Calli. This is taking too long. I'm going into the woods. I'll call Deputy Louis and Antonia and invite them to search with me."

I am not the most intuitive of men, as I have clearly shown through my many years on this planet. However, I do know numbers; I do know that the probability that someone known to us has abducted Petra and Calli is much higher than the possibility that a stranger has done this. I also know that Griff Clark can be a scary man. I have seen Mr. Clark many times in passing and he has always been pleasant and courteous. But I had a glimpse, albeit brief, of another side, a brilliantly poignant view of Mr. Clark one evening. It was parent-teacher conference night at the elementary school last March. The meetings were behind schedule, but I didn't mind. It gave me the opportunity to walk around the halls of the school, to look at the children's artwork taped to the walls, to view how other parents interacted with their children. It was a comforting scene to watch. I was not so unlike the other parents. Older, yes. I knew I looked more like Petra's grandfather than her father, but I could see many kinds of families in those hallways. Single mothers holding their children's hands as they received a grand tour around the building, and fathers being shepherded from classroom to classroom by beaming kindergarteners.

Petra was explaining to Fielda and me how their first-grade classroom conducted experiments on how far those little plastic sports cars, Hot Wheels, I think they are called, could travel, when we came across the Clark family huddled in a small, out-of-the-way corner of the school building. Griff Clark's face was purple with rage as he berated Calli and Antonia.

"Do you know how goddamn embarrassing it is for me to come to these things and hear how Calli don't talk yet?" he hissed. Calli had her head down, staring at her feet, while Antonia was trying, unsuccessfully, to hush Griff.

"Don't shush me, Toni," he growled, his voice not raised above a gruff whisper, but menacing still the same. He grabbed Calli under the armpit. "Look at me, Calli." Calli looked at her father. "Are you retarded? You can talk, I know you can. You gotta stop this goddamn game and start talking.

"And you—" he turned on Antonia "—you let her get away with it. Pussyfooting around it. 'Oh, we can't push her, we can't force her to talk,'" he said in a mock falsetto voice. "Bullshit!"

At that moment Calli's eyes fell on Petra's and I saw such a completely resigned, helpless look on Calli's face. No embarrassment, no anger, nothing but pure acceptance. Petra gave Calli a meager, half-hearted smile and wiggled her fingers at her, then pulled me away from the sad scene.

Later, at the Mourning Glory, Lucky Thompson brought over sundaes piled high with toppings. He ruffled Petra's hair and asked what we were celebrating.

"We are celebrating my genius daughter's glowing conference," I told him, and Petra blushed with pleasure.

"Why don't you join us, Lucky?" Fielda invited.

"Oh, I don't know," Lucky said, looking over his shoulder. "I've got a lot to do."

"Please," Petra begged. "I'll share my sundae with you. You made it way too big!"

"Okay, then," Lucky said, sliding into the booth next to Petra. "How can I resist that invitation?"

I asked Petra, "Do you think it is always like that for Calli?"

Petra knew exactly to what I was referring. "When her dad is there, I think so. When he's gone, it's okay. Her mom is real nice," Petra said around a spoonful of turtle sundae.

"I do not want you going over to the Clark house when her father is there. Do you understand, Petra?" I said sternly.

She nodded her head. "I know. But sometimes I feel like Calli needs me even more when her dad is home, you know? It seems too bad that I have to stay away from her then. That's when she's the saddest, when he's home." She shrugged her shoulders.

"Are you talking about Griff Clark?" Lucky asked.

Fielda nodded. "Do you know him?"

"No, not really. I've just seen him around, you know. When

I've gone out with the guys. He's a pretty rough character," Lucky said.

"Do you think that her dad hurts her? You know, hits her when he gets mad?" Fielda asked with concern. I prayed that Petra would say no, that she did not think that Griff hit Calli and Ben or Antonia for that matter. I had visions of having to call the Department of Human Services and inform them of abuse, not an enviable position to be in.

She shrugged her shoulders again. "I don't know. She doesn't talk, you know. She just seems sadder when he's home."

"Do you feel the same way about me?" I asked Petra. "Do you feel sad when I'm around?" I made a pouting face at Petra.

"No, silly," she responded, shaking her head and grinning. "I'm happy when you're around."

Lucky was looking wistfully at the three of us. I knew he hadn't had an easy life. He always sidestepped questions about his family. He had told me a number of times how much he would one day love to have a family like mine. I told him I almost never had it myself. That if Fielda hadn't thrown that muffin at me, I would most likely be a lonely old man. He laughed at that, but his smile didn't reach his eyes.

"Can I have that?" Petra indicated the maraschino cherry that Lucky had pushed to the side of the sundae.

"Of course," he answered and he scraped it up with his spoon and popped it into her open mouth. "Yeah," Lucky said, shaking his head as if remembering something, "I wouldn't let Petra anywhere near Griff Clark."

I readily agreed. In that brief moment in the school corridor between Griff Clark and his family, I saw that one percent of meanness that people like him accidentally show to the world at large. It frightens me, what he could be capable of, what he may have done to my daughter. I shiver, something I think is impossible in ninety-degree weather. But then, of course, anything is possible now.

I make my way back to Mrs. Norland's home, trying to compose the words I will need to say to Antonia and to Deputy Louis in order to convince them to accompany me into the woods.

CALLI

"Calli." She heard the voice, calm, almost loving, but the same fear that pressed against her throat moments before returned. Griff was standing over her, gray-faced and ill-looking.

"Calli, let's stop this nonsense. Come on over here. Let's go home. Don't you wanna see…" His voice trailed off as he stepped closer to Calli and he ingested the scene in front of him. First Petra's battered head, discolored face and neck. He looked again to Calli.

"Jesus, what happened? Jesus, Calli, what happened to her?"

Calli stood silently, weighing her options. Which way to go? The deep ravine behind her, Griff in front of her, barring her passageway.

"Calli," he barked sharply. "What happened here? Tell me!" He roughly grabbed her shoulder, but let go when he noticed something among the thistles. He bent down to retrieve it, held it in his fingers, a dirtied ripped rag, white with dainty yellow flowers.

"Jesus," he said, looking to Petra again. His eyes traveled down her motionless form, the dirty blue pajama top, her naked bruised legs, speckled with blood.

"Jesus," he repeated. Griff turned swiftly and retched, bitter, yellow bile spewed from his throat. He breathed in deeply, but gagged again, loud, croaking, dry heaves followed, but nothing more came forth.

Calli took this opportunity, with Griff hunched over clutching at his cramping stomach, to slide down the bluff and steal past him, but not retreating into the forest.

"Calli," wheezed Griff. "Calli, who did this? Do you know who did this?" He absently wiped his hands with the sullied yellow-flowered rag. Realizing what he was holding, he flicked it to the ground as if it seared his hand. He stumbled over to Petra and placed a trembling hand at her wrist and then at her throat, pressing, feeling for her pulse. He shook his head.

"I can't tell." He fell to his knees, laid his ear to her chest, and then lightly held his finger under her nose, searching for a warm current of breath.

"Calli." He looked toward her. "Who did this to her?"

They both heard the rustling through the trees, heavy, lumbering stomps.

"Calli! Calli!" Calli and Griff both recognized Ben's voice as he crashed through the brush and placed himself between Griff and Calli. "Leave her alone. Get away!"

"Ben, what're you doing here?" Griff asked, genuinely surprised.

"Get away from her!" Ben shouted again, searching around him for something to grab, a stick, a rock.

"Ben, shut up!" Griff yelled as he stood. "We need to get help up here."

Ben's eyes flicked to Calli, then Petra, and back to Griff. "Run, Calli," he whispered. "That way." He indicated the trail from which he came. "Go down, all the way down. It will lead you to Bobcat Trail. Run, Calli, don't stop."

"Ben, shut up," Griff said. "You don't know what happened here. We have to get outta here. Maybe we should carry her out," he said, looking down at Petra. "But maybe we shouldn't move her." Griff bit his lip in indecision. "We can't leave her here." He looked up at Ben again. "You stay with her. Calli and I'll go down the trail and get help."

"No," Ben said.

"What'd you say?"

"No, I'm not letting you go anywhere with Calli."

Ben reached behind him for Calli, never taking his eyes off his father. He found Calli's hand and pulled gently toward him so that her cheek lay against his back.

"Ben, we don't got time for this. I think Petra's dying. You go then and get help. I'll stay with her."

"No, Calli will go," Ben said. "We stay with Petra."

"Who made you boss?" Griff scoffed. "Who's she gonna tell? What'll she do, mime it? You stay. Me and Calli will go." Griff began to walk past Ben to take hold of Calli, but Ben stepped to the side, blocking his path.

"Ben, I will knock you silly if you don't get outta my way. This isn't a game." Griff made to move past Ben again, but Ben sidled in front of him.

"No, Calli's going down to get help. I'm not leaving you alone with Petra."

Griff blinked. "What? You think I had something to do with this?"

Ben said nothing. He stared warily at his father, his arms stretched out to the side, a wall between Griff and Calli.

"What? You really think I did this, Ben? I'm your dad."

"I know," Ben said, walking backward, trying to ease Calli toward the trail that would lead her downward. "Why are they even up here?" Ben asked, sweeping his arm to indicate Calli and Petra. "Why are you even up here? You never go up here."

Griff faltered, stammered, said nothing.

"You're here, they're here, Petra's hurt bad and Calli's a mess. What am I supposed to think?"

"Don't think, Ben. You might hurt yourself. Now get the hell outta my way. Calli, let's go." Griff reached around Ben and snatched Calli's arm and began dragging her toward the trail.

"No!" Ben exclaimed. "Keep your hands offa her!" Ben shoved at Griff, who stumbled backward, caught surprised.

Ben moved quickly and swung around to Calli. He grabbed her shoulders and lowered his nose to hers. "Go, Calli, get help. I'll take care of Petra. Run. You run as fast as you can. And you tell 'em. You tell 'em where we are."

Calli hesitated, but Griff had recovered and was lunging back toward them. She turned and was gone.

BEN

Dad looks crazed as he gets back to his feet. What the hell have I done?

"Ben, you stupid son of a bitch. Why the hell did you do that? Now she's gone. Once we get outta here I'm gonna beat the crap out of you."

"I don't care," I say as I move to get away from him. "You're gonna stay here with me until the police come."

"The hell I am," he laughs. He is always laughing at someone.

"Go ahead, laugh, I don't care," I say, sounding like a stupid son of a bitch.

"Stay here with her. God knows the sick fuck who did this is prob'ly still hiding behind a tree, but you stay here, and I'll go get help," he says.

"No, you're not going anywhere." I stand my ground.

"Fuck that," Dad says and he runs at me and stiff-arms me right in the chest.

I think I shocked him by not falling over and crumpling

into a little ball like a baby. I'd grown a lot this summer, gotten a lot stronger. He bounces offa me like a spring and falls backward. He looks funny, the surprise on his face. I would laugh, if the look on his face didn't scare me to death.

"Little fucker," he whispers as he struggles to get to his feet.

For once in my life, I think my dad looks old. Not ancient old, like an eighty-year-old man, but just tired old. Like a middle-aged man who spent too much time drinking and being mean to others, time sits on his face like some Halloween mask.

He comes at me again, this time more prepared. He swings his right arm as if to smack me in the head, but lunges at me down low, hitting me in the stomach, and lands on top of me. My air is instantly gone. I try to suck more in, but can't and I fight wildly to get him off of me. I pound on his back, at his face, even pull his hair, I'm embarrassed to say, anything to get him away from me so I can breathe again. He tries pinning my arms down above my head but I am flailing around like a maniac and he can't quite get a good grasp on me.

"Ben, goddammit, stop it. Hold still!" he shouts.

But I won't. I can breathe again and it's a few seconds before I realize that he is trying to get off of me, but I won't let him go. He is trying to get away from me. He is trying to crawl over the top of me, but I have hold of his leg and am holding on with all my might. He stands on one leg and sorta drags me along with him a few feet, but like I said, I'm a pretty big kid and he can't get too far. He falls backward on his butt. That is just enough to loosen my grip a bit, and he pulls his foot back and then kicks forward, hitting me smack-dab in the nose. I think we both hear it break. I don't see stars like they always show on Saturday morning cartoons, but I think I see what looks like a few fireflies blinking at me. We both freeze for a second, I honestly don't think he can believe he did this to me and I can't, either, though he sure has hit me enough. Blood comes rushing outta my nose and it feels like someone pinched my nose off with pliers.

"Goddammit, Ben," he says. "What'd you have to go and do that for?"

He means it, too; this is my fault, like I broke my own nose. I have never felt like killing something before, not even Meechum. But I feel like killing my own dad, right now in these woods. Instead I wallop him in the side of the head with my bloody fist.

"I know you think I had something to do with this, but I didn't. I really didn't, Ben." He tries to reason with me as he moves to block my blows.

"I don't believe you. I'm gonna tell, I'm gonna tell what you did to Petra and to Calli!" My hands are slick and slimy with my blood and my punches slide uselessly off him. He crawls away from me. I don't go after him, but I stand and wipe my bloody hands on my shorts. Ruined.

"Ben," he gasps, "you want me to go to jail? You want me to get sent away for something I didn't do? 'Cause that's what'll happen. They'll send me away, prob'ly forever." He rubs his face; I see that his hands are shaking. "Jesus, Ben. I think Petra's dying. We gotta get her help."

"Calli will get help. She's probably near the bottom now, she'll get help up here," I insist.

"Christ, Ben, she hasn't talked in four fucking years!

You think she'll talk now? How's she gonna tell what happened?"

I don't answer him. I am too worn out and my nose hurts, but I watch him carefully through my swelling eyes.

When I was five, I remember thinking that my dad was the biggest, strongest guy around. I would follow him around the house when he was home; squeeze in next to him when he was sitting in his La-Z-Boy chair. I would watch his every move, the way he stuffed his hands into the front of his jeans when he would talk to one of his friends, the way he held his beer in his right hand and popped the top with his left. I would watch the way he would close his eyes, take big drinks of the beer, roll it around in his mouth and swallow. I was amazed at how much pleasure I would see on his face when he drank his beer, the way that all of us—Mom, baby Calli, and I—would just seem to disappear when Dad was drinking.

During the first two or three beers he would be nice and funny, even, playing tickling games and pulling Mom down onto his lap to hug her. He might play card games like Go Fish or Old Maid with me or he might hold Calli, her back on his thighs, holding her little feet singing, "Bicycle, bicycle, cruise…" as he moved her legs like she was pedaling a bike.

But after that fourth beer it started to change. Dad would pick on Mom for stupid stuff, for not hanging up his shirts just right or the kitchen floor wouldn't be swept good enough. He'd yell at her for spending too much money on groceries and then yell at her for not making anything good to eat. He would get bored playing cards with me and quit in the middle of the game, even if he was winning. Dad just plain ignored Calli after beer number four.

Now after beer number seven he'd get all impatient and not want to be touched. When I'd try to snuggle in next to him in his chair, he'd push me away, not hard, but a person could tell he wanted to be left alone. Mom would take Calli and me upstairs to read stories. I'd get in my pajamas, I remember they were white and had these grinning little clowns holding balloons all over them. I wouldn't tell any of my friends this, but I loved those pajamas. It was like sliding into something happy when I put those on after a bath. One time, though, after beer number seven, Dad said I looked like "a goddamn sissy" in those pajamas and that he should burn 'em. I didn't wear them after that; I wore an old T-shirt of Dad's to bed. But I didn't throw the pajamas away, either. They're still folded underneath my winter long johns in my bottom drawer. Personally, I don't think they're sissy pajamas, I just think they were happy. Every five-year-old kid should have a pair of happy pajamas.

After beer number twelve we left. If it was during the day and it wasn't raining Mom would take us for a walk in the woods. She'd put Calli in this harness thing that hung in front of her and we'd head off into the woods. She'd show me all the places she played when she was a little kid, Willow Wallow, Lone Tree Bridge, and, of course, Willow Creek. She'd take us down to where the creek was wide and had these big boulders sticking out like steps. Mom would lift Calli out of the harness and lay her in a blanket in a shady spot and then she'd show me how she could cross the creek using those boulders in twenty-five seconds. When she was younger, she'd be able to make the trek in fifteen seconds flat, three seconds faster than her friend would. Her friend, I knew, was

Deputy Louis, though she'd never call him by name. He was just her "friend."

One time, after beer number twelve, before we up and left the house, Mom said something about Louis, something about when they were kids, like nine, and Dad hit the roof. He started ranting about Mom, calling her all these horrible names, threw a beer can at her. So Mom doesn't talk about when she was little anymore around Dad.

After a couple of hours clomping around the woods, after Dad had a good chance to get up to beer number who knows what, she'd take us home. Beer number who knows what was usually followed by a long sleep. We could make as much noise as we wanted to; Dad would be completely passed out. But we didn't, we stayed quiet, didn't even watch TV when he was like that. I was always a little worried that he'd wake up when I was caught up in some old rerun and he'd smack me upside the head when I wasn't ready for it.

I used to walk around, holding my pop can the way Dad held his beer can. I'd hold it in my right hand, popping the top with my left, even though I'm a righty. I practiced tilting it back to my lips, taking a big gulp and swishing it around in my mouth before swallowing hard, then tossing the can to the floor when I was finished. Mom caught me doing this once. She looked at me long and hard and I thought for a minute that she was gonna get mad at me, even though I never saw her get mad at Dad for doing it. But she didn't. She just looked at me and said, "Benny, let me get you a glass of ice for your pop next time, and a straw. It tastes so much better that way."

And she would—every time I had a pop, out came the

frosted glass, ice, and a straw. She was right, though, it did taste better that way.

Sometimes, after beer number who knows how many and the long nap, Dad would wake up and still be real nervous-like. Then he'd go into his bedroom clothes closet, dig around in there for a while and then pull out a dark bottle of something. The minute Mom saw him searching through his closet for that bottle, we were outta there. Mom would stick us in her car and off we'd go. If it was evening time, she'd take us out to eat over in Winner, which was a bigger town and had a Culver's. We'd get hamburgers and French fries and share an order of onion rings. Calli'd sit in her high chair and Mom would break off tiny pieces of her food and lay them on the tray in front of Calli. It was funny watching Calli try to pinch those tiny bits of food between her fingers. Sometimes she'd miss, but still stick her fingers in her mouth, hoping to get a taste of something. Afterward, before we'd leave, Mom would buy me a big thick Oreo shake all my own. She'd buckle me into the backseat and I'd settle for the long ride home, sucking on my shake. Winner wasn't all that far from Willow Creek, but Mom would take what she called the scenic route and we'd drive and drive and drive.

One night after driving and driving, I was jerked awake when our car bounced down the side of the road, in and out of a ditch. Mom stopped the car on the edge of the road and turned back to Calli and me.

"You okay?" she asked. I nodded yes, even though she couldn't have seen my face in the dark.

"I spilled some of my shake, though," I told her.

She handed me some napkins to wipe up my pants and then

laid her head on the steering wheel. "I'm sorry," she said, but not really to me. "I'm sorry, I'm just so tired."

Then she started the car up again and we went on home. Dad was sleeping in his chair, beer cans everywhere. I bet if I had counted them there would have been at least twenty-one, plus the dark brown bottle sitting on the end table. Mom didn't bother picking up all those cans that night. She walked right on past them, saying something about how "he can just pick up after himself from now on," and took Calli and me on up to bed.

From then on, if Dad started digging around for his bottle from the closet, he could never find it. This made him furious, but after a while he'd just stagger around until he found another beer in the refrigerator and then he'd settle back into his chair. Once in a while, when Dad started acting kind of scary, Mom would put us in the car and take us over to Winner, but we never drove around for as long as we did that one night she went off the road. She'd pull into a park area, lock our doors and close her eyes for a while. "Just resting," she'd tell us. On one really cold winter night we got to stay at a motel in Winner. It didn't have a pool or nothing, but it had cable and Mom let me flip through all the channels as much as I wanted to. Mom just sat on the bed with me, holding Calli, trying not to cry.

I hope I'm not doing the wrong thing. I hope that Petra doesn't die because of what I am doing; I hope that she isn't already dead.

Now Dad and I are just sitting here, all bloody, looking at each other, waiting for the other one to make a move, but we don't. Not yet.

ANTONIA

Ben has not returned yet, so on top of everything else, I need to worry about him, as well. The comments from the Gregorys didn't help matters, either. I know Ben, he wouldn't hurt the girls, and I know Griff, he just plain doesn't find kids interesting enough to spend very much time getting mad at them. Besides, the number of beer cans strewn around the house this morning was much less than normal, well short of his mean drinking. If he'd gotten to the mean drinking stage I would have been much more concerned.

Louis has not returned my call. I know he is busy with other aspects of this case, as well as his other duties, but I am surprised that he isn't here. Louis has always been there for me, except when he left for college. Even I know that me asking him to stay was asking too much. Louis was there when a fifth-grade bully was terrorizing me when we were nine, he was there when I had a panic attack about presenting a speech for my tenth-grade literature class, and he was there when my mother died.

Even though my mother and I were so different, had so little in common, Louis knew that the loss of her was the biggest thing that had ever happened to me. He knew that those hours that my father and I spent nursing her while she lay in bed, rotting from breast cancer had left a deep-seated imprint on me. Louis would drive me to the public library in order to check out whatever book my mother had requested I read to her, while a morphine pump deadened some of the pain.

My mother was a great reader. I was not. I liked books; I just didn't have time for them. Between school, working at the convenience store and spending time with Louis, I never made the effort to read. My mother was always placing books on my bedside table, hoping that I would pick one up and have a wonderful discussion about it with her. I never did, not until she got sick. Then, out of guilt more than anything, I began to read to her. One day, near the end, my mother asked me to find her old copy of *My Ántonia* by Willa Cather. I had seen this book before; my mother had set it on my bedside table many times. I had never taken the time to read it, even though my name was chosen because this was my mother's favorite book. I could not imagine what I could possibly have in common with the Antonia of Willa Cather's world, so long ago. But at my mother's request I began to read. I tumbled, reluctantly, into the turn-of-the-century Nebraska, and loved what I found. Louis would often sit with me while I read aloud to my mother. I was so self-conscious at first, not used to the sound of my own voice in my ears, but he seemed to enjoy it and my mother often had a weak smile on her face as I read.

One afternoon, about three weeks before my mother died, she patted the mattress on the hospital bed that we had brought in when we knew that she was going to die. I lowered the metal bar that prevented my mother from falling out of bed and gingerly sat next to her.

"Come closer, Antonia," she said to me. My mother never called me Toni, it was always Antonia. I moved in closer to her, careful of the tubes that ran into her arm. It was so hard looking at her like that. My beautiful, beautiful mother who always smelled of Chanel before. Now a different smell, sour and old, hung around her. Her hair, once a golden-blond, now was dun-colored and lay lank on her shoulders, her face pale and pinched with pain.

"Antonia, my Antonia," she whispered. I secretly loved it when she called me that. "I just wanted to tell you a few things, before…before—" She swallowed with great effort. "Before I die," she finished.

"Mom, don't say that," I squeaked and before I knew it the tears were falling. How I hated to cry.

"Antonia, I am going to die, and very soon. I just didn't get enough time with you," she sighed. "The boys, they'll be all right, but you, you I worry about."

"I'm okay, Mom," I sniffled, trying not to let her see me cry.

She took my hands in hers and I played with her wedding ring like I did when we were sitting in church when I was little so many years before. The ring spun loosely on her ring finger, she had lost so much weight. Her hands looked as if they belonged to a much older woman, the blue-tinged veins thick and protruding.

"Louis is a nice young man," she said.

"Yeah, he is," I agreed.

"Antonia, I won't be at your wedding…" she started.

"Mom, please don't say that," I begged. My nose ran thickly and I had to pull a hand from hers to wipe it. "Please don't talk like that."

"I won't be at your wedding, so I want to tell you a few things about being a wife and a mother." She waited patiently until my sobs became quiet, wet hitches of breath. "People say that being a mother is the most important job you will ever have. And it is very important. But it is even more important, I believe, to be a wife, a good wife."

I must have looked at her skeptically, because she started to chuckle at me, but the laughter caused her too much pain.

"I don't mean you have be a floor mat. That's not what I mean at all. I mean, who you choose to walk with through life will be the most important decision that you will ever, ever make. You will have your children and you will love them because they are yours and because they will be wonderful. Just like you." She wrinkled her nose at me and grinned. "But who you marry is a *choice*. The man you choose should make you happy, encourage you in following your dreams, big ones and little ones."

"Did Dad do that for you?" I asked. Night was settling in and the shadows made my mother look much softer, much younger, and less like she was dying.

"He did. I had such simple dreams, though. I just wanted to be a wife and mother. That's all, really. You must remember that, Antonia. In the end, I have had everything that I have ever wanted. My dear, sweet husband and my dear, sweet children. I just wish I had more time with you." She began crying quietly.

"It's okay, Mom, it's okay," I tried to soothe her. "I'll remember what you said, I promise." She nodded and tried to smile, but her pain caused her lips to curl downward. I picked up the book that lay next to her bed.

"How about a little Carson McCullers?" I asked.

"Yes, that would be just fine," she answered.

I began reading and my mother fell asleep within minutes. For the first time that I could remember, I bent down and kissed her while she slept. Her lips felt thin and papery, but warm. Underneath the odor of disease and the sheer exertion of trying to live, I caught her true scent. And I closed my eyes and willed myself to remember. But I went and forgot, didn't I? I forgot everything she had told me.

I was sitting in World History class one afternoon, when the principal came to my classroom door. The teacher stopped writing on the chalkboard and he went over to where the principal stood; they whispered with their heads close together for a moment and then both looked in my direction. I remember my chest tightening in fear and thinking to myself, *I haven't had enough time with you yet, Mom, I haven't had enough time with you, either.* I slowly rose from my chair, leaving my books and things behind. I remember Louis following along behind me, gripping my elbow, walking me to his car and driving me home. He stayed with me long into that first terrible night without my mother. We didn't talk—we didn't have to—and now I think we had much the same friendship that Calli and Petra have.

After my mother died I continued to read. Before I went to bed each night I would read a few pages of a book aloud to myself. It took me forever to finish a novel, but it didn't seem right to me to read silently to myself anymore. Odd, I know. Griff made fun of me when I read children's books that I would find at garage sales to Ben when he was in my womb. I learned not to do that when he was around, but I loved cradling my huge stomach with one arm while holding a book in the other, reading to my tiny fetus. I firmly believed Ben could hear me in there, rocking back and forth, maybe a tiny little thumb in his mouth. It was much more acceptable reading aloud like that after my children were born. Even now, I read each night to Calli and even Ben, once in a great while, will let me read part of the book he is reading. When Griff is out of town, I will crawl into my bed and read myself a bedtime story until I fall asleep, book in hand.

Louis asked me a few times, after my mother died, if I would read to him, but I was too self-conscious and wouldn't. He gave up after I told him impatiently not to ask me again. Louis was always there for me, until, of course, I wouldn't let him be. Even when my father passed away. Griff and I had been married for three years; Louis sent me a sympathy card. I could tell it was from him without even looking at the return address. I had memorized his small, neat printing back when we were in first grade. I never showed the card to Griff, Louis had signed the card *Always, Louis* and I did not have the energy to try to explain that to Griff.

Sometimes I dream of Louis. Of he and I together as we once were, when we were sixteen. In my dreams we are always in Willow Creek Woods walking hand in hand. I can feel the texture of his palm against mine, the brush of his fingers. Even now, when I think back to these dreams, if I sit completely still I can feel his touch. In my dreams, when Louis kisses me, the rush of air that we exchange into each other's mouth remains on my tongue hours after I've wakened. In the back of my mind, even as I am dreaming, I am saying to myself, *You're married, Antonia, what about your husband? What about Griff?* And in my dream I would force myself to pull away from Louis, to sweep away the feel of his touch. I would awaken then, sometimes with Griff next to me, but more often than not with Griff a thousand miles away in Alaska, my skin hot and my brain addled.

Still I could go for days, even weeks, without thinking of Louis. But then I would see his police car parked downtown or I'd see his pretty wife in the grocery store with their little boy situated in the grocery cart, kicking his fat little legs and I'd think, *That could be me, that could be my life.* Then I'd get disgusted with myself and shut down that corner of my mind for a while. Griff wasn't always so bad. He didn't start drinking really hard-core until after Ben was born. And he didn't hit me for the first time until Ben was three. I don't even remember what it was that I had done to make him so mad, but he hit me so hard that I didn't leave the house without sunglasses for a month. He didn't hit me again for at least a year, but he did get smarter about it. He never hit me in a place where someone would see the marks. But even so, he could be so wonderful. So funny and sweet. And the stories he would tell about his adventures on the pipeline always made me laugh so hard. Even Lou could never make me laugh like that. If only he could stop drinking, things could be so different. No, I know Griff loves me and he's my husband. He was my choice, just like they say, for better or worse.

I need to go and look for Ben now, with or without Louis.

I am used to Griff not being around for me. That was one thing that I could count on, Griff not being reliable. I decide I am not coming out of the forest until I have Ben for sure. I'm not confident that Calli is in the woods, but it makes sense that she would be. I will bring her home, too. Mrs. Norland tries to talk me out of leaving, but in the end places several bottles of water into my backpack and gives me a hug. As I loop the backpack through my arms and settle it onto my back I see Martin Gregory trekking his way toward Mrs. Norland's house.

"Now what?" I wonder and I open the door to meet him halfway.

DEPUTY SHERIFF LOUIS

I walk Mary Ellen McIntire to the exit, open the door for her and once again the heat of the day nearly takes my breath away. I tell her that I will let her know if she can be of any assistance to the Clark and Gregory families and watch her make her way to her car. She looks defeated, broken, and I wonder if this day will ever end. I see Tucci waving me over to him and I close the door on the oppressive heat outside. "Who was the guy that was brought in a minute ago?" I ask him.

"The tall guy with white hair?" Tucci asks, but continues without waiting for my answer. "That was Charles Wilson, the counselor over at the elementary school. And guess where they picked him up at?" This time Tucci waits for my response.

"Where?" I ask, but think I already know the answer and I feel my stomach clench.

"Willow Creek Woods," Tucci says, smacking his hand on his desk. "Says he was out walking his dog. But guess what? No dog. Park ranger noticed him roaming around Tanglefoot Trail and called us. Bender and Washburn went out and picked him up."

"What's he saying?" I ask.

"Nada. Nothing. He's lawyered up. The minute the little girls were mentioned, he clammed up," Tucci says triumphantly. Already he thinks that Wilson is the one who took the girls. Maybe so, but what about Griff?

"Do you think he would talk to me?" I ask Tucci.

"No way. He said he wanted his lawyer, right away. He's sitting in the conference room waiting for her. We got nothing on him. His lawyer will have him out of here in the next hour." My phone rings and I sit back in my chair to answer it.

"Louis, it's Martin. Antonia and I were wondering if you could come over to Mrs. Norland's home."

I sit up straight in my chair. "Did something happen?" I ask.

"Nothing you don't already know about. They found those footprints in Antonia's backyard, but we want to talk to you about searching for the girls."

"Martin, a few officers made a sweep of the woods near your home and found nothing. A larger scale search is being planned with dogs and a helicopter," I say. I consider telling him about Charles Wilson being brought in, but decide against it. I know too little, and I don't want to get his hopes up for nothing.

"I know. I understand you are doing what you can, but time is passing too quickly. Please come over to Mrs. Norland's house. We need your help. Please," Martin pleads.

"I'll be right over, Martin. Don't go and do anything until I get there, okay?"

"We'll be waiting. Please hurry."

I hang up the phone, not a little bothered that Toni hadn't been the one to call me. I wonder what it meant. Is she losing faith in me, doubting my abilities as an officer? I hope not. There are few leads. Maybe the school counselor is the guy. Doesn't feel right, though. Tanglefoot Trail, where he was picked up, is nowhere near the girls' homes. We still can't seem to locate Lucky Thompson, the college kid who works at the Mourning Glory. He hadn't shown up for his afternoon shift at the café. So many questions. My hand rests on the phone's receiver, and I am debating whether to call my wife. I should have checked in with her by now. I leave the police station without calling her. As I pull away, I switch my radio to F2 so that only Meg, our dispatcher, can hear me.

"Meg, this is for your information only," I tell her.

"Go ahead," she responds.

"I'm checking out the woods along Bobcat Trail for our missing girls. I'll be back in contact shortly."

"Ten-four."

ANTONIA

Louis is on his way over. It seems so simple now, for us to just go out into the woods to look for the girls. I don't plan to come home until I have Ben, Calli and Petra back with us.

"How do you think we can get past the press or the other officers without them knowing where we are going?" Martin asks.

"I don't know." That same question has been nagging me, as well. While getting as many people as possible looking for the kids would be a good thing, the idea of a camera following us around did not appeal to me. Besides, I wonder how Calli would react if there were a bunch of strangers in the woods looking for her. I think it would frighten her, that perhaps she would hide, making it much more difficult to find her.

Earlier, I had thought there was no way I would survive this day. A hundred emotions have traveled the course of my body and I am exhausted. But now the day is ending and the less sunlight we have, the more difficult it will be to locate the children. I wish we had set out hours earlier and I find myself resenting Louis and Agent Fitzgerald for snatching precious time away.

"He's here," Martin says, seeing Louis through Mrs. Norland's curtains.

I open the door to let him in even before he can knock.

"Hi," I say. "Thanks for coming."

"Sure. Martin sounded urgent." Louis reaches out to shake Martin's hand in greeting. Who did that anymore, I wonder. It is so formal, especially in our circumstance.

"We want to go looking for the children," Martin informs him. "I know that's not really in the plan that Agent Fitzgerald laid out, but we feel we need to do this."

Louis listens, showing no reaction.

"It's going to be dark in a few hours, Louis," I tell him. "I cannot stand the idea of them being out there in the woods at night. I have to go looking for them."

"I know what you're saying. I don't disagree with you. I just think that we would be able to cover a lot more ground with the organized search tomorrow. We'll have the search dogs and all the people we could ask for."

"We can still do all that tomorrow, if we need to." Impatience fills Martin's voice. "Right now, Antonia and I are going out looking for them, with you or without you. We're hoping you will be able to go with us or at least help us avoid the media as we set out." Martin and I both anxiously await Louis's decision. He has the same look on his face that he'd get when we were kids. That look of indecision right after I would dare him to do something he knew would either get him in trouble or hurt. In the end, Lou always took the dare.

"All right. Where do you want to start?" Louis asks with a sigh.

Martin looks to me. "I'm not familiar with the forest. I wouldn't know where to begin looking, I am afraid."

"Ben said he already tried Willow Wallow and the places on the edge of the woods. Let's head in deeper right away. How about Old Schoolhouse Path and then Bobcat Trail? Maybe the girls tried to find the school and got lost," I suggest.

Old Schoolhouse Path is a winding, mostly overgrown trail only recognizable to those who know the woods well. Settled about three miles into the woods is a small one-room schoolhouse, at least one hundred years old. No one knows why someone would choose to build a school in such a remote, difficult place to reach. Some people who had lived at the edge of the forest believed that a small group of settlers had made their home in the woods and as a community had built the school. It was difficult, however, to keep a teacher interested in staying in such an isolated area. So eventually, the people of the wood moved closer into town and abandoned the school made of limestone and oak. The sturdy little school was still standing, but engulfed by weeds. The small windows were broken out and many woodland animals had taken up residence there.

I had taken Ben and Calli there once a few years ago and we had talked of cleaning up the schoolhouse, maybe making a fort out of it, our own personal hiding spot. But it was too far into the woods, the hike too tiring for Calli, and we discarded the idea. Maybe Calli and Petra had decided to find the old school and investigate. This idea was much more comforting a scenario than the one that included Calli's footprints in the dust. Calli being dragged off somewhere.

"What about the reporters?" Martin asks.

"Could we distract them somehow?" I wonder. "Tell them that there is going to be a press conference at the sheriff's office, send them there?"

"That's all fine and good until they get there and there's no press conference. You don't want to piss them off, Toni. You may need them later on," Louis says.

"I think I know what we can do," Martin remarks. "May I use Mrs. Norland's telephone?"

"Of course," I answer. "Who are you calling?"

"Fielda," he responds. "She was planning on speaking with a reporter from Channel Twelve anyway. I don't think a few more reporters will matter."

"I think I know how we can keep the reporters happy for even longer," Louis adds. "If Fielda wouldn't mind, I know of someone who wants to help in any way that she can. Mary Ellen McIntire is in town." Louis looks at us expectantly.

"You mean the lady whose little girl was murdered? You don't think the same person who did that to her daughter had anything to do with this, do you, Louis?" I ask, my voice cracking.

"I don't know, Toni. I hope not. It's different in many ways, but Jenna McIntire was somehow lured from her home and into a wooded area. There's just enough of a similarity for Agent Fitzgerald to be interested and for the press to be all over this. It will keep the media occupied for a while."

Martin and I look at each other. "I'll call Fielda and explain what we are doing. Louis, call Mrs. McIntire and have her drive over to my mother-in-law's home. Antonia, go outside and tell the reporters that there will be a press conference at the Mourning home in—" he looks at his watch "—in fifteen minutes."

BEN

I am so tired and I keep nodding off. My eyes are nearly swollen shut and my head is throbbing. Dad looks like he is sleeping, so I relax a little bit. Through my slits for eyes I see Petra move, just a little bit. So she's not dead, thank God. I stand from where I am sitting, using a tree to steady myself. I feel dizzy and so, so tired. All I want to do is take a drink of water, ice-cold, and crawl into my bed and sleep for days. I stumble over to where Petra lies; she has tucked herself into a little ball, her arms covering her head so I can't see her face, which is prob'ly a good thing. My stomach isn't feeling so great; I don't think I can stand to get too close a look at Petra's face beaten to a pulp. But I need to get her to talk to me, to tell me what happened while Dad is sleeping.

"Petra," I whisper. "Petra!" I say a little bit louder. I kneel down and place my hand on her shoulder. My fingers are covered with dried blood and no amount of wiping them on my shorts will clean them off. Petra curls up tighter into her little ball.

"Petra, it's Ben. Please wake up. I gotta talk to you."

She moans a little bit as if it hurts her even to hear my voice.

"It's okay, Petra. You're safe now. I won't let him hurt you anymore." I glance over to where my dad sits, still sleeping. Petra moans again and I pat her on the arm.

"Mommy," she cries softly.

"You'll see your mom soon, Petra." I try to make her feel better. "Petra, did my dad do this to you?" No response. "Come on, Petra, you can tell me. Did my dad hurt you? Who brought you here?"

No answer. I sigh and sit back on my butt. At least she said something; she isn't going to die this instant anyway. Petra is okay for a seven-year-old. And she is real good to Calli. I gotta give Petra some credit. It couldn't have been easy having a kid who didn't talk, ever, for a best friend. It didn't seem to bother her any, though. Those two would just play like any first-graders, except that Petra'd do all the talking.

"Ben," she'd say when she was over, "Calli and I were wondering if we could borrow your baseball glove and bat?" or "Calli's not feeling very good, is your mom around?" It was pretty amazing, come to think of it. As long as Petra was around, I didn't worry too much about Calli.

Those two would go off together with their heads bent toward one another, looking like they were having this serious conversation. It made me wonder sometimes if Calli just wouldn't talk to us. Maybe she and Petra really talked all the time. I asked Petra once. I said, "Petra, has Calli ever talked to you?"

"We talk all the time," she said all casual-like. "But not out loud. I know what she is thinking and she knows what I am thinking."

"Weird," I had said.

"Yeah, I guess," she said.

"But a good kind of weird," I said quickly. Having Petra around made my life easier and I didn't want her to go thinking she was nuts to be Calli's friend.

"Yeah, a good weird," she agreed and then skipped off to where Calli was waiting for her.

It's a mystery to me. I pat Petra on the shoulder again and she cringes at my touch. She begins crying softly and moaning again.

I look back to where Dad is, do a double take. He's gone. I stand up real quick and look around me, spinning in a circle. Not there. He has gotten away. I feel tears burning my already sore eyes. *I let him go.* Had Calli gotten down to the bottom yet? I'm not sure how much time has passed. She is fast, though, faster than I would have been, but did she have enough time to get to help before Dad got to her? I didn't know. Maybe he's just hiding behind a tree somewhere, waiting for me to turn my back, then he can finish both me and Petra off. I feel only a little bit of shame in thinking that Dad would kill me, but he had broken my nose and Petra was lying there half-dead. I don't feel so big and strong just now. I can almost hear Dad laughing at me, "Oooh, the big hero, Ben! What'cha gonna do now? Them tears, Ben? A crybaby on top of it all."

Then the tears really come pouring out and I can't stop them. What if Dad got to Calli? I let her down again. I was tired of being the big brother, tired of taking the licks for everything. What should I do? Do I stay with Petra until help comes or do I go on down the bluff looking for help myself? I don't know what to do. I am twelve years old and I shouldn't have to make these decisions. What would Mom do? I think about that as I settle to the ground next to Petra, my back resting against a large rock. Not the Mom who was around when Dad was home, but the Mom who was there when Dad wasn't. The Mom who single-handedly whacked down the bat that flew down our chimney one night with an umbrella, and then carried it out to the woods to get rid of it. The Mom who, when I was eight and fell out of a tree and cut my head on a rock, wrapped a towel around my bleeding head and held my hand while the doctor put five staples in my skull. She didn't even cry or get sick. She just sat there, made me look at her, and told me it was going to be okay while they shot those staples into my head. What would that Mom do in my place? I chew on that for a while and finally decide that Mom would stay with Petra until help came. That would be the right thing to do, I could keep Petra safe. That is what I'm going to do. I will stay and hope that Calli made it down the bluff by now. But what would she do when she got there? How would she let them know where we were? I just have to trust her. She'd tell them. In her own way, she'd tell them.

DEPUTY SHERIFF LOUIS

Antonia is describing again to me Calli's favorite spots in Willow Creek Woods, and I am writing them down in my notebook, though I don't need to. I know these places; we both grew up here and played in these woods since we were kids. I know each hollow and gully as I know the curve of Antonia's face. I know the trails as I have known the map that is Antonia's skin.

My cell phone rings and I consider ignoring it, but it might be someone with info on the girls. I answer it and hear my wife on the other end.

"Loras, what are you doing?" she asks impatiently.

"Working," I tell her, turning away from Toni and Martin.

"You weren't even supposed to work today," she reminds me. I don't answer, knowing she has a lot more to say to me.

"Lou?" Toni asks, coming up behind me and placing a hand on my shoulder. "Is there news?"

"Who is that?" Christine asks. "Is that Toni Clark? Loras, what's going on? Are you with her?"

"I'm working," I repeat. I know I'm acting cold toward my wife. But this is serious. Two girls are missing, even if one of the girls belongs to my ex-girlfriend.

"Loras, you need to come home," Christine's voice is dangerously low. "You haven't spent time with Tanner in days."

"I can't do that at this time," I say, my voice professional. I could be talking to the dispatcher. Why am I acting this way? It's as if I don't want Toni to know I'm speaking with my own wife.

"Loras." Christine is on the verge of tears. "You're talking to your wife, not another deputy. I need to know what's going on!"

"That's just not possible at this time. I'll contact you later."

Christine explodes. "Dammit, Loras, knock it off! Don't you care?" Her voice shrieks from the cell phone, and I know that Toni and Martin can hear her. They both look down, embarrassed for me. "You are throwing this marriage away!" she rants on. "You're with her, aren't you? You are going to fucking ruin our marriage over that sad, stupid woman who can't keep her husband from drinking or even look after her own kids."

I feel Toni's hand on my arm and I look over at her, expecting her to try and yank the phone from me and give Christine hell. But she doesn't. Instead she points toward the trees. I follow her outstretched finger and hang up on Christine without even saying goodbye.

Tearing out of the woods is Calli. Seeing the anguish fall from Antonia's face when she realizes her daughter is coming toward us sends a burst of relief through me. I cannot stand to see Antonia in pain of any sort; she has carried around too much of her fair share anyway. Calli and Ben are Antonia's life, even if her no-good husband doesn't have the same priorities, his being a bottle of beer and a place to flop.

Calli is out of the woods and I see Martin looking behind Calli hopefully, searching into the hawthorne trees that edge Bobcat Trail. No one is coming behind Calli, not yet. As she stops beside me, Calli appears unharmed. She could be any seven-year-old playing a running game, but for two things. In her right hand she is holding a silver necklace with a charm in the shape of a musical note. The necklace, I know, belongs to Petra because her mother described it to me in perfect detail when she called me at four-thirty-five this morning to tell me that Petra was missing from her bedroom. As is procedure, I also got a photograph of the girl and a full description of the clothing she was wearing when she was last seen. Short blue pajamas, white underwear with yellow flowers, and of course, the necklace. Petra's white tennis shoes were also reported missing. Martin has seen the necklace, too, and briefly collapses, but he is up quickly. In long, purposeful strides he approaches. I have seen this look before, a tortured, keening need to know brushed raggedly on the face of a desperate parent, most recently on the parents of ten-year-old Jenna McIntire.

Calli clutches at my sleeve and I stoop so as to be face-to-face with her. I expect no words; Calli hasn't spoken for years. Perhaps she will point and lead us to Petra. Hopefully to a positive end. But she doesn't indicate with a finger or lead me by the hand to the woods. She speaks. One word. As Antonia steps closer I see both confusion and relief. Martin is crying, great inconsolable sobs. And I see what they both do not. Bunched up in Calli's other hand is Petra's white underwear with yellow flowers.

MARTIN

I turn when I hear the rustle in the trees. I see Petra's little friend, Calli, running down the path. It is what is in her hand that I am drawn to. From so far away it glints as it swings from her hand. It has never been off Petra's neck, and my stomach seizes and the strength rushes from my limbs and I stumble to my knees. I look to her face, and on it I see fierce determination, not fear, not terror. A smile almost plays on her grimy face. A moment of hope. I look behind Calli and do not see Petra following. She's cleared the brush now and I stand up, my hand already outstretched to take back my child's necklace. The girl stops in front of her mother and the deputy sheriff, her breath coming out in ragged puffs. This mute little creature who never speaks, and I feel desperation roiling up in me. I need to find my Petra, now. I am running to where the girl stands, ready to shake her bony shoulders. "Tell me! Tell me!" I will scream, my nose touching hers.

I stop a few steps from her. She is tugging on the sleeve of the deputy sheriff. He bends down, his ear level with her mouth. One word crashes into me, and I weep.

ANTONIA

In the woods, through the bee trees whose heavy, sweet smell will forever remind me of this day, I see flashes of your pink summer nightgown that you wore to bed last night. My chest loosens and I am shaky with relief. I scarcely notice your scratched legs, muddy knees, or the chain in your hand. I reach out to gather you in my arms, to hold you so tight, to lay my cheek on your sweaty head. I will never wish for you to speak, never silently beg you to talk. You are here. But you step past me, not seeing me, you stop at Louis's side, and I think, *You don't even see me, it's Louis's deputy sheriff's uniform, good girl, that's the smart thing to do.* Louis lowers himself toward you, and I am fastened to the look on your face. I see your lips begin to arrange themselves and I know, I know. I see the word form, the syllables hardening and sliding from your mouth, with no effort. Your voice, not unsure or hoarse from lack of use, but clear and bold. One word, the first in over three years. In an instant I have you in my arms and I am crying, tears dropping many emotions, mostly thankfulness and relief, but tears of sorrow mixed in. I see Petra's father crumble. Your chosen word doesn't make sense to me. But it doesn't matter, I don't care. You have finally spoken.

CALLI

Calli ran on legs that she could no longer feel, just a heaviness below her waist, but the need to move forward kept her going. For Ben. For Ben who always came through for her, who took beatings and cruel words that in all rights belonged to her. Calli gripped more tightly to the items in her hands, Petra's necklace and her underwear. Why Petra wasn't wearing them, Calli did not understand, but she knew that they were important in all of this. Petra, hurt so badly, he had said she might die. Oh, God, would that be her fault, too? Out of the corner of her eye she saw a straw-colored lump among a patch of brown-tipped ferns. Calli stopped abruptly. The dog. The dog she had seen earlier, wandering playfully through the woods. Dead. Lying there in a heap, its long, pink tongue poking from between its pointed teeth. Its eyes open wide and unseeing. The dog's collar had been removed. Calli had the unnerving feeling that something was watching her and she turned away from the dog and continued her trek down the bluff. Faster, faster, not even watching the ground in front of her for rocks or roots that could cause her to stumble. Ben said to go down, go down to find help, and she would. That man. That scary man, up there, too. His dog. Yes, that was his dog. Daddy, she thought, Daddy, he was so angry with her and he would take it out on Ben, she knew, and Petra, maybe. *Ben, Daddy, Petra, that man, Ben, Daddy, Petra, that man, Ben, Daddy, Petra, that man...* The words spiraled through her mind. Then she could see it, the end of the trail, where the trees abruptly stopped. *Ben, Daddy, Petra, that man, Ben, Daddy, Petra, that man.* She ran out into the clearing, saw an unexpected sight, her mother, oh, her mother, and Deputy Louis and Petra's daddy! She could stop running now. She did what Ben had told her to do, get help. *Ben, Daddy, Petra, that man, Ben, Daddy, Petra, that man, Ben, Daddy.* Who to go to? Deputy Louis, yes, he would get help right away, get that man, get Daddy. She was at the deputy's side, her mother's arms stretched out toward her... *Ben, Daddy, Petra, that man, Ben, Daddy, Petra, that man, Ben, Daddy, Petra, that man...*

"Ben!" The name erupted from her, it didn't feel like it came from her mouth exactly, but somewhere deeper, from just below her breastbone. She didn't recognize her own voice, it sounded so strong, so clear and she wanted to say more...*Ben, Daddy, Petra, that man, Ben, Daddy...* But then her mother's arms were around her, rocking her. She was so tired, so thirsty, they were all moving now, and she went silent once again.

MARTIN

Calli is still holding Petra's necklace, surrounded by her mother and Deputy Louis. Through my tears I go toward her to get it back. Ben? Ben did this? I could not believe it, though, yes, it crossed my mind when Fielda had broached the subject hours ago in anger. Ben? I try to pry the charm from Calli's fingers, but Louis steps between us.

"Martin, give her space," he orders.

"Where is she?" I croak. Calli has her face buried in her mother's stomach; my hands are shaking in desperation.

"Martin," Louis says gently, "we'll find her. I'm calling for backup right now."

I can see Louis fumbling and retrieve something from Calli's hand, not the one holding the necklace. I crane to see what it is, but cannot. He crumples the item into his fist, so I cannot tell what he is holding, and then he lopes off to his car to call for help.

"Calli, tell me, is Petra all right?" I ask as soothingly as I can. "Did you just come from her? Please tell me. Is Ben up there with her? Did Ben hurt you?"

Antonia gives me a searing stare and shields Calli from me. As if I am the dangerous one here. "Listen, I don't know what you're thinking, but Ben had nothing to do with…" Louis hurries back to us, interrupting Antonia's angry reproach.

"I've called for more officers to help us go up after Petra and Ben." He pauses and looks Calli up and down. "And for an ambulance. The medics will check Calli over and will be available if Petra and Ben need assistance," Louis tells us. He bends down to face Calli. "Calli," he says soothingly, "is Petra okay?" He waits for a response from her. Slowly, she shakes her head no and I moan and head toward the trail.

"Martin, wait! We need more information before we go up there! There are three trails—we need to know which one to take!" I stop and return to them, agitated.

"Ask her, then, ask her where they are! She can talk, she said, 'Ben!' Ask her!" I shout, spittle flies from my lips and both Calli and Antonia cringe at my outburst.

"Martin, go stand by the road," Louis orders. "Stand there and flag down the ambulance so it knows that we are here. I'll talk to Calli. She'll let us know exactly where to go." His voice softens as he adds, "It will save us time this way. I promise. Now go, wait for the ambulance and the other officers."

I do as he says, however petulantly, and he returns to where Calli and Antonia stand, holding on to each other. The injustice of it stings me. I should be hugging Petra, reassuring her, not still wondering where she is, alive or dead. I tromp over to the road, where gravel meets the pavement and wait, scanning the distance, searching for the ambulance. Not yet.

I lean against the police car, its metal still exuding the day's monstrous heat, and I leap away.

Antonia calls back to me, hesitation in her voice. I must have frightened her. "Martin, can you grab a water bottle for Calli? They're in the backseat."

I hear Louis yell, "No, wait!" and he comes running toward me.

I open the back door, behind the passenger's seat and pull out three water bottles, two for Calli and one that I will bring up with me when we go to find Petra. I, frankly, do not care about Ben at this point. Had he done this? As I begin to pull myself out the car I see them. Stained in dirt, but I recognize them, I had folded them myself just yesterday when I pulled them from the dryer. White with little yellow flowers. I snatch the plastic bag that held them and inspect them closely, by now Louis is at my side.

"Martin," he says helplessly. I shove the package into his chest, not able to look at it anymore.

"I am going after my daughter," I tell him simply, calmly, despite the terror clutching at my chest. And I run, all fifty-some years of me, up that trail, with Deputy Louis calling after me.

"Martin, wait! Wait! We need to wait for backup."

I ignore his pleas and run.

DEPUTY SHERIFF LOUIS

"Damn," I mutter to myself as Martin dashes past me and heads up the trail. God knows what he will find up there. "Toni," I bark. "Wait here for the other officers and the ambulance. I'm going with Martin." I scan her worried face. "It will be okay. I'll go up there and bring Ben down, safe and sound. Don't worry. We'll take Hobo Hollow. Tell them the trail on the left, where it forks."

She nods and squeezes my hand.

"Thank you, Louis." Her voice trembles. I squeeze back and follow Martin into the woods.

It doesn't take me long to catch up with him. He is stopped near the edge of a trail and is examining something lying off to the side. He is breathing heavily and does not turn as I step close to him at his elbow.

"It's dead," he says matter-of-factly.

I reach down to touch the dog's flank. "He's still warm," I observe. "He hasn't been here long."

"What do you think happened to it?" Martin asks fearfully.

"I don't know." I keep my voice level and calm. "Martin, you need to go back down now. You're going to get both of us in a lot of trouble if you go up there."

"I'm going up," Martin says firmly.

I sigh in resignation. "Let's take it somewhat slower, though, all right? It will do Petra no good if one of us gets hurt before we reach her. Okay?"

"Yes, fine," he says, gazing down at the dead dog. "We need to hurry, though, please. Let's hurry."

We continue upward. Dusk is only an hour or so away, but close enough for me to begin to worry that we won't get Petra, Ben and whoever else was at the top of the bluff down. A rescue mission down the bluff would be difficult enough during daylight, but in the dark of night, it would be complex. I requested that several all-terrain vehicles be brought to the trail to expedite matters. I had also told the dispatcher to have a helicopter from Iowa City on standby in case of serious injuries.

"Petra isn't dead, Martin."

He looks at me. "Did Calli tell you that?"

"Not in words, but I questioned her. She indicated that Petra was at the top of Hobo Hollow and she was hurt, but she couldn't say how badly."

"Did she tell you who did this?" Martin says through gritted teeth, wheezing with the exertion of the climb.

"No, I didn't get that from her. That was when you found… Do you need to sit and rest for a moment, Martin?"

"No, I'm fine." We continue forward in silence.

"I could kill whoever did this, Louis. I really and truly could."

"That wouldn't solve anything, Martin. It would make things worse, so much worse."

"You have a child, a son." It wasn't a question.

"Yes. His name is Tanner, he's four."

"And you would do anything for him?" Martin asks, concentrating on the ground in front of him.

"Yes, I think I would."

"Then you could kill someone who hurt your child, in that way," he says resolutely.

I take a sidelong glance at Martin. His face is waxy. A sweaty sheen covers his forehead and he mops at it with a handkerchief that he pulls from his pocket. "I would probably feel like killing someone who would hurt Tanner, but I don't actually think I would. Especially if the police were already there to help."

"She said, 'Ben,' and she was holding Petra's necklace and her underpants in her hands. What do you suppose is going through my mind?" He stops for a fraction of a second, shakes his head and then hurries onward. "We need to get to the top, and then we will go from there."

I take a moment to use my walkie-talkie to convey where I am and to get an update on what was happening at the base of the trail. The ambulances have just arrived. One to transport Calli and Toni to the hospital, another standing by, waiting for further direction. Two officers on four-wheelers and several on foot and horseback would be joining us shortly. I remind everyone that we had no suspect and no description of a suspect. Just that everyone needed to be on the lookout for Petra and Ben. Most of the officers knew them by sight, but pictures were circulating.

We are nearing the fork in the trail and I use my arm to specify the direction we would take. "Whatever we find up there, Martin, you must let me step forward first. Your first thought will be to go to Petra, but don't." I step in front of him in order to make him stop. "Do you understand me, Martin? You can't just barrel up there. Someone dangerous may be at the top. Hell, someone dangerous could be watching us right now. You need to let me determine what we do next. We shouldn't even be up here right now without other officers."

"You couldn't have stopped me," Martin says.

"No, that's why I'm up here with you. I don't want you getting hurt, or you hurting someone else, for that matter. When we get up there, you wait. You wait until I tell you what to do next. You stay behind me at all times. Got it?"

Martin purses his lips and looks prepared to argue, but he doesn't. "I understand," he says and keeps walking. I am surprised by his stamina. He is still going strong, and even my legs are beginning to ache with the effort of trekking up the bluff. I am sure that adrenaline has a lot to do with Martin's endurance. He will be a very sore man tomorrow morning.

CALLI

Her mother had taken one look at her torn and bleeding feet and picked her up, holding her as she would a toddler, chest to chest, Calli's chin resting on her shoulder. Petra's father had scared her. The look on his face, the terrible sound in his voice. Much different from her father's, but even more insistent. They had left so quickly, but that was good, they were going up to get Ben and Petra, get help, which was what Ben had told her to do. And she had done that, gotten help. Everything would be okay now. She was so tired now, so sleepy. The water had tasted good; she drank and drank from the water bottle her mother pressed to her lips. But now she felt sick to her stomach, the water was gurgling around in her empty middle.

She was vaguely aware that she had spoken. One word. *Ben.* She had said her brother's name and she was so surprised that nothing bad had happened when she spoke the word. Her mother was still there holding tightly to her, she hadn't been ripped from her, nothing bad had happened. Calli thought that she might like to say more, but she was so very tired. The feeling had returned to her damaged feet and they burned. All she really wanted to do was sleep, sleep with her hands linked around her mother, her head tucked into the soft groove that was her mother's neck. In the distance she could hear the wail of an ambulance coming closer.

In a quiet, half-asleep nook of her mind, the thought that she perhaps should have said more to Deputy Louis flitted at her like a dragonfly. What had she said? *Ben*. But there was so much more she should have said. *Ben, Daddy, Petra, that man, Ben, Daddy, Petra, that man, Ben, Daddy, Petra, that man*. Petra's daddy had looked so frightened, but she had only said *Ben*, that wasn't scary. Then Petra's daddy had run and then Deputy Louis ran after him. To help. *Ben, Daddy, Petra, that man, Ben, Daddy, Petra, that man, Ben, Daddy, Petra, that man*. Calli soundlessly mouthed the words *Ben, Daddy, Petra, that man, Ben, Daddy, Petra, that man, Ben, Daddy, Petra, that man…* She was too weary and her mouth stilled.

The siren from the ambulance came to an abrupt stop and Calli could feel her mother laying her down. She struggled to stay in her mother's arms, plucked at her shirt, trying to take hold, but her fingers felt weak and boneless and she was only able to feel the fabric slide through her grasp like water.

Her mother's face drifted above her and she heard her say, "It's okay now, Calli, I'm staying with you. I won't leave. Sleep now. Just sleep."

She felt her mother's own fingers rest lightly on the side of her cheek and her mother kissed her, her lips warm and dry, like paper. And Calli drew in the scent that was her mother and let sleep take her.

BEN

I hear something in the woods crashing toward me. Oh, God, I think, Dad is coming back. Oh, God, he will kill me this time. I jump to my feet and ready myself for him. I tilt my head to hear better, I can barely see and I run my hands over my face, it feels puffy and sore. I reach for a nearby branch. It isn't very thick or sturdy, but it has sharp points. I may be able to hold him back with it. Aim for the eyes, I tell myself.

The noise from the forest comes closer and it sounds too big to be Dad, it sounds like it is running on more than two feet and my next thought is coyote. And that freaks me out more than my father for some reason. Maybe because, with Dad, I know his ways, the way he moves, how he fights. A coyote would be a whole different story and I look around for a bigger stick. Then the noise is here, right here, and my next thought is of Petra. A coyote might go right for her, she is so little and helpless. She looks hurt bad. A big old coyote could just drag her off, eat her up in three big bites. I hurry over to her and spread my arms out wide, holding the stick ready for battle, waiting.

I'm not sure what is more surprising, me not seeing a coyote or my dad smashing out of the woods or seeing Petra's dad and the deputy sheriff. I keep my eye on Mr. Gregory, because he looks so dang mad. I see him see Petra lying there and then he sees me holding this big old stick and I know right away what is going through his mind. Before I can even say anything he is flying at me. This old, real proper man flying at me. I see his feet actually leave the ground and I think, *Well, crap, he thinks I did this to Petra.* For the second time that day I get the wind knocked outta me, and let me tell you, it hurts a heck of a lot more the second time round when you can see what's coming.

Then Mr. Gregory is on top of me, screaming something I can't understand, and the whole time I'm not breathing so I can't tell him what really happened, that they should be out there looking for my dad. But the only thing that comes outta me is a big "oomph!" Suddenly the deputy is there and he yanks Mr. Gregory offa me.

"Martin!" Deputy Louis screams. But Mr. Gregory is still trying to pound on me, saying something about pervert and how he is going to kill me. "Martin!" he screams again. "Martin, look at him!" And finally, Mr. Gregory drops his fists and looks at me, really looks at me and then at Petra.

Mr. Gregory looks down to where Petra is lying and he bends down. I can see him check to see if she is breathing. Mr. Gregory starts crying then. And I think I never saw a man cry before, really cry. I stand up and try to see what he is seeing. And my second thought is, she's died. I let her die. I was supposed to take care of her until help came and she died. So then I start crying.

"Thank God, thank God," I think I hear Mr. Gregory whispering over and over and I try to stop my blubbering to listen more closely to him. "Thank you, God," Mr. Gregory says even louder.

"Is she okay?" I ask him, trying not to sound like a little kid, but my voice sounds all squeaky, so that it's pretty clear that's all I am.

"Ben, what happened?" Deputy Louis asks me. "Are you all right? Who did this to you?" And I know just then that at least the deputy doesn't think I hurt anybody.

"My dad," I whimper, giving in to the mess of it all. "My dad did it," I cry. And in an instant, Deputy Louis has his arms around my shoulder, telling me that it's gonna be okay. But how could it be?

"Petra needs a doctor, right now," Martin says. "We need to get help up here right now."

Deputy Louis gets on his walkie-talkie and says a few numbers that I take to be secret police codes and then I thump right back down on my butt, because all the fight has gone outta me and I can't do one more thing. My legs feel like rubber, my face hurts and I figure Mr. Gregory broke something in me when he tackled me.

"A helicopter is coming in from Iowa City, but we need to get Petra to the nearest clearing, which is at the bottom where we came up from, Martin," Deputy Louis tells him.

"I don't think we should move her," Martin says worriedly. "How are we going to get her down the bluff?"

"An EMT crew is coming up with the officers. They can

check her out and recommend how this should be done." Deputy Louis looks at his watch. "It will be dark any time now. We need to move fast."

I look up to the sky and can see the pink and orange colors that come out right before the sun sets.

"I think she needs medical care as quickly as possible. Please," Mr. Gregory implores, "we need to get her help now." Mr. Gregory is not looking at me. I'm not sure if he feels bad about knocking me down or if he still isn't sure what part I had in all this.

Now we can hear the low rumble of engines. The four-wheelers are almost to us. They come one by one to the top of the bluff. Two people, a man and a woman who I think must be the paramedics, hop off and rush over to Petra and immediately check her over. I scoot over to the far side of where the action is, trying to stay out of the way. Deputy Louis is busy talking to a group of police officers and to Ranger Phelps, who has come up on horseback. I sit back and just watch for a while and try to keep my eyes open, but keep dozing off.

I open my eyes and I can hear the *chop, chop* of a helicopter coming closer. It is night now. I can see stars, sharp little pinpricks of light above me, and I feel cold even though everyone else looks like they are sweating. Everyone is fussing around Petra, and everyone seems to have forgotten about me. I'm not the one hurt real bad, but I feel lonely sitting in my own little corner of the woods, with everyone hustling to make sure Petra is okay. I wonder about Calli. She musta got down the bluff and got help. I wonder where she is now and I look around for someone who doesn't look too busy for me to ask. But they are all running around, so I just wait and watch. Watching Petra being strapped to that stretcher and dangling from the helicopter down the bluff is just about the scariest sight ever. The helicopter looks like a big old bird and Petra looks like something clutched in its talons. But I saw a lot of scary things today. I can't see Mr. Gregory, but I imagine it is all he can do to not jump up and try to drag that stretcher right on back to solid ground.

We all watch as the helicopter takes her on down the bluff. She'll only be in the air for a minute, then they will put her in the helicopter and carry her off to Iowa City. I wonder how we will get down the bluff.

ANTONIA

I insist that I go in the ambulance with Calli. I am not going to let her out of my sight again. I have mixed feelings leaving Ben behind, but I know that Louis will bring him to me safely. Poor Ben, he is always the one left to fend for himself, it seems. I feel a flash of anger at Griff for always leaving me in this position, the one to parent all on my own; he is never there when I need him.

Calli immediately falls asleep when she is laid in the ambulance, despite the paramedics poking at her, taking her pulse and blood pressure. One of the paramedics, a kind-looking older woman, gives me a reassuring smile.

"She'll be okay," she tells me. "All her injuries appear to be superficial, but they will give her a thorough examination at the hospital and get her cleaned up. We need to give her an IV, she's showing signs of dehydration." I watch as the paramedic swipes Calli's arm with alcohol and expertly inserts the IV, Calli barely stirs at the procedure. I give a sigh of relief and the woman looks at me questioningly. "What happened up there?"

"I'm not sure. Something very bad," I tell her and I look down at my Calli, knowing that right now, at least, she is the only one who can tell me exactly what happened up on Hobo Hollow. I wonder if she will speak again or if she will go back to her silence. "Can you go any faster?" I ask the paramedic. She shakes her head no.

"We don't put on the lights unless it's a life or death emergency," she says apologetically.

"My son is still up there. The sooner I get Calli taken care of, the sooner I can get back out to the forest and find out what's happening with Ben."

"Is their father in the picture?" she asks, and I listen closely to her voice, searching for any judgmental undertones. I don't hear any.

"He is, but he's away on a fishing trip. I can't get a hold of him," I explain.

"Oh, that's too bad." She resumes attending to Calli. "How old is your boy?"

"He's twelve," I respond, inching closer to Calli.

"People are up there looking for him?"

I nod. "And another little girl. What would you do?" I ask this kind woman who is taking an interest in me.

"You have any family here in town?"

"No, it's just the four of us."

"Friends you can call?"

"No," I whisper, and once again loneliness presses in around me and for the first time I am truly aware of the isolation I have found in my own hometown.

"My name is Rose Callahan. I'm off at ten," she tells me. "Once the doctors and nurses get Calli checked over and settled in, I'd be glad to sit with her. I'm sure they will keep her over for observation. She may be pretty dehydrated after being up in the woods all day. You see how when I pinch the back of Calli's hand, the skin doesn't immediately lay flat again? That's called skin turgor, a sign of dehydration. It's easily remedied, but we need to keep a close eye on her. I really would be glad to sit with her if you need to be somewhere else."

I hesitate and do not respond to her offer.

"Everyone at the hospital knows me. I have three grandkids of my own, but they live out west."

"I don't know," I begin.

"If you need me, you call me. I'll give you my phone number. And please call me. I don't have anyone here in town anymore, either. Are you from Willow Creek?"

"I was born and grew up here." We pull into the ambulance unloading area; Rose jots her number down on a scrap of paper and hands it to me.

"You call me, understand? If you need anything, you call me."

"I will, thank you," I tell her as some attendants come, gently lift Calli from the ambulance and wheel her into the hospital emergency room as Rose and her partner fill them in on Calli's situation.

"This is Toni Clark, Calli's mother," Rose informs them.

"Please come with me, Ms. Clark," a male nurse instructs me and I follow him into an examination room. I turn back to wave at Rose, but she is already gone. "Tell me what happened here with Calli," he asks.

"I'm not really sure what happened. She wasn't in her bed

this morning, and we couldn't find her. Another little girl, Petra Gregory, is still on the bluff. The police have been looking for them all day. She came running down from the woods, like…this," I say, indicating her scratched legs and bleeding feet, her dirty nightgown.

"Was she able to tell you what happened?"

"No." I shake my head. "But she said her brother's name, 'Ben.' He's still up there."

The nurse looks confused. "Both your children were missing?"

"No, just Calli and her friend, not Ben. He went looking for them. Calli came out, Ben didn't. Not yet." I am so tired; the entire story makes little sense even to me. "The police are up there looking for them."

"I'm sure a police officer will be here shortly," the nurse assures me. "He or she will most likely question Calli about what she remembers about today. We will get her checked out and cleaned up before that happens."

"All right, thank you," I tell him.

"Dr. Higby will be right in." The nurse leaves me in the brightly lit examination room, alone with Calli, and I try to brush her matted hair away from her forehead.

Calli tries to curl herself up into a tight little ball, but this is difficult as the examination table is narrow. She shoves a grimy thumb into her mouth and every few moments her eyelids flutter, as if trying to open, but they remain closed. I hear the door open behind me and in steps a man, the doctor, I assume, as he is wearing a white lab coat. He is completely bald, his head gleaming underneath the fluorescent lights. He wears glasses with red frames and a tie decorated with smiley faces.

"I'm Dr. Higby," he introduces himself. He holds his hand out to me and I shake it. He has a powerful grip and I am struck by how much his hand looks like Griff's, strong and coarse from manual labor. "Tell me about who we have here," he says, looking down at Calli who is trying to warm herself by pulling the sheet that covers her more tightly about her.

"This is Calli Clark. I'm Toni, her mother. She's been out lost in the woods all day. I don't know what happened to her."

"Was she found like this?"

"She came out of the woods on her own, but she was exhausted. She fell asleep the moment she was off her feet."

Dr. Higby refers to the notes in a chart he holds. "Her vital signs look strong. Let's check her over and see what we have here. We're going to have to wake her up, Mrs. Clark," he says apologetically. "Having her awake and able to tell us where it hurts will help us treat her. Would you like to be the one to wake her? She would probably find it frightening to wake up to this scary mug of mine." He smiles at me.

"Calli, honey." I go to her side and rub her shoulder. "Calli, I need you to wake up now." I gently try to pull the sheet from her and her eyes open, instantly awake, her eyes dart around in panic. "It's okay, Calli, Mom's here," I croon. "You're at the hospital. We need you to wake up so you can let us know where it hurts. This is Dr. Higby. He's going to help you feel better."

Dr. Higby steps into Calli's line of vision and she watches him carefully for a moment, taking in the red glasses and his tie.

"Hello, Calli, I'm Dr. Higby. Just like your mom said, I'm going to check you over to see if you are hurt anywhere. I hear you've had a pretty scary day."

Calli gives no response, but continues to observe the doctor.

"I want you to know, Calli, that you are completely safe here," Dr. Higby assures her. "Nothing bad is going to happen here. We all are here to help you, okay?" Calli does not answer.

"Dr. Higby, may I speak with you a moment? Calli, we'll be right out here. You okay?" She nods and Dr. Higby follows me out into the hall.

"Calli doesn't talk. I mean, she spoke for the first time in four years today. She said her brother's name. It's all she said, but that's huge for us. I'm not sure what to expect now, if she'll talk all the time now or what."

"Calli's a selective mute?" he asks. "There's no physical reason for her not talking?"

"That's what we've been told. I'd almost given up hope in her ever talking again, but she did today. She said her brother's name." I feel a renewed sense of excitement and hope in telling Dr. Higby this.

"It is very good news that Calli spoke. I have a very limited experience with selective mutism, Mrs. Clark, but we have a psychiatrist on staff who may be more informed on the subject. Would you like for me to call her and have her visit with you?"

"Calli isn't crazy," I tell him, my initial liking of the man fading quickly.

"No, of course not. I didn't mean to imply that. Dr. Kelsing is a medical doctor with a wide expertise. She could be very helpful." Dr. Higby waits patiently for me to mull this over.

"You think she's good?" I ask. "You think she could help Calli?"

"I implicitly trust her judgment, Mrs. Clark," he responds.

"All right, then, I'd like to meet her," I say as I notice two police officers come through the emergency room doors.

"I'll call her immediately and then we'll get to work on fixing up Calli." He pats my arm and goes to contact Dr. Kelsing.

The two officers confer with the emergency room receptionist and make their way over to me as I peek in the examination room to check on Calli. She waggles her fingers at me in a halfhearted wave and I smile at her and hold up a finger to tell her that I'll be right back. I meet the officers back in the hallway. Their faces are familiar to me, and I recognize them as being several years behind me in school.

"Mrs. Clark?" the taller officer asks. I nod. "I'm Officer Bies and this is Officer Thumser. I think you went to school with my sister, Cheryl."

I nod distractedly. "Did you find my son?" I ask anxiously.

"Yes, Mrs. Clark. He's on his way now to be checked out here at the hospital."

"Is he okay?" I ask, my heart thumping.

"It appears he's fine, Mrs. Clark. He should be here within the next hour or so. We need to talk to your daughter, ma'am."

"Did you find Petra? Is Petra okay?"

"I'm sorry, I can't share any information about Petra Gregory at this time. Mrs. Clark, we really need to see your daughter. She is crucial to this investigation."

At this moment Dr. Higby reappears. "Hello, Mike, Russ. What can I do for you tonight?" he asks.

"We were just explaining to Mrs. Clark that we need to visit with Calli about what happened to her today."

"We need to make sure that Calli's condition is stable before anyone speaks with her. You can understand that."

"Yes, we understand. How long till you think she can talk to us?"

Dr. Higby and I look at each other and I nod to him, giving him permission to share Calli's situation.

"Calli's a reluctant speaker. She may not be able to tell you what you want to know. We have a consultant coming in to help us. We are going to need to proceed very slowly with her."

The officers' disappointment is apparent, but they are wise enough to say nothing. "Could you give us a call when you feel she's ready to see us? It really is important. And, Mrs. Clark, we'll need to visit with your son after he gets checked out. And you, as well."

"Me?" I ask. "Why me?"

"Just follow-up questions. We finally located Roger Hogan, your husband's fishing buddy. Mr. Hogan didn't offer much, but your husband wasn't with him. Good luck, Mrs. Clark," the tall officer tells me. "I'm glad your little girl is back safe and sound."

I freeze for a moment, trying to process that news. Griff isn't with Roger? Where is he, then? I don't allow myself to consider what it means. Dr. Higby and I return to Calli's side. Calli is wide-awake now, trembling from the cold of the room.

"I know it's cold in here, Calli," Dr. Higby says. "We'll get you all fixed up and nice and cozy soon. We'll tell you exactly what is going to happen before it happens, okay? That way, if you have any questions, you can ask."

A young nurse enters the room. She has a cheerful smile and wears pink scrubs. "Hi, Calli, my name is Molly. I'm going to be your nurse while you're here. I'll be with you every step of the way." Calli looks quickly to me and snatches at my hand.

"Don't worry, honey, your mom can stay with you the whole time," Molly assures her.

Dr. Higby pats me on the back and excuses himself. "Sometimes the patients feel more comfortable if only females are in the room. I'll check back in with you soon." He gives me a sympathetic smile and leaves us.

I bend down to kiss her and for the first time that evening I notice the smell of urine on her. My stomach clenches at the thought of what happened today.

"Now, the first thing we need to do is get you out of that nightgown and into this lovely gown." Molly carefully removes Calli's pink nightgown and places it in a plastic bag. Calli loves this nightgown; I often find her wearing it in the middle of the day. I think she likes the way that it swirls around her as she moves. When she doesn't know that I am watching, I see Calli dancing in her pink nightgown to music that only she can hear. She is graceful and delicate and when she dances she reminds me of the dandelion fluff we catch and then release to make wishes. I always make the same wish on her as she leaps and twirls—*please speak to me, Calli, please speak.* I silently vow to buy Calli the most beautiful nightgown I can find. One that feels like silk next to her skin and flows like water around her as she moves.

"Now, Calli, I'm going to give you an exam. Do you know what an exam is?" Molly asks. Calli gives a slight nod of her head. "Oh, of course you do. How old are you? Sixteen? Seventeen?" Calli smiles, shakes her head and holds up seven fingers.

"Seven?" Molly asks. "I'm shocked. You seem so much older." Again Calli smiles. I like this Molly right away. "Now, Calli, I'm going to go from the tip-top of your head right down to your little piggy toes and ask you if anything specifically hurts. You just let me know yes or no, okay?" Again Calli nods.

"I can tell you're going to be a super patient. Okay, let's get started. First of all, does your hair hurt?" Calli wrinkles her nose and looks at Molly in disbelief. "Well, does it?" she asks again.

Calli shakes her head no.

"Good! That's good news. How about your head, does anywhere on your head or neck hurt?" Again Calli shakes her head no. I can see Calli is enjoying this game and by the time Molly gets down to Calli's piggy toes, we have learned that the only places Calli feels any pain are in her stomach and in her feet.

Molly quietly explains that she would have to collect evidence from Calli. When she says the words *rape kit* my stomach lurches.

"Is that necessary?" I ask numbly.

"We need to rule out any assault that may have occurred and we need to gather any evidence that may have been left behind. I'll be very gentle. And you can stay here with her," Molly assures me as she pulls on a pair of latex gloves.

Molly takes a long oversize Q-tip and asks Calli to open her mouth. She swiftly swabs Calli's cheeks and horrific thoughts charge through my mind. I try to push them away. Methodically, carefully, Molly moves down along my daughter's body, combing, scraping and collecting the grime and dreadfulness of the day. I force myself to watch, to watch what my inattentiveness has caused. I force myself to watch now because I have not watched my child closely enough; she has spent the day in the forest running, running from something terrible. Did he catch her or was she fast enough? *Please have been fast enough,* I silently recite over and over. When the exam is finally complete I have read every furrow in my daughter's face, the confusion and the unasked questions. I have no words for Calli. I cannot think of one useful, com-forting word for my daughter during this intrusion and we are both silent.

"I don't see any obvious indication of sexual assault, but we'll send the swabs to the lab." I close my eyes and take a deep breath. Maybe it will be okay. Molly continues, "They'll let us know for sure. Her feet are cut up pretty badly. After we take X-rays, we'll clean them and wrap them up tight," she explains to me. To Calli she says, "You'll feel a lot better, I bet, after you have a bath, won't you, Calli? We'll also get you something good to eat after X-rays. Sound good?" Calli bobs her head yes. I am hopeful that she will answer in words, but she does not. I need to be patient. At least now I know she can talk when she really needs to and I hold on to that fact.

Molly situates Calli onto a gurney and we make the journey toward X-ray. I notice that night has arrived in full force as we pass by the emergency room doors and I think again of Ben and Petra up on that bluff. I stop at the emergency reg-istration desk to see if they had any word on Ben and the woman behind the counter tells me that Ben will soon be on his way to the hospital.

"He'll catch a ride in the back of a police car and doesn't need to be transported by ambulance. That's good news," she informs me. "He must be doing quite well, Mrs. Clark."

Relief shoots through me. "That *is* good news. Can someone come find me when he gets here? I'm going to X-ray with Calli now."

"Sure thing. And sometime, when you get a few moments, there is some paperwork for you to fill out. Don't worry about it until you get everything settled with your children."

"Thank you," I tell her. Everyone is so kind here and I briefly wish to be admitted here myself so people can fuss over me.

As Molly pushes Calli down the hallway, I see Dr. Higby with a woman coming our way. She is an older woman, perhaps in her early sixties, with iron-gray hair, glasses and beautiful skin. My mother's skin had looked that way before she became ill, but I had never taken the time to appreciate it.

"Mrs. Clark, this is Dr. Kelsing," Dr. Higby introduces me to the woman. "We share Dr. Kelsing with the hospital in Winner."

"Nice to meet you, Dr. Kelsing."

"I'm pleased to meet you, as well, Mrs. Clark. I understand that Calli has had a pretty rough day."

"Yes, she has." I suddenly feel shy under Dr. Kelsing's gaze. Her eyes are sharp and intelligent and I have the feeling that few could pull anything over on her.

"Families who experience extremely stressful events such as yours are typically very hesitant to accept outside help. Most often they try to pull their family unit more tightly together in order to deal with the experience, try to deal with the effects on their own."

We are outside the X-ray room when Molly says to Calli, "Calli, honey, we need to take your pictures now. We would like your mom to stand out here, because we don't need to take her picture today. Just yours. You'll be able to see her through this window, though, okay? You all right with that?" Calli nods yes.

"I'll be right out here, Calli, watching you through the window," I assure her. Molly wheels Calli into the X-ray room and I watch as they situate my little girl on the table, bending her arms and legs in different directions, trying to get the best angle for the picture. Calli looks so small, so young. The reality of it all burns at the back of my eyes and I press my fingers to my eyelids. I do not want to cry in front of these strangers.

I turn back to Dr. Kelsing. "I know I can't do this on my own. Can you help us? Can you help Calli continue to speak?"

"I can't promise you anything, Mrs. Clark, but we can work together to do what you decide is best for Calli. I have had some experience with selective mutism. I have information about it that may be useful for you, if you'd like."

For some odd, unknown reason, I decide to trust this woman who has skin like my own mother's. "I'm scared," I tell her, struggling not to cry. "I'm so scared to find out why she stopped talking in the first place. But I'm even more scared…" The tears spill over and I bite my lip, willing them to stop. Dr. Kelsing does not speak, but waits for me to compose myself, and I like her even more for it. "I'm even more scared to find out what happened out in the woods that caused her to start to talk again."

Deputy Sheriff Louis

I watch as Martin struggles to keep it together as his daughter is lifted away by the helicopter. After she is out of sight and we can only hear the hum of the helicopter blades, he turns to me and says, "I have to get off this bluff. I need to get to Fielda and tell her that Petra is going to be all right."

"We'll ride the four-wheelers down. It will be quicker, and then I'll drive you to Fielda first thing," I tell him.

Awkwardly, Martin straddles the four-wheeler and clasps his arms around the officer who will transport him down the bluff. The officer gives Martin directions over his shoulder to hold on tightly to him, then the two are off into the thick of the forest. I hope that all will be well with Petra. She didn't look good to me and I knew the stress of the transfer in the helicopter could be more than her little body could take. I walk over to where Ben is resting against the trunk of a tree. I can't tell if he is sleeping or not, so I squat down next to him and shine my flashlight near his face to check. He is awake. The beating he has taken hits me full force as I take in his discolored cheek and swollen nose and eyes. Splattered blood stains his torn shirt and he is holding his side gingerly.

"Ben, how're you doing? You ready to go down now? You think you can ride down on a four-wheeler?" I ask him.

"I think so," he answers and I help him to his feet. "Can I ride down with you?" he asks. I look at my fellow officers and they nod in assent. The two of them climb onto one four-wheeler while I assist Ben in getting on the other.

"You hold on real tight, okay? Wrap your arms around me. If I go too fast and you want me to slow down, just squeeze me tight. I know you're in a lot of pain, Ben, so let me know if you need to rest, all right?"

"All right," he answers. "I just wanna get home and see Mom and see if Calli's okay."

"I'll get you down there as soon as I can. Ready? Hold on." I slowly ease my way into the forest. It is dark, probably much too dark to be traveling by four-wheeler, but we have little choice. We need to get Martin to Fielda and then to Petra, and we need to get Ben back to his mother. I have a feeling that Martin may have busted a few of Ben's ribs when he tackled him. I hope that Toni will be able to forgive Martin that. It was a horrific sight, seeing Ben standing in front of Petra, holding that stick. If I hadn't known Ben, I think that I would have jumped to the same conclusion that Martin had.

The light from the four-wheeler does little to illuminate the trail and I think that we might be better off ditching the quad and walking our way out, but we are making decent time. I know that the trail will become more even, less steep, the farther we go. I am sure that Ben can feel the pounding of my heart as he leans against my back. I have no clear vision of what is ahead of us and I can't hear any noise except that of the engine and of sticks snapping as they crush beneath the wheels. I feel that I am both blind and deaf and I am more frightened than I care to admit. If what Ben has told us is true, then Griff is somewhere in these woods hiding, perhaps waiting to pounce. In my mind he is capable of most anything. I remove one hand from the handlebars and pat my revolver, double-checking that I have quick access to it.

"What about my dad?" Ben says over the engine.

"We're just worrying about you and Petra and Calli right now," I call back, hoping that Griff isn't lurking behind some tree, overhearing what I'd just said. "It will be very difficult to find him tonight. We'll go back out full force in the morning to find him. Don't worry, Ben, I won't let him hurt you."

"I'm not worried," he says. But I hear the drop in his voice, the uncertainty in his tone. I pat his hands that are wrapped around my waist, and I speed up; we are minutes now from the bottom.

Out of the corner of my eye I see something. The glow from the headlights of the four-wheeler shine briefly on a figure crouched among the trees. For an instant I think it could be a mountain lion, but that doesn't make sense; mountain lions have not been seen in these woods for decades, well before I had even moved to Willow Creek. The angles and posture of the form are too human and I briefly consider stopping, but Ben is clinging to me and my first responsibility is to get him safely out of the forest. I take the four-wheeler up a notch and feel Ben tighten his grip around me.

I don't think he has seen what I have, but I'm not going to bring up the subject; Ben is going to have enough nightmares as it is, he doesn't need me fueling more fears. I radio in a message that would be cryptic to Ben and any average listener, but the gist of it is that I need backup for when I return to the woods, after I drop Ben off at the bottom.

At the base of the bluff I hand Ben off to Deputy Roper, the same deputy who is Griff's good friend. Logan knows that we are on the lookout for Griff, but he doesn't know that Ben has told me Griff is in those woods, was the one who had beat him senseless, who most likely hurt Petra Gregory.

"Logan, can you transport Ben here to the hospital in Willow Creek? We need to get him checked out. His mother is there waiting for him."

Logan looks at me suspiciously. "You got a suspect back in there?"

"Maybe. Tucci, Dunn and I are going back in to check a few things out. How 'bout it? Can you take Ben to town?"

"Sure," Logan answers. I can tell he doesn't want to, but he can hardly refuse to help the son of one of his good friends. "Ben, boy, you really got messed up. Who did this to you?" Logan asks.

Ben knows enough not to tell Logan that Griff, in fact, had been the one to mess him up. He just shrugs his shoulders and then winces at the pain the movement causes.

I see Ben settle into the back of the cruiser and I poke my head into the open door. "Your mom is waiting for you at the hospital. So is Calli. You don't worry about things out here. We'll take care of everything. You just look after your mom and sister. They're really going to need you now, Ben."

"Okay," Ben says softly and I pat his shoulder before I close the car door. Poor kid, I think, then stop myself. I had hated it when people whispered that about me. It got to be so that I could tell when people were just thinking *poor kid,* could tell just by the sad look in their eyes after my dad had died. I open the car door again and lean forward. "You're a strong kid, Ben," I tell him. "I'm proud of you. Your mom and Calli are very lucky to have you." He doesn't respond, doesn't even look at me, but I see his shoulders straighten slightly. He'll be fine.

"Ready?" I ask Tucci and Dunn as Logan pulls away with Ben. They are, and we head back into the forest, this time on foot and with flashlights in hand.

MARTIN

Too quickly, the sound of the helicopter has disappeared. My Petra is gone. I had found her, and then had to let her go again. I am at a loss as to how I had ended up on the back of a four-wheeler, crashing through the forest with my arms wrapped around a perfect stranger.

And now I am in a police car, traveling at a maddeningly slow speed to my mother-in-law's home. The kind officer has offered to go and tell Fielda on my behalf so that I could arrive more quickly at the hospital in Iowa City, but I say no and thank him. I want to tell Fielda that Petra is alive, hurt, but on her way to a place where the medical personnel can help her. My daughter is being carted off to a hospital that I have never visited, in a town that I have never entered before. The number of people I am entrusting my daughter to is stagger-ing: pilot, nurses, doctors, and I know eventually the police officers will want to question her about what happened today. I wonder if she has awoken. She was not conscious when I first found her, her beautiful face so bruised and distorted that if I had not seen her curly, black hair, matted with what I now know to be blood, I might have mistaken her for another unfortunate child. Her breathing was regular, and that was all that really mattered to me, that she was living. The cuts, the contusions…the damage that was done to her, I can cope with, even though I push the very thought of what may have happened, what I will to not have happened out of my mind. She was breathing, sweet, warm breaths and I will send her mother to her. Fielda will make it all better; she will be a comfort to Petra. I, on the other hand, will return to the forest. I will return and find the monster that has done this to my family. It will not matter that the man is Calli and Ben's father, or Antonia's husband. That will be of little consequence to me. I will find him and I will kill him.

ANTONIA

Dr. Kelsing remained by my side as Calli finished with her X-rays and says she will return after Calli is all cleaned up and settled for the evening. I thank her and ask if I should try to get Calli to talk.

"No, just be with her for now, just be her mother. Talk to her as you always have. Ask her questions, but don't expect verbal answers. She needs to feel safe. Knowing that you are with her will go a long way to making her feel safe. I'll check back with you shortly."

Molly begins gently to clean Calli's cut feet. Her feet are coated with dirt, dust and dried blood and it is difficult at first to tell the extent of the damage to them, but as Molly lightly begins to wash away the filth it is quite apparent that Calli will need stitches, and that it will be a very long time until her feet are fully healed. I try not to gasp at the sight of the deep punctures and gouges in the bottom of Calli's feet and at the livid red welts that crisscross the tops of her feet. The nail of her big toe is torn clean away. Calli goes rigid and begins to shake in either cold or in pain, I suspect both. She begins to cry silently.

"It's going to be okay, Calli," I tell her, finding my voice, stepping in front of her line of vision so she will not have to see what Molly is doing down there. I rub her arms to try and warm her.

"Calli, I'm just getting your feet cleaned up so you don't get a nasty infection in them. I know it's no fun. Just hang tight, okay?" Molly explains.

Calli nods bravely, wraps her arms around my neck and squeezes.

"That's right, Calli," I whisper in her ear. "Hold tight. I'm right here."

Calli's back arches and she begins kicking and struggling to pull away from Molly.

"Whoa, Calli, I need you to try and stay still. I know it hurts," Molly says soothingly, despite the fact that Calli's foot strikes her in the chin. As much as I like Molly, I feel relief that Calli still has some fight left in her.

Dr. Higby enters the room, comes over to Calli and smiles at her and moves to ruffle her hair. Calli cowers and buries her head in my chest and Dr. Higby pulls his hand back.

"That's okay, Calli. I guess I wouldn't want anyone rubbing my head if I felt the way you do right now, either," Dr. Higby says jovially. He washes his hands in the small sink in the corner of the room and pulls on a pair of latex gloves. "Calli, I'm going to give you a little medicine right now. It will help your feet take a nap."

Calli peeks up at Dr. Higby doubtfully.

"Well, they're not going to start snoring or anything." Calli's mouth twitches at this. "But they will feel numb," Dr. Higby continues. "You won't feel any pain in them at all in a few minutes." I feel Calli relax slightly in my arms.

As Dr. Higby and Molly mend Calli's feet, I speak to my daughter. I whisper to her all the favorite stories she loves to hear and I love to tell her. I tell her about the night she was born and the incredible thunderstorm that blew into town the minute I went into labor.

"It was the strangest storm for October. The day began gray, but warm. You weren't due to arrive for three more weeks, but I felt the familiar twinges, the slight pulling across the top of my abdomen, the ache in my back. It was just like it was with Ben, but this time I knew more of what to expect. Daddy was home from Alaska and he was so excited for you to arrive. He kept fidgeting around the house, trying to find things to do. I swear he oiled every squeaky door in the house, caulked the bathroom floor and cleaned the leaves out of the gutters. He kept asking me if I was all right, if the baby was coming now and I would say no. Not for a long time, I told him.

"Finally, I had to shoo him away because he was making me so nervous. He took Ben over to the park to play catch with the football and I went in the bedroom to lie down. It wasn't ten minutes later when I saw the flash of lightning and heard the enormous boom of thunder, and at the exact, the very same moment that it began to rain, not just rain but pour, torrential rain, my water broke and I knew you were on your way."

Calli smiles slightly at this story I have told her so many times. Her limbs have relaxed completely in my arms, but her eyes are still alert, as if she's ready to leap from the table if need be.

"I didn't know what to do. Your daddy had left with Ben in the car. I had told him it would be hours before we would need to go to the hospital. The rain began pouring down in buckets; I could hear it pounding on the roof and the wind was blowing so hard that the windows rattled. And it seemed that with every clap of thunder I would have a contraction, your way of telling me, 'Look out, I'm on my way.' I called my doctor and he told me I should get to the hospital as quickly as possible. I threw some clothes in Ben's school backpack, and in your yellow blanket I carefully wrapped the little outfit I was going to take you home from the hospital in, and put that in the backpack, too. I thought about calling Mrs. Norland next door, but I figured she wouldn't want to go out in the storm, so I decided to drive Daddy's truck to the hospital. This very hospital, actually. Problem was, I couldn't find where Daddy left his car keys. He never put them in the same place twice. So I spent twenty minutes looking for them. Finally I found them in the front pocket of a pair of jeans he had tossed by the washing machine. I grabbed the backpack and opened the door. The wind caught the screen door and pulled it right off its hinges. I remember feeling sorry for your daddy because he had spent so much time that week oiling those hinges to get rid of the squeaks, now he wouldn't even be able to enjoy the silence of opening and closing it anymore.

"I hoped that Daddy and Ben were on their way back home and just as I hoisted myself up into the truck—not any easy thing to do when you're pregnant, even tougher when you're in labor—I remembered I hadn't left Daddy and Ben a note. So I got back out of the truck, waddled in the house like a duck, and wrote a quick note. All it said was *BABY!!!* in big letters. Then I went back out into the storm and got into the truck. Now, I had driven a stick shift only, like, two times, and both times Daddy was with me, helping me along. Somehow, I don't know how, I got that thing started and off onto the road. It was raining so hard that the windshield wipers couldn't keep up and I had to drive slowly just to make sure I was staying on the road. I prayed that another car wouldn't suddenly come up behind and rear-end me because I was moving like a snail. But thankfully I didn't see one other car until I got into town. Every few minutes or so I would have to pull over to the side of the road when a contraction overtook me and I would have to keep my feet pressed down on the clutch and the brake so I wouldn't stall the truck. I was determined to get to that hospital. I said right out loud, even though you were the only one who could have possibly heard me, 'I am not going to have my baby in this rusted out old truck!' I just slowly kept on creeping forward until I finally made it to the hospital, and I left the truck parked right in front of the emergency room entrance. I didn't find out until later that I had left the door open, the lights on and the keys in the ignition. I wasn't thinking so much about those details at the time, though, was I?

"The nurse barely got me onto a bed and the doctor just stepped into the room when you came. In three pushes you were there, giving this mighty cry! And then suddenly you were in my arms, this perfect, beautiful, little baby girl with a head of dark hair. I apologized to you first thing. I said, 'I usually don't look like a drowned rat, I hope I didn't frighten you too much.' You just kept crying and crying. You sounded like a little lamb bleating."

Calli smiles at this part of the story, just as she always has. When she was three, before she stopped talking, she would chime in with a high-pitched "baaaaa" and I would laugh because it was just what she had sounded like. She makes no noise now, though; I was hoping that Calli would come in on her part. Molly and Dr. Higby are still working on Calli's poor feet; I hear words like *antibiotics* and *tetanus,* but I try to ignore them for now.

"The nurse took you from me for a few moments and she weighed and measured you. Six pounds, two ounces, and nineteen inches long. You were perfect. When she handed you back to me you were wiped clean and wrapped in a blanket. The nurse had pulled a little pink hat over your ears and you were still crying. Oh, you had so much to say to me!" I look at Calli carefully, worried that my last sentence may have bothered her, but she gives no indication that this is so.

"After a while you sort of just cried yourself out and fell asleep. I just looked and looked at you. Your face was so peaceful. Then Daddy and Ben burst into the room! They were both completely soaked from the rain. Their hair was matted down and water dripped off their noses. I could hear their feet squelching on the hospital floor.

"*'Did I miss it?'* Daddy asked. It was pretty funny because there I was holding what was clearly a newborn in my arms.

"*'It's a girl,'* Ben observed, seeing the pink hat on your head.

"*'A girl,'* Daddy breathed as if it was the most amazing thing in the world. And he and Ben walked hand and hand up to us and looked and looked at the new beautiful girl in their lives. Daddy looked down at Ben and said, *'Benny, you have a sister. A little sister. You're the big brother now and you have to look after her when I'm not around.'* And Ben nodded. He looked so serious. Ben reached out one finger to touch your cheek. *'Soft'* he said. And then you opened your eyes. And I swear, though no one who wasn't there to see it believes me, I swear you smiled at him."

Here, in the cold, white, hospital examining room, Calli smiles a true smile.

"Later, when Daddy and Ben were all dried off, they took turns holding you. Daddy paced and paced the hospital room saying, *'My Calli-girl.'* It was still thundering and lightning out, and the power went out so the hospital had to use their backup generators. They let Ben and Daddy stay with us at the hospital room that night, though technically they weren't supposed to. It was a perfect night, Calli, the day that you were born."

Calli closes her eyes as if she is remembering. I wish she could remember that day. It was truly perfect. At least the way I told the story it was perfect. I remember feeling so hopeful that the birth of Calli would be the catalyst to a new beginning for our little family. But of course it wasn't. Nothing is perfect, not even the perfect day, though I have set into Calli's and Ben's minds that it was so. What I have left out from the story was that while Griff was carrying around Calli, singing softly to her, his hands were shaking so badly that I feared he would drop her. I remember being ready to leap from the bed to catch her if she fell. I remember asking Griff to hand her back to me, making every excuse as to why I needed her back in my arms. She needed to try nursing, she was tired, he looked tired. He wasn't fooled, though. I could see it in his eyes, the flash of hurt in the fact I didn't quite trust him holding our baby.

He hadn't taken one drink in the week that he had been home before Calli was born. Before he had left for Alaska the last time it had been bad, so very bad. He had crossed a line, one of many that I had drawn out for him through the years. That first night he had come home before Calli was born he had lain by my side in our bed, his hand on top of my huge belly and had promised to change. He had cried softly into my shoulder and I'd cried along with him. I'd believed him. Again. He could do it, he could stop drinking with my help, he had promised.

But the night that Calli was born, with his hands trembling so fiercely as he held my baby, I knew that was a promise he couldn't keep, not yet anyway. He left the hospital in the dark corners of the morning while Ben and I were sleeping and Calli slept in the nursery. He left and came back hours later. There was a glassiness in his eyes, they couldn't quite focus, and I could smell the liquor on his breath as he kissed my cheek. He held Calli firmly and capably that morning and his hands had stopped shaking.

"There you are, Calli," Dr. Higby tells Calli. "All done. The worst is over. Now we'll just finish getting you all cleaned up. You, Calli, are a very lucky little girl."

I see Calli's tranquil face freeze for a moment, then it changes. Her eyes begin to bulge and her skin fades to a sickly chalk color. Dr. Higby looks back at Molly and she lifts her hands and shoulders. She hadn't been touching Calli's feet. Calli's mouth twists into an ugly grimace as if she is screaming; she is shaking not from cold or pain, but from complete terror. I look around helplessly as her silent shriek clangs around my head.

"What's wrong?" I ask her. "What's wrong, Calli?" But still she thrashes almost convulsively. Molly and I hold her so that she won't fall off the table. "What's wrong?" I whimper as tears collect behind my own eyes. I notice that Molly's and Dr. Higby's eyes aren't focused on Calli, but are settled on a spot just over my shoulder. Keeping my grip firmly on Calli, who is kicking and writhing, I turn to see what they are looking at. There stands my Benny, beaten so badly, his clothes bloody and ripped. My knees go weak at the sight. He is looking at Calli with fear in his eyes.

"What's wrong with her?" he asks me over Calli's head. His voice sounds so young.

I don't answer him. I want so badly to go to him and draw him close to me. I wave him toward me with one hand, but he stands rooted to his spot.

"I'm going to give her a sedative, Mrs. Clark," Dr. Higby says. It takes several moments for the shot to have any effect on Calli, but soon she calms and her shaking subsides and her eyes begin to close. She still clutches at my shirt, pulling me close to her. She seems to be trying to speak to me, but her lips are slack and can't form the words.

"What, Calli? What is it? Please tell me," I whisper into her ear. But she has fallen asleep and whatever has frightened her so badly has crawled back into its hole and sleeps, too, at least for now.

MARTIN

When we pull up to the front of my mother-in-law's home I see that the reporters have gone, but one strange car remains in the drive. I thank the officer and he offers to stay until we are ready to travel to Iowa City. He will escort us, get us there quickly and safely. Again I thank the officer and say no. We will be fine. We will get to Petra just fine. My legs feel heavy as I make my way to the front door, already they ache from the day's exertion. My pants are dirty and I have some of Ben's blood on my shirt collar. I try to tame my hair by pressing my fingers against its wiry texture, but know it does little good. My glasses are set crookedly on my nose and I take them off and try to bend them back into the correct position. I see a rustle at the curtains; Fielda must have heard the car pull up in front of the house. I see her peek through the window briefly, then the front door is open and she hurries to greet me. Behind her are her mother and a woman I do not know.

"Did you find her, Martin, did you find Petra?" She seizes

my arm and her voice has the same hysterical tone that I heard her use with Agent Fitzgerald. I wonder what has happened to him; I have not seen or heard from him in hours.

I gather Fielda in my arms and hold her tightly to me. I feel her body sag against me and instantly I am aware of my mistake.

"She's alive." I cannot bring myself to say that she is fine, no; I cannot say that to my wife.

Fielda screeches with relief and joy. "Thank you, God, thank you!" she exclaims, still clutching on to me. "Thank you, Martin, thank you for finding her. Where is she? Where is she?" Fielda looks around as if Petra is off playing a few yards from us in the front yard.

I clear my throat. Tread carefully, I tell myself. Do not alarm her. "She's at the hospital."

"Oh, of course." She squints her eyes at me. "She's going to be all right, isn't she?"

"I think she'll be fine. You need to go to her," I tell her.

"What do you mean, you think she'll be fine? What happened, Martin? Let's go, let's get in the car and go."

"They took her to Iowa City, to the hospital there. The medical personnel thought that the hospital in Iowa City would be the best place for her to go."

"Iowa City? What's going on?" Fielda steps away from me and crosses her arms in front of her. The woman I do not know makes her way toward us and rests a hand protectively on Fielda's shoulder.

"Fielda?" the woman says. "Fielda, is everything okay?" she asks.

"I don't know," Fielda says in a voice too loud for the quiet of the night. The cicadas have even stopped chirping. "I don't know," Fielda says again. "Martin?"

I take Fielda's hand and pull her along with me, leaving the woman behind.

"You tell me what's happening right now!" From the porch light I can see that tears are brimming in Fielda's eyes. I need to tell her now and I need to tell her everything.

"We found Petra at the top of the bluff. She was hurt..." I swallow hard. "She was hurt in many ways, but she was breathing. She had cuts on her head and bruises. A helicopter took her off the bluff. They have flown her to Iowa City. She's there by now. You need to go to her now, Fielda, she needs you."

"Is she going to die?" Fielda asks. "Is my little girl going to die?" There is steel in her voice almost daring me to tell her that death was a possibility.

"No!" I say with more conviction than I feel. "Can you drive to Iowa City on your own?"

"But why?" Fielda looks confused. "Why don't you come with me?"

"I can't, I need to help with the investigation," I say, hoping that she will ask no more questions.

"Investigation? Do they have the person who did this? Who did this, Martin? Do you know?"

I nod. "I do know. You need to go now. Can you drive on your own, Fielda?"

Fielda looks at me as if she wants to ask more, but something on my face causes her to pause.

"I can take her," the unknown woman tells me as she approaches us, and for the first time I look at her carefully.

"I'm Mary Ellen McIntire." She holds her hand out to me and I recognize her from the television news, from when she had begged for the safe return of her daughter.

I take her hand. "I've heard about you, your family. I am very, very sorry."

"I'll drive Fielda and her mother." She looks to Fielda to see if this is acceptable to her. Fielda nods, but is examining me carefully.

"What happened to you, Martin? Is that blood?" She points to my stained shirt.

"I'm fine. Now please go. I'll join you as soon as I can. Tell Petra that I love her and I'll see her soon." I kiss Fielda on the forehead and turn to Mrs. McIntire. "Thank you for looking after my wife. I am grateful."

"I'm glad to help. Fielda and I have become fast friends."

"I'll go get my purse, oh, and Snuffy," Fielda says as she hurries into the house. Snuffy is Petra's stuffed anteater, which she sleeps with each night.

Mary Ellen leans in close to me. "You know who did this, don't you?"

"I think I do, yes." I do not look her in the eye.

"He did terrible things to Petra," she states. I notice it is not a question.

"Yes, he did."

"You're going after him, aren't you?"

"Yes, I am." I now look her straight in the eye, trying to determine if she will tell Fielda, who would rail against my foolishness.

Mary Ellen McIntire and I stand in the shadows of the porch; she briefly touches my arm, but says nothing.

Fielda and her mother emerge from the house, purse and Snuffy in hand. She kisses my lips, tells me she loves me, then gets into Mrs. McIntire's car and drives away. I stand for a long time, watching until the red glow from the car's taillights disappears, and then I trudge up the steps, into the house, and flick off the porch light. I sit in the dark at the kitchen table, trying to gather my thoughts.

Then I stand stiffly, my muscles protesting, and I go upstairs to my mother-in-law's extra bedroom. I open the closet door and reach high behind the photo albums and behind Mrs. Mourning's wedding gown, the very same dress that Fielda wore for our wedding. The gown is wrapped in paper and sealed in a box, tied with a blue ribbon. I stand on the tips of my toes and fumble around for the wooden box. My hand grazes the container and I am able to nudge it toward me. I pull the box down and lay it on the bed. It is not locked. I lift the top and hear the slight creak of its brass hinges. Inside is a gun. I do not know the caliber or the brand name. I have never been interested in firearms. The gun that I have set before me belonged to Fielda's father who had passed away many years before, long before I had met her. Fielda's mother does not know why she keeps it; guns scare her, but she cannot bring herself to give it away, and most likely has forgotten that it is up here. I take the gun out of its velvet-lined box and am surprised at its heaviness for such a small gun. One lone bullet rolls around in the box and I pull it out and hold it tightly, warming it within my sweaty palm. I glance at my watch and know that I am short on time. I need to hurry.

ANTONIA

I look at Calli as she sleeps. Her dirty face isn't peaceful, unlined and untroubled as a seven-year-old little girl's face should be in sleep. Deep grooves have settled in the space just above the bridge of her nose and her lips are pinched tightly. On another examining table, next to Calli, sits Ben. Dr. Higby and Molly are now tending to him, collecting more evidence. His face is a mess. I have avoided asking Ben the question that has rested on my tongue since I first glanced at him when he entered the hospital. *Who did this to you?* I am afraid of the answer.

I dip the washcloth that Molly has given me in a basin of warm water and begin to wipe the dirt from Calli's body. I start at her face, beginning at her hairline, trying to gently smooth the channels that travel along her forehead. I move down behind her ears, along her cheeks and under her chin, carefully lifting and lowering her head as if she is an infant. I see her nearly naked form on the table, except for her hospital gown and the thick white gauze that is wrapped around her feet; the number of bruises that dot her arms once again startles me, even though I had watched Molly take pictures of them earlier. These are no childhood bruises caused by a careless tumble or by an accidental bump into a sharp corner. I gently fit my fingers around the even arrangement of the marks and shudder.

I continue my washing of Calli, now focusing on her hands, trying to rinse away the dirt that has collected in the little wrinkles that form her knuckles and in the valleys that score the inside of her palms.

I trace the lines on her palm, now pink from my scrubbing, and I wonder at her future, my little damaged girl. And I wonder about Griff. Where is he?

"Well," says Dr. Higby, "we've got one broken nose and what appear to be three broken ribs on Ben here. You'll live, Ben, but you won't be playing any contact sports for a while."

Ben snorts a little at this and looks sadly at me.

"We're going to get Calli settled into her room for the night. You two are welcome to stay with Calli tonight or you are free to go home," Dr. Higby tells us.

"Stay," Ben and I say at the same time and we smile at each other. We both know we need to be with Calli.

"I'd like to run home and get a few things. Some clean clothes, Calli's blanket and stuffed monkey," I tell Dr. Higby.

"That's probably a good idea," Dr. Higby says. "Calli is going to need all the comfort she can get in the next few days. And, Ben, no offense, but you could use a shower and a clean shirt."

Ben laughs and I am glad. Whatever happened up there wasn't enough to take Ben's laugh away.

"Do you have a way to get back to your house?" Molly asks.

I frown. No, I don't. My car is back at the house, I am stranded at the hospital. I very much want Calli to wake up with her yellow blanket and monkey. I think of Rose, the nice paramedic, and her offer to help out in any way that she was able.

"I think I do," I tell Molly.

DEPUTY SHERIFF LOUIS

Tucci, Dunn and I retrace the path that Ben and I came down on the four-wheeler. We pause for a moment at the carcass of the dog that Martin Gregory and I had found earlier in the evening. I wonder if the dog had anything to do with the events of the day and make a mental note to suggest that the forensic team investigate. "Did Charles Wilson, the school counselor, ever find his dog?" I ask.

"Don't know," Tucci answers. "We had nothing to hold him on. His wife said she woke up at about seven this morning and that he left sometime before then to walk the dog on the trails."

"Do we know where Wilson is right now?" I ask, wondering if we hadn't let Wilson go prematurely. From the glow of my flashlight I see Tucci shrug his shoulders. "Call into dispatch and check on it. We need to cover all bases." Suddenly I feel foolish tracking some unseen being in the forest in the dead of night. I don't know what made me think that I would be able to find whomever I had seen crouched among the trees. I guiltily admit to myself that perhaps I hoped that, I, the fearless hero, Antonia's hero, would bring Griff in. Ben had told me that it was Griff up there on top of the bluff. It was Griff who beat him, and it was Griff who left Petra and Ben up there all alone.

"Do you see anything?" Tucci asks after we had been walking for about forty minutes.

"Naw," I say, disgusted with myself.

"He's probably long gone now. We may as well go back. We'll organize a search for daybreak. He could be anywhere by now," Dunn says.

The radio at my hip crackles and the dispatcher lets me know that I have a guest waiting for me down at the bottom of the bluff. Agent Fitzgerald.

"Let's go," I tell Tucci and Dunn, convinced that Griff is still out here, waiting, for what I'm not sure.

When we step out of the forest I can see Fitzgerald deep in conversation with a man and woman dressed in civilian clothing. The headlights from two cruisers light them up from behind. I figure the two people that Fitzgerald is talking to are other agents from his office. When we approach the group they stop talking and look at us. I can tell by the look on Fitzgerald's face he isn't happy with me.

"What the hell do you think you were doing?" he spits at me. Tucci and Dunn shift uncomfortably behind me.

"Have you gotten word on Petra Gregory's condition?" I ask, ignoring Fitzgerald's obvious anger.

"She's still unconscious, but stable. There's evidence of sexual assault," the woman next to Fitzgerald tells me and my stomach clenches as I think of Calli. "I'm Special Agent Lydia

Simon. This is Special Agent John Temperly. We're here to help with the investigation involving the two little girls. I understand you've had quite an evening."

"You could say that," I tell her, still eyeing Fitzgerald warily, waiting for his next burst of anger.

"You took two civilians—worse, two of the victims' parents—on an unauthorized search," Fitzgerald says in a threatening voice. Agent Simon places a hand on Fitzgerald's arm and he instantly quiets. I get the sense that she has great influence over Fitzgerald, is perhaps his senior in their department.

"You found the two girls and the boy?" Simon asks me.

"Actually, Calli Clark found us. We were standing right about here when she came out of the woods. She was carrying Petra Gregory's necklace and underwear. We figured out that Petra and Calli's brother, Ben, were still at the top of the bluff."

"You let Martin Gregory go up the bluff," Fitzgerald says accusingly.

"There was no way I was going to stop him." I can't keep my own irritation out of my voice. "I called for an ambulance and backup and followed him up the bluff. He thought that Ben Clark had something to do with what happened to Petra and he was going up there, ready to kill anyone at the top that might have hurt his daughter!"

"You should have followed procedure and waited for backup," Fitzgerald shoots back at me.

"Hold on now," Agent Simon says. "Let's just all get up to speed on the investigation and go from there. We can't change what has happened and the girls are safe. Let's focus on finding who did this."

"Ben Clark, Calli's brother, said that Griff Clark, their

father, was the one," I say, trying to make my voice sound professional again.

"Ben saw his father up there with the girls?" Agent Temperly asks.

"Yeah, said his dad was the one who beat the crap out of him up there. He was pretty messed up. He was standing guard over Petra when we got to the top. Ben said he tried to keep his dad there, but he got away."

The three agents ponder this for a moment. "What does Calli Clark say about what happened?" Agent Simon questions.

"Calli hasn't spoken in four years," I tell her. "Until today. She said *Ben* when she reached us at the bottom of the bluff. And that was all. I don't know if she's said more. She's at the hospital in Willow Creek. Her brother should be there by now, too." I look at my watch. It is a little after eleven. I am exhausted, but my night is just beginning.

"Why would she say her brother's name if it was her father who did all this?" Agent Temperly asks. "Why didn't she say *Dad?* Could the brother have been lying? Could he have done this?"

"Absolutely not," I say. "Ben Clark is a good boy. He did nothing but spend the day looking for his sister and Petra."

"Well, you tend to have a soft spot when it comes to the Clark family, don't you?" Fitzgerald says snidely. "Does Antonia Clark know that her husband is now the major suspect in this case?"

"I don't know." The reality that the man that my Toni had married has done some truly horrific things hits me hard. I don't want to be the one to tell her.

"We need to talk to that little girl," Agent Simon says with finality. "We need her to tell us what she saw up there on that bluff. Let's go on over to the hospital and see if we can speak with her."

Ben

I feel better now that I've taken a bath in the little bathroom in your hospital room. I had to be real careful not to get the tape that was wrapped around my ribs wet, not too easy. Dr. Higby gave me some green scrubs to put on. I'm also feeling a little light-headed from the medicine that the nurse gave me for the pain in my nose and ribs. Mom just left to go back to the house to get some stuff. I asked her if she could bring back my Green Bay Packers pillow, not that I needed it to sleep, but when a face hurts as much as mine does, a guy needs something extra soft to lay his head on. Mom borrowed the car of some lady named Rose and asked her if she would keep an eye on us while she was gone and Rose promised she would. She's gone down to the cafeteria to get some food to smuggle in for me. I requested chips and a Mountain Dew, but Rose said I wouldn't want anything too salty or too sweet with the cuts I had all around my lips. I had to agree with that, I guess.

I lie in the hospital bed that is next to you and click through the channels on the TV that is attached to the wall above us. I keep the volume down low so as not to wake you, but from the looks of things you won't be waking up for a while. The way you screamed earlier when I had walked in still clanks around in my head. I wonder if how I looked scared you, I looked pretty monstrous, if I do say so myself. Mom told me that you had said my name when you found them at the bottom of Bobcat Trail, and at first I felt pretty good about that. Then I got to thinking, Calli, why did you go and say my name? Why didn't you say Dad's name? He's the one who caused this big old mess in the first place. I'm hoping you don't think I had something to do with it all; it was pretty confusing up there. I look over to where you're sleeping. What were you thinking, Calli? I want to ask. Why did you say my name?

Calli, when you were born, I was so sad and happy at the same time. I was five and the chore of sharing you with Mom turned my stomach sour. When I first saw your tiny little toes, no bigger than jelly beans, I knew that my mom wasn't just mine anymore. You had a cry that could wake the dead. And how you wailed! She would carry you around for hours on her shoulder, patting your back and whispering in your shell-shaped ear, "Hush now, Calli, hush now." But you wouldn't. She would stumble around, half-sleeping, her eyes all shadowed, her hair sticking up and wild. Even after all your fussing, covered with spit-up, foul and stinky smelling, she'd still be all patient with you. She'd say, "Ben, we have a feisty one here. She's going to keep us on our toes. Big brother, you need to look out for our little whirlwind."

And I have, time and again.

Dad was the only one who could quiet you down. When

he'd come home from the pipeline I'd hear the squeak of the back door and the thunk of his green duffel hitting the floor, and I'd think, now Calli will shut up. He'd snatch you right out of Mom's arms and say all sweet like, "Stop that squallin', Calli-girl." And you would. Just like that. Your red, squinched-up face would go all smooth, and you'd look at Dad big-eyed, like you were thinking, "Who is this man?" Then you'd rub your little peanut nose into his chest, grab his big, sausage finger with your tiny hand and fall into this deep sleep.

It was as if the house just wasn't big enough for two centers of attention, and when Dad came home you knew it was time to sit back and watch awhile. I think that Mom felt sort of bad that you'd stop your howling for him and not her. I mean, she was the one who would change your shitty diapers, and feed you that nasty green gunk from a baby food jar. And she's the one who about went crazy from worry when you were two months old and had a fever of one hundred and five degrees. It was Christmastime and forty below outside, and the walls shook with the force of the wind. But Mom still filled the tub with freezing cold water and stripped the two of you bare naked and climbed into that popsicle water. You both had goose bumps the size of footballs and blue lips, but she just sat there holding you, the two of you shivering so hard little waves sloshed over the side of the bathtub. She sat there rocking you in that tub until the fever was gone and you started screaming like normal, your crying pinging off the bathroom walls.

I couldn't sleep, what with your fussing echoing through the house, so I made Mom chocolate milk and found her favorite socks, the rainbow striped ones with little slots for each toe to slide into, for her to put on. I climbed over the bars of your crib and pulled out your yellow blanket and that goofy sock monkey Mom made you. I tucked them in Mom's big bed, because I knew she'd lie with you there that night. She sat for what seemed hours, watching you breathe, every once in a while putting her finger beneath your nose just to feel that small rush of warm air coming out. I wonder if she ever does that with me. Creep into my room, even though I'm twelve now, and check to see if I'm still breathing, watch the rise and fall of my chest. I'd like to think that she does.

So I think that Mom's feelings were hurt that Dad was the only one to calm you. I know that you didn't mean for her to feel that way. I know that having Dad home filled up each corner of the house, kind of like someone sitting on your chest. It's real hard to make sounds when each breath just goes into breathing. Funny how Dad was the only one who could quiet you and in the end was the only one who finally got you to speak.

ANTONIA

I hurry down the hallway and to the elevator. Rose Callahan
is so kind to let me borrow her car. I'm not sure of how I
am going to thank her, but I will certainly find a way when
this is all over. I jangle her keys in my hand as I wait for the
elevator door to open. Ben and I still haven't had the conversation that is needed. I haven't asked him who had beaten
him so badly. Once again my lack of proper mothering
skills is shining through. Wouldn't most mothers exclaim,
"Who did this to you?" I'm not ready to ask that question
yet. I'm not prepared to hear that Ben's own father has
been responsible for this and so much worse. My stomach
churns at the prospect of all the devastation Griff doled out
this day. But maybe not, though, no one had come right
out and said Griff did all this, he could be off in some bar
somewhere for all I know. I just want to go home and get
my children some clean clothes and items of comfort. The
elevator door opens and I step in, push the button for the

main floor and lean back against the wall. I close my eyes and try not to think. The doors open again and I step out. Then I have the urge to retreat into them, given the scene unfolding before me.

There seems to be half a dozen police officers. I see Agent Fitzgerald talking with two people I've never seen before. A few reporters occupy a corner of the main entrance waiting area and Louis looks to be in a heated discussion with Logan Roper, Griff's old high-school friend. Then I see the doors to the main entrance open and in stomps Christine Louis. Louis's wife. Great, I think. She doesn't look so happy. I look around for an exit to take unseen, but it's too late. Christine spots me, gives me a searing look and goes over to her husband.

"Christine?" Louis says looking off behind her. "Where's Tanner?"

"He's out in the car, Loras," she says shortly. She is the only person I know who ever calls Louis by his first name. "He's sleeping."

"You left him out in the car alone?" Louis says in disbelief. "Christine, there's a kidnapper out there somewhere. You just can't leave a child unattended in a car."

"You—" she pokes a finger at him "—gave up any say in what I do with my son the minute you decided that *her* children were more important than Tanner."

"What the hell are you talking about?" Louis says, taking Christine by the arm and pulling her out of earshot.

I take that opportunity to exit quickly through the hospital doors, searching for the red Civic that is Rose's car. As I unlock the car door and start to climb in, Agent Fitzgerald and the two strangers he was speaking with surround me.

"Mrs. Clark," says Agent Fitzgerald, "I'm pleased to hear that your children have been found and are safe and sound."

"Yes, me, too," I say brusquely. I want to get out of there before Christine tries to pull me into her argument with Louis.

Agent Fitzgerald introduces me to the two as his colleagues, Agents Temperly and Simon. I smile at them in greeting and settle myself behind the wheel.

"We need to talk to your children, Mrs. Clark," Agent Simon says to me.

"I know you do. Should we set up a time for sometime tomorrow?"

"You don't understand," says Agent Temperly. "We need to speak with Calli now."

"No, *you* don't understand. Calli's had a horrible day, she's sleeping right now. No one is asking her any questions tonight," I declare firmly.

"We don't need your permission to speak with a witness, Mrs. Clark," Fitzgerald informs me.

I wonder whatever made me trust this man. "No, but you do need the doctor's permission to speak with her. And if he says my children aren't ready, then you will not speak to them!" I climb out of the car again and march right back into the hospital to let Dr. Higby know that under no circumstances is anyone to talk to my children until I get back.

DEPUTY SHERIFF LOUIS

I pull Christine to a more private corner of the hospital waiting room. Here we go again. Christine threw her little public fits about twice a year, then she would calm down and say she was sorry and we would carry on as usual until the next time.

"What is going on?" I ask her through clenched teeth. "I'm working here."

"That's half the problem," she cries. "You're working all the time. We never see you!"

"It's my job!" I say, louder than I intend. I can feel many eyes on us. I glimpse Toni hurrying out of the hospital and wonder where she is going. Did she know that Griff was somewhere out there?

"And she's the other half of the problem," Christine's voice breaks as she tosses her chin toward Toni. "You hung up on me, Loras! You were with *her*. Whenever she needs something, you go running. Right now, even, you're looking at her, when I'm trying to tell you that we are leaving."

That pulls my gaze back to Christine. "What do you mean, you're leaving? Is Tanner really out in the car?"

"Yes, he's sleeping. I locked the doors. He's fine," Christine growls.

"What if he woke up and climbed out? Jesus, Christine, use your head. Let's go out there."

"Yes, let's go out there, Loras. You can say goodbye to him then. I'm taking Tanner back to Minnesota."

"What? Like, for a vacation?"

"No, not *like for a vacation,*" she mimics me. "For good. We're moving in with my parents until I get settled and can find a house."

"You can't just take Tanner and leave!" I explode. "You can't keep me from my son."

"I have no intention of keeping you from your son. You do that well enough on your own. We'll work out those things later. Come say goodbye if you want."

"Why are you doing this now, Christine?" I ask helplessly.

"I'm *finally* doing this, Loras. I am sick and tired of walking in her shadow."

"You don't have to leave, though. We can work it out. We always do," I say unconvincingly.

"Do you know what it has been like for me?" Christine asks me. "Living in this town? With your history with her? You won't get away from it and I can't get away from it. I'm done, Loras. I am done."

She walks away from me and into the hospital parking lot toward our station wagon. I follow, knowing I need to give my son a kiss goodbye.

Martin

As I creep from my car, which I have parked well down the road, I can see a police officer sitting in a squad car. He's a reservist, a man from my own church. The interior light from the car casts shadows on his face; he is sipping from a coffee cup, reading. I steal past him unnoticed and move to the back of the Clark home to wait.

I settle behind a small copse of what my father would have called junk trees, thin, craggy things with trunks no bigger than my wrist. The night is still warm, but a soft breeze tinged with a bit of northern air has cooled things considerably. In fact, I am quite comfortable. Under any other circumstances I would be apt to doze off, but the weight of the gun in my lap is a hard enough reminder of why I am here. In the daylight hours I would be easily seen, but in the dark of night I have become an extension of the Clarks' backyard, at least that is my hope. I have a good view of Antonia's and Griff's vehicles, both parked in the driveway near the back door.

From my vantage point I also see into the Clarks' kitchen. The house is black. If the reservist discovers me, I can just say that I thought I saw a prowler and I came to investigate. A weak excuse, I know. I am also waiting for my good sense to return, but as of yet, it has not. I am a logical man. I know that it makes no sense for me to be stalking my child's kidnapper and abuser by hiding outside his home with a gun. I am waiting for my good judgment to return to me, that I will suddenly realize that this is not how college-educated, reasonable men behave. But for the moment it does not matter that I am the head of the economics department at St. Gilianus, nor does it matter that for the past fifty-seven years I have been firmly ensconced in the conviction that capital punishment is inherently wrong. Anger rests in my belly like a buzzing colony of bees, scraping at my skin from the inside out.

So I wait, and I do not have to be patient for long. From where I sit I see a figure emerge from the woods, broad but moving in a stilted, uncoordinated manner. Should I go forward, confront the skulking being? Should I slink away, back to my mother-in-law's, place Fielda's father's gun back into its velvet-lined box and hide it behind dusty old treasures? I pause too long for any of those scenarios to be an option, because just as I am going to make the choice, a choice that would surely change my life forever, a car appears and pulls in right behind the other two vehicles and out steps Antonia Clark. The shadow that came from the woods suddenly stops, then quickly retreats. Antonia steps from the car and moves to the front of the house, I hear soft murmurs of a conversation and then silence. I sit for what seems an eternity, listening to my own heart pounding, watching, my eyes darting from the woods to the house, back and forth, waiting.

I startle as the light above the back door comes on. The door opens and I see Antonia step out into the backyard, a bag on her shoulder, in her hands a green pillow and a stuffed animal. I watch as she squints into the darkness and then walks to the area where hours earlier the state crime unit was so intent. I expect Toni to turn and leave, but she doesn't. She begins to walk toward the woods. In that moment, another choice is offered to me, one that unequivocally will change several lives forever. What will I choose? To warn Antonia or to sit in silence?

ANTONIA

I drive the familiar road back to the house. Our neighborhood looks abandoned, what with the press and all but one
police car gone. We have no streetlights along our road and
no lights burn in the Gregory home, or mine, for that matter.
Hadn't I turned a light on before I left this afternoon with
Martin and Louis? Maybe one of the police officers switched
off the lights when they left. I send a silent wish of good
fortune on to the Gregory family. I hope that Fielda and
Martin are sitting next to Petra right now, holding her hand.
I am so fortunate to have my two back safely, damaged for
sure, but physically whole. I am still hopeful that a long string
of sentences will soon accompany Calli's one word. I sit for
a moment behind the wheel of Rose's car and look upon my
home as if I am a stranger, an outsider. It is so dark, I can see
little, so I close my eyes and visualize the home that had been
mine in childhood, and now as a wife and mother, as if it is
daytime. It is a narrow two-story structure, simple, but with

good bones. I picture the peeling white paint that bubbles and blisters on the outside and that lay in crispy shards on the lawn. The flower beds are beautiful, those look well-tended. I love my home; no matter the dark days I have had here, it is my home. I wonder what Ben and Calli think of this house. Are all their memories sad? Surely they must have good thoughts, too. I will have to ask them when this is all over. Do they want to start fresh, somewhere new or stay put?

I slide out of the driver's seat and begin to make my way toward the police car. The officer steps from his car and greets me.

"I'm so glad to hear that your kids are safe, Mrs. Clark," he tells me.

"Me, too," I say. "And thank you for all you've done. Is it all right if I go in the house now to get a few things for the kids?"

"Sure," he replies. "We've gotten everything that we need from the house. Do you want me to go in with you?"

"No, thanks, I'm fine. I'll be out in just a few minutes." The officer smiles at me and climbs back into his car. I trudge up the front steps. I am so tired. I open the door and quickly go upstairs. I stop first at Calli's room and switch on her light. It's hard for me to imagine that just hours earlier strangers had been tromping through this room, gathering evidence, looking for traces of violence, dusting for fingerprints. I am surprised at how undisturbed her room looks, the crime scene officers were very conscientious, cleaning up after themselves, replacing toys and books to their proper spots. Only Calli's bed looks wrong, stripped of bedding, naked. I grab some clothes, shove them in Calli's backpack, and pick up her stuffed monkey and yellow blanket. I do the same in Ben's room and hurry down the steps. As I put my hand on the knob of the front door, I pause. I turn and head back to the kitchen. I flick on the outside light over the back door, open the door, and step out into my backyard. Looking out across my large, beautiful yard, visions of the day swim in front of my eyes. Would I ever look at these woods in the same way? Would I ever be able to find comfort in a place that swallowed up my children and spit them back out at me damaged and broken? I walk closer to the dark, towering trees until I feel a strong hand clamp onto my arm and my heart stops in alarm. But just as quickly I recognize Martin's smooth, cultured voice, hushed to a whisper.

"Antonia, quiet. Someone is in the woods. Come on." And he pulls me silently to the side of the yard, next to the shed behind a snowball bush where we are well-hidden.

"Martin," I murmur, "what are you doing?"

"Shh," he orders and points toward the woods. I see nothing.

"What is it?" I whisper.

"Griff, I think," Martin says. I can't help but notice how lifeless his voice sounds.

"Good," I respond in a normal voice. "I need to ask him a few questions about where he's been today." I begin to step from the bush toward the woods. Martin yanks me roughly back.

"No," he demands. "Stay here, listen to me." I stop and he releases my arm from his grasp.

"Have you talked to Ben about what happened up there?" Martin speaks again in a low, hoarse whisper.

"No," I admit. "We really haven't had the chance. I'm just so glad they're okay. What about Ben?"

"He was up there when we found Petra. He told us what happened, who hurt Petra and Calli. It was Griff."

"Ben said this?" I ask.

"He did. Ben said that Griff was up there when he got to the top of the bluff. That Griff was standing over Petra and was going after Calli." Martin's voice breaks when he says his daughter's name.

For the first time I notice that Martin holds something tightly within one hand.

"What is that?" I ask and reach out to it, my hand brushing against the cool metal. "My God, is that a gun? Martin, what are you doing?"

"I don't know," he says in a small voice. "I don't know. I thought…I thought…"

"You thought you would come over here and shoot the man who you think hurt your daughter? Without even speaking with him first, without the police questioning him? Martin, I know Griff has troubles, but he would not have hurt Petra."

"How do you know that? What about the bruises your son has? Your son was up there, Antonia. Are you saying he is the liar? Who did this, then? Was it Ben? Was it your husband? Which one, Antonia? Which is it?" Martin hisses.

"Yeah, Antonia, which is it?" an oily, familiar voice asks conversationally. My heart seizes in my chest. It is Griff. He smells of sweat and his face looks haggard and tired. "Who you gonna believe? Me or Ben?"

"Griff, I don't know what happened. I don't know. Ben and Calli are in the hospital. Petra is, too, she's hurt really bad. I don't know what happened."

"But you think I coulda done something, don't you? You'll

believe that little bastard, but you won't believe your own husband…" Griff, the man who sent me sweet notes every year on the anniversary of my mother's death, steps toward me.

"Get away!" Martin yells.

"What the hell?" Griff shouts. "You've got a gun? You've got a goddamn gun. What? You two come here to shoot me? Jesus, Toni!" In one powerful movement Griff slaps the gun from Martin's hand toward me. I scream as the gun goes off with a loud blast and I cover my face as the bullet explodes into the ground, sending up chunks of dry dirt. Both Griff and Martin scramble for the gun, but Griff is faster and reaches it first. With one hand he picks the revolver off the ground and swings it with a sickening thud against Martin's skull. He crumples immediately to the ground clutching his head.

"Griff, don't!" I scream. "Please don't!" I cry as I kneel down by Martin.

"He was gonna shoot me," Griff says in a dazed voice. "You were here to shoot me."

"No, no. I didn't know he was here. I didn't know," I sob. "I was here to get some pajamas for Calli, to get her monkey!" I point to the sock monkey on the ground; it is smiling up at us. Griff has the gun aimed shakily at me, but he glances down at the toy and then at Martin's now motionless form.

"I don't believe you." His hands continue to tremble, whether from nerves or lack of drink, I don't know.

"Please, let's talk about it, please," I beg. "Tell me what happened, Griff. Tell me." Where was that police officer, I wonder, looking through the darkness for him.

"I didn't do it." His voice is full of emotion. "I know it looks like I did, but I didn't, I didn't hurt that girl!"

"But why were you up there? Why were you in the woods with Calli?"

"I don't know. I don't know. It was stupid. I took her into the woods. We got lost. And then Calli was gone and Petra was there all bloody. And Ben, Jesus, Ben. He kept coming at me and I hit him. I hit him. God, and her underwear."

I feel as if I have been socked in the stomach. My husband had taken Calli into the forest; he had hurt Ben and Petra, poor little Petra. I force the bile that has crept into my throat back down.

"God, my head hurts!" He presses his fingers to his eyes and in that instant I run. I duck behind the shed and run for the woods. If I could just get to the woods then I could hide. I know these woods. I keep expecting gunfire, but none comes. But despite the pain in his head and his trembling hands, Griff is still quicker than I am. Before I can step into the safety of the trees, he is here, his arms around me in a crushing bear hug. I try to kick him away from me, but he holds on tightly. We hear the sirens at the same time; we both freeze midstruggle for a brief moment. Then, before I can scream or break away, Griff drags me into the forest.

Deputy Sheriff Louis

I watch as Christine pulls away from the hospital parking lot, and I momentarily consider chasing after her, jumping in the car with her and Tanner and driving off to Minnesota. It is a brief thought, however, because I spy Toni, head down, rushing once again out of the hospital. I begin to go toward her, but notice Fitzgerald and the other agents observing me through the tall windows that line the front of the hospital. I make a beeline back toward the main doors, back to the investigation.

Fitzgerald is waiting as the automatic doors open and cold air from the air-conditioned main lobby once again strikes me in the face. My uniform is dirty from my trek through the woods, I stink of sweat and am perspiring heavily again after my heated conversation with Christine.

"She won't let us talk to the girl, or the boy for that matter,"

Fitzgerald says as I walk to a vending machine to buy a bottle of water.

"Who won't?" I ask, slugging the whole bottle back in one gulp.

"Antonia Clark," Fitzgerald replies. "She says Calli isn't up to talking now and she doesn't want Ben talking to us, either. I think she's hiding something."

"What would she be hiding?" I ask as I thread more change into the machine, this time choosing a soda full of caffeine and sugar. It is going to be a long night.

"I think she knows something about her husband. I don't buy that she didn't know he didn't go on that fishing trip today. Maybe she's covering for him," the agent named Temperly says.

"That's bullshit," I say, looking him in the eyes. "Have you even talked to Toni Clark? Have you even had one conversation with her that makes you believe this?"

"Just the one we had a few moments ago, when she absolutely refused to cooperate with us," Temperly says snidely. "I don't know, I guess if my child was kidnapped and my son beaten to a pulp, I'd want to know who did it."

"And so does Toni," I say in an even, low tone, trying to keep any anger out of it. To be thrown off this investigation was the last thing I needed. "She just wants to keep her kids safe. She'll let them speak with you when they're able."

"Yeah, she really kept them safe, didn't she?" Temperly mutters under his breath.

Agent Simon steps forward, a good thing because Temperly is pissing me off. "Let's talk to the doctor, see how long he thinks it will be before Calli will be able to speak with us. Then we can go from there."

"Where was Toni off to, anyway?" I ask the three agents. They all shrug and look at one another.

"Her crazy husband is out there and you just let her leave?" I ask in disbelief.

The agents raise their eyebrows at each other. "Let's go find the doctor," Simon says.

As we walk past the receptionist's desk the clerk calls out, "Can one of you speak with a Fielda Gregory? She's on the phone, very upset about her husband."

"I got it," Fitzgerald says before I can grab the phone. I step as close to him as I can, hoping to hear what is happening with Martin. Fitzgerald listens for several moments before he tells Fielda that he will get back to her shortly. "Jesus Christ," Fitzgerald mumbles. "What next?"

We all look at him expectantly. "It appears that Martin Gregory is now the next person to go missing out of our two little families."

"What do you mean? I had Jorgens take him home. He told me that Martin said he and Fielda were heading over to Iowa City together to see Petra."

"Gregory never went with them. Fielda drove to Iowa City with her mother and Mary Ellen McIntire," Fitzgerald explains.

"Jenna McIntire's mother?" Temperly asks.

"Yes. Let me finish," Fitzgerald says impatiently. "Petra needs surgery and Mrs. Gregory doesn't want to consent to the operation until she speaks with her husband. But she can't find him. She tried at home, at the police station, here at the hospital, friends, family, everywhere with no luck. Then Mary

Ellen McIntire piped up that she might have an idea where Martin Gregory is."

I wait for a moment for Fitzgerald to continue. Then it clicks. "Jesus, he went looking for Griff," I whisper.

"Yeah, he did. Mrs. McIntire said she and Martin had a brief conversation and that he alluded to the fact that he was going after whoever had done this to his little girl," Fitzgerald says grimly.

"As far as we know, Griff Clark is still up in those woods. Would Martin go back in there at this time of night?" Agent Simon asks, looking to me.

"If I know Griff Clark like I think I do, he's probably taken off for good. Right after he gets a few drinks into himself." A horrible thought skitters across my brain and I turn to the receptionist. "Can you tell me where Calli Clark's doctor is?"

A few minutes later Dr. Higby introduces himself to us and quickly makes it clear that under no circumstances are we to try to speak with the Clark children.

"No, no," I say. "It's Toni Clark. Do you know where she went, when she left a little while ago?"

"She went home. Said she wanted to get some clean clothes for the kids. Why, is there a problem?" Dr. Higby asks as a look of genuine concern creases his face.

"I don't know yet," I answer as a transmission comes over on my walkie-talkie. We all stop to listen as a dispatcher relays a report of a disturbance at 12853 Timber Ridge Drive. The reservist stationed at the house had reported that he heard angry voices at the back of the Clark home and what could have been a gunshot.

BEN

Rose has come back with a tray full of food. Pudding, Jell-O, soup, ginger ale. All soft food, she says, so I won't hurt my face chewing. I have to smile at that. She is a nice old lady. She leaves me alone so I can eat; she says she'll be sitting out in the waiting area if we need her. Says she knows I probably don't want some strange lady sitting in our room watching us. She's right. I just want to lie in bed, eat my mushy food and watch TV.

Calli, you're still sleeping. I keep looking over at you, wishing you'd wake up. Because even though I don't want Rose sitting in here with me, I'm still pretty lonely, and it seems like it's taking Mom forever to get back here. Your nurse stopped in a few times to check on you, taking your pulse, checking your IV, feeling your forehead.

I try not to think of Dad. I'm beginning to feel a little bit guilty about what happened up on the bluff, but what was I supposed to think, with Petra all hurt and you looking so scared? I don't think that I can ever look him in the eyes again after what happened. I hope Mom understands. I couldn't even tell her that Dad was the one to break my nose, but I think she knows, deep down.

I remember, Calli, before you stopped talking, you'd lie at the end of my bed, waiting for when I'd come home from school. Every day I knew that you'd be up there. I didn't mind so much. You always left my stuff alone—you did like to play with my rock collection, but you couldn't hurt a rock collection, could you? I'd open up my bedroom door and you'd be sitting there sorting out the rocks. You'd have a pile of black ones, of shiny metallic-looking ones, of pink feldspar and of yellowish calcite. You didn't call them by their scientific names, though; you had your own names for each one.

"This is Magic Cat's Eye," you'd say about my black obsidian. Or you'd hold up my shiny quartz. "This is Ice Rock. If you bury it in the backyard, everything will all turn to ice."

Sometimes I thought you'd never shut up. And now that you haven't talked for so long, I can hardly believe that you ever will again. I miss it now. I never would tell anyone this, but I still talk to you, and in my mind you talk back. Of course I'm still the older, smart one, and you're still my little sister, who couldn't possibly know as much as me. In my head you'd say, "Ben, do you think that Daddy will ever stop drinking?" And I'd say back, "I just don't know, Calli, but I suppose anything's possible." Or we'd just talk about stupid, everyday stuff like what we're having for supper or what we're going to watch on TV. I wish you'd wake up right now and say, "Ben, I want to watch channel seven, give me the remote!" But you don't. Never once have I asked you why you don't talk. I know it's got something to do with the day Mom lost the baby, though. I came home from Ray's house and there Mom was on the couch. Someone had put a blanket over her, was it you? Someone had put a blanket over her, but the blood was seeping through. I asked you what happened over and over, but you didn't say a word. You just sat on the floor by Mom, rocking back and forth, holding on to your stuffed monkey, and I called Louis and he called an ambulance. I thought for a minute you might say something when the baby came out. For the life of me I still don't know why they let us two kids watch that. When the baby came outta Mom and they wiped her clean, and you reached out to touch her red hair, I thought you were gonna say something. But you didn't. You just held your monkey a little tighter, rocked a little faster, until someone noticed us and called Mrs. Norland over to take care of us. At first, I thought it was because it must have been so scary seeing Mom fall down the stairs, but I watched you. I watched you real close after it all. I watched you when you were around Mom and when you were around me. And I watched you when you were around Dad, and I could see it real clear then. Your little face would go all stiff and you'd curl your fingers up real tight when he would come into the room. It wasn't real obvious, but I knew something was up. I think Mom did, too, but she never said anything. Sometimes I think that's what's wrong with Mom; she doesn't say what she should when she should.

I think you might be waking up. You are kind of wiggling around, trying to open your eyes, but you can't. You're so tired. I'm half-afraid that when you do finally open them up you're going to start hollering like you did when you first saw me. I start to go for the nurse's buzzer, thinking maybe you're hurting somewhere, but then you stop moving around and fall back asleep. I finish eating my chocolate pudding and keep flicking through the channels and when I look back at you, you are awake, just staring at me, like you can't quite believe I am here. Then you smile, just a little bit, but it's a smile anyway. I climb out of my bed and come over to your side.

"You okay?" I ask and you nod yes. "That's good," I say. You look at me kind of funny and I hurry up to say that I am okay, too. Then you do something that surprises me. You pull back your bedcovers and pat the space right next to you. I climb in next to you, being careful of the tube stuck in your arm, it's a tight fit in your little hospital bed, but I squeeze in.

At home, at night, sometimes you'd climb into my bed with me if you couldn't get to sleep and I'd tell you some story. Lots of times I'd tell you the regular fairy tales, Red Riding Hood, the Three Little Pigs. But sometimes I just made something up, like you and Petra being princesses and going on these great adventures. You liked them, though, those lame stories. And I figure you want me to tell you one now. I don't know where to begin. It seems stupid to tell you a story about the Gingerbread Man after what happened today. Then I get an idea. Probably a really dumb idea, and if Mom had known I was going to start telling you this story, I'm sure she probably would ground me for life. But it just sorta begins to spill out of me.

"Once upon a time there were two princesses, one named Calli and one named Petra. These princesses were both beautiful and smart and they were best friends. They didn't really care about being beautiful, though. They thought it was more important to be smart and brave. And they had many wonderful adventures together fighting dragons and witches and trolls. The thing was, Princess Calli didn't talk. No one knew why she didn't talk, but she didn't. She was still smart and brave. Plus she had Princess Petra to talk for her. They were quite a team, the two of them. Petra would say the magic words and Calli would wave her magic hands and the fire-breathing dragon would fall over dead and the mean old witch would be turned into a slug." You smile up at me at this part, that is one of your favorite stories, the one about the witch being turned into a slug.

"One day, though, Princess Calli and Princess Petra got lost in the woods." I stop and look over at you during this part. You look up at me like you aren't sure what I am doing, but you don't act like I should stop, so I don't. The door opens and the doctor comes in, the one with the crazy tie. I think maybe I should stop telling the story, but he tells me to keep on going, that he is just going to check you and me over quick.

"So Princess Calli and Princess Petra were lost in the woods and the thing was they didn't go into the woods on their own, Princess Calli's dad took them there." I look at you again and you are frowning, like what I am saying is all wrong, so I try again. "Princess Petra and Princess Calli went into the woods by themselves?" Again you shake your head no. I try again. "Some stranger took Princess Calli and Princess Petra into the woods?" Again, no. My idea isn't working so good and I look at Dr. Higby, who sits down in a chair in the corner of the room, in a spot where you can't see him. He gives me a nod like he wants me to keep trying.

"Only Princess Calli was taken into the woods by her father, who was under the spell of some nasty potion?" Calli nods hard at this and I sigh. Now I am getting somewhere.

MARTIN

My hands go to the tender spot where Griff had hit me with the gun. I can hear the police sirens getting closer and I am relieved. Such a stupid thing I have done, coming here, thinking that I could mete out justice like some all-knowing demigod. I could never actually shoot someone, even the most vile, evil of men. I am just an angry, silly, weak man, who once again has let things get beyond his control. I scan the ground before me, looking for the gun that Griff knocked from my hand. It is gone and so is Antonia. I have failed her, too. I feel dizzy and nauseous from the lump on my head and I lean against Antonia's shed for support.

When the sirens are upon me and I see a number of officers spill from their cars I call out to them, not wanting to be mistaken for a criminal. Actually, that is exactly what I am. An inept vigilante. Within seconds I am surrounded by police officers, one of them being, to my relief, Deputy Sheriff Louis.

"Where's Toni?" he asks me immediately. "Where did he take her?"

"The woods," I say, pointing in the general direction I had seen her run. "She tried to get away, but he was too quick. They went into the forest." Without another word, Deputy Louis is gone and behind him a gaggle of officers follows him, including Agent Fitzgerald.

A woman in a blue suit much too formal for the situation, I absurdly think, steadies me by holding my arm. A man takes my other arm and they gently settle me to the ground.

"An ambulance is on the way," the woman assures me. "Are you Martin Gregory?" she asks.

"I am," I say weakly, still holding my throbbing head.

"Let me see." She shines her penlight on my head and winces at what must have been an awful gash. Her companion fishes a handkerchief from his suit jacket and presses it into my hand.

"I'm Agent Simon and this is Agent Temperly. We're assisting in the investigation of your daughter's abduction. Can you tell us what happened?"

"I made a mistake. I made a big mistake," I say, feeling very sleepy. This must have been how Petra felt, I thought, with the gash that I had seen on her head. I'm in pain, this is certain, I have an incredible urge to just sleep, but what Petra has to be going through is so much worse.

"What happened?" the woman asks me again.

I sit for a long time saying nothing, not sure of the way to tell them, to share my ridiculous story of selfishness. Finally, Agent Simon rescues me by saying, "What happened to Antonia Clark?" This I can answer.

"Her husband took her into the woods." Again I point in the direction that I saw Antonia run.

"Did he have any weapons? There were reports of gunfire," the agent named Temperly asks.

"A gun," I say, knowing now that I could not postpone the inevitable. "I think he picked up the gun from the ground and took Antonia into the woods." Blood has seeped through the handkerchief that Temperly handed to me. I fold it, trying to find a clean spot to hold against my head.

"What gun from the ground?" Agent Simon asks, I think already knowing the answer.

"My gun. I came here with a gun," I admit. "Then Antonia arrived and I couldn't let her go in the woods where he was. Not after what he did to my daughter. So I warned her. We hid and he found us."

"Did you threaten him with the gun?" Agent Temperly asks.

"No, no, but I was holding it. That was threatening enough, I think. He knocked it from my hand and it went off, into the ground." I show them the damaged ground where the bullet had impacted. "He hit me with the gun and Antonia tried to run away. He caught her and pulled her into the woods. They could not have gone far. It's not loaded, though. The gun. I only had one bullet and that one was used."

"It's not loaded," Simon says, her voice oddly grave.

"That's a good thing." I look at her in confusion.

"It's a good thing if you're Antonia Clark. It isn't a good thing for Griff Clark and the officer who may shoot him because they both think the gun is loaded." Agent Simon turns to her partner. He nods and he walks away, I am sure to try to contact the officers who have dashed into the forest.

"You know coming out here was not a smart thing to do, don't you, Mr. Gregory?"

I nod miserably and wince at the movement. My eyelids grow heavier. Sleep is what I crave.

"Your wife has been searching desperately for you."

Immediately my sleepiness vanishes. "Petra," I gasp. "Is Petra okay?" I try to stand, but my quick movement sends a wave of pain and dizziness through me and I sit hard upon the ground.

"Hey, stay put, you need a doctor. I don't know exactly what is happening with your daughter, but your wife needs to speak with you. We'll get you to a phone as soon as possible, Mr. Gregory, I promise." Once again the piercing sound of a siren fills my ears. An ambulance. For me, I suppose. Hopefully just for me and not Antonia. Surprising myself, I think, hopefully not for Griff Clark, either.

ANTONIA

Griff is dragging me through the woods and I am screaming at him to stop, to please stop. Finally he does.

"I'm not gonna hurt you, Toni! Jesus. Do you really think I would do those things to Petra? Do you?"

He looks so pathetic and sad that I almost feel sorry for him. I have known Griff long enough for me to know how to handle him. I reach out to him with my other hand, slowly, no sudden movements, and gently remove a leaf that is stuck in his hair. "No, Griff, I don't think you would have done anything to hurt Petra. I am just trying to understand what happened." I let my hand rest on his shoulder. In one hand he still holds the gun. With the other, he holds tightly to my upper arm, and I think I know where Calli got her bruises. He drops his head onto my shoulder and coughs out a dry sob.

"Calli was up early this morning. We went for a walk in the woods and got lost. We got separated…"

I bite back a response to Griff's obvious omission of important details, like why Calli was only wearing her night-gown and no shoes on this walk and why he hadn't left a note telling us where they were.

"I swear I never even saw Petra until I found Calli on top of the bluff. Then Ben came up and saw—saw Petra. She looked so bad. But I didn't hurt her, I was trying to help her, God, I swear, Toni. I didn't do anything to her." I can feel Griff's tears on my neck. I wonder if they are real as I pat his shoulder.

"We'll just tell everyone that, we'll tell everyone that you didn't do it, Griff." I cup his face in my hands and make him look at me. "Griff, they have tests to see if someone really committed a crime, they do DNA testing. When they run those tests they'll know you didn't hurt her."

"I know, Toni, Jesus, I'm not an idiot," he snarls at me. "But I felt for her pulse, I tried to help her! I practically threw up all over her up there. They make mistakes. The police make mistakes all the time. You gotta tell them. You gotta tell them I was with you or something. That I couldn't have done this!" He is gripping my arm even more tightly, the gun in his hand resting on my shoulder.

"I will, Griff, I'll tell them. Don't worry, I believe you!" I say convincingly. "I'll tell them you were with me, that you went up there to look for the kids and Ben made a mistake. Don't worry."

Griff looks relieved and he lets go of my arm. "Thank you, thank you, Toni. You won't be sorry. I'll stop drinking, it will be good now, I promise. I know I've made some bad mistakes, but it will be better now." He smiles at me gratefully. "Do you remember what it was like before? It'll be like that again, like

when Ben was little. It was good then, wasn't it? I'll quit the
pipeline, get something here in town. Or maybe we'll just
move, start all over in a new place. Won't that be better? We
could go to the ocean. You've always wanted to see the ocean.
We could go live by it, get a house right on the beach."

I nod. "Yeah, that'll be good. It'll be good." I'm surprised
that he remembers this about me. "Come on, let's go back
now. We'll talk to the police, they'll understand."

"I don't know." Griff hesitates. "I think that I might have
hurt Martin. I hit him pretty hard. God, I shouldn't have hit
him so hard."

"What were you going to do? He had a gun, remember?
You were scared. You were protecting yourself. Come on, let's
go home. They'll be looking for us, it'll be better if we go to
them, Griff. Please, let's go, the kids need us."

"I don't know, I don't know," Griff frets. "Let's keep going.
You know the woods better than anyone. Let's keep going,
then when things calm down we'll go get the kids."

"Keep running?" I ask. "But why? I told you I would
cover for you. It's okay, we need to get to Calli and Ben.
Please, Griff," I beg.

"You're always takin' their side. Jesus, Toni, just do this one
thing for me, please, then we'll get the kids. We can get to
Maxwell by morning if we can get over to Highway Eighteen
in the next few hours. Then we'll make sure the coast is clear
and go get the kids."

"Griff, Calli's feet are all bandaged up. She's not going to
be able to travel for a while, and Ben's got some broken ribs.
We can't just start dragging them around the countryside."

"Then we'll come back for them in a week or so, when

they're doing better. Toni, come on, they'll be coming in here soon after us." He sounds desperate.

"You go on without me, then. I'll tell the police everything. How you were with me, how you didn't do anything but take Calli for a walk this morning. I'll tell them that you just want them to know the truth before you come home. They'll understand that, I'm sure they have arrangements like that all the time. You go on to Maxwell. I'll make sure the kids are okay, then meet up with you soon."

"You're lying," Griff says in a wounded voice, grabbing my arm again.

"No, I'm not, I'm not," I assure him.

"Jesus, you're lying to me!" His face twists in grief and he begins to drag me deeper into the forest.

"Griff, you're hurting me, please stop, please!" I try to pull away from him, but he waves the gun in my direction.

"You're coming with me. We'll get to Maxwell, then we'll get the kids."

I begin to cry noisily and brace my feet against the dry earth. He easily tows me along behind him like a child's pull-string toy. "Shut up!" he orders. I can't stop my sobbing; my cries come forth in loud brokenhearted jags.

"Shut up!" he bellows. "Goddammit, Toni, they're gonna hear you. Shut up!"

Panic has overtaken me and I can't catch my breath. I begin hyperventilating. My fingers are tingly and I have a strange numb sensation around my mouth. I look up at Griff helplessly.

"I can't breathe!" I try to tell him, but all that comes out is a hiss of breath as I try to gulp in more air.

"Shut up! Shut up, Toni, they'll hear you!" He grips me by

the shoulders and thrusts me up against a tree, my head striking the rough bark. "Shut up, shut up! If you don't be quiet you will never see Calli and Ben again, do you hear me? They'll find us! I will not go to jail for something I didn't do! Shut! Up!"

"Please," I whisper, catching enough breath to speak. "Please let me go."

He leans in close to me, puts his lips close to my ear and murmurs, "If you say one more goddamn word, I will shut your mouth for good. Now shut up."

I go still, not because of his threat, but because I had encountered this very same scene, in a different time and a different place, as an outsider looking in, but the same nevertheless. Poor Calli, I thought. Poor little four-year-old Calli, watching her mother fall down a flight of stairs. His screams of "shut up, shut up" causing Calli to cringe, not able to stop crying. I remember lying on the couch, covered in a blanket, watching Griff screaming at his little four-year-old daughter. I remember Griff bending down to whisper into Calli's ear something, something. And for four years, she has only spoken one word. One lonely word.

"Oh, God," I gasp in his ear. "It was you, it was you!"

BEN

"So Princess Calli was taken prisoner by the king, who didn't know what he was doing because of the potion he had drunk. The princess tried and tried to use her magic, but it wouldn't work on the king because he was too strong."

I look over at Dr. Higby, who is sitting all quiet in the chair. Standing right beside him is that nice nurse, Molly. She puts a finger to her lips and looks at you, Calli. You are only looking at me, looking up at me like you want me to keep on going.

"Princess Calli and the king became lost in the big, dark woods and Calli's feet hurt because she didn't have any shoes on, but still they kept walking through the woods together. She was hot and thirsty, she wanted her mother, the queen, and her brother, the prince, but she didn't know where they were. She couldn't figure out why they weren't coming for her, she thought maybe they forgot about her. But they didn't, they spent all day trying to find her. Her brother looked and looked and the soldiers of the kingdom started to look for her, too. And finally, her brother found her, on top of the bluff with the king and her friend Petra. Only Princess Petra was hurt real bad. The king had done a really bad thing and hurt her so bad that now Petra was the one who wasn't able to talk."

I feel Calli go all stiff next to me and I look down at her. "Isn't that how it goes, Calli? Isn't that how it went?" I ask her. She sits stock-still, her face serious as if she is thinking real hard. Slowly she shakes her head from side to side. I see Dr. Higby lean forward in his chair. "What happened, Calli?" I ask her. "You finish the story, I can't. I wasn't there, not for all of it. You finish the story."

MARTIN

They won't let me climb into the ambulance on my own, but insist that I lie down on a stretcher and lift me into the vehicle.

"I'm fine," I maintain, but no one appears to be listening. A paramedic begins dabbing at my forehead, his face smooth and unreadable. Very professional, I think. I know I will need stitches, but before that happens I need to get to a phone.

"Please, I need to use a phone. I need to call my wife," I say.

"Someone from the hospital will contact your family, sir, don't worry."

"No, please. My daughter is the one who was airlifted to Iowa City. My wife has been trying to contact me. Please, I must talk to her. I have to find out how my daughter is doing." I struggle to sit up, but the paramedic firmly presses on my chest to keep me in a prone position. I must have looked amply distressed because suddenly I have a cell phone in my hand and a few moments later I am speaking with Fielda, who breaks down upon hearing my voice.

"Martin, Martin, where have you been? Are you all right?" she weeps.

"Yes, yes, I'm fine." I will tell her about my shabby stab at heroics later. "How is Petra? Is Petra okay? They told me that you said she needs surgery."

"She's in surgery right now. I'm sorry, Martin, I couldn't wait any longer for you. I had to make a decision. They needed to relieve pressure that was on her brain. I said yes."

"Of course you did, Fielda. That was exactly what you should have done. I'll be there soon. I have to take care of some things here, but I will be there with you as soon as I can. I should have gone with you in the first place. I am so sorry, Fielda, I am so very sorry." There is a pause on the phone line.

"Martin," Fielda begins cautiously, "you didn't go and do something that you're going to be sorry about now, did you?"

I thought of Antonia out in the forest with that desperate, sad man and I say, "I hope not."

She sighs and tells me she loves me, no matter what, and to hurry up and get over to Iowa City.

When we arrive at Mercy Hospital, as I am wheeled into the emergency room, a police officer keeps stride with the gurney and speaks with me. "We're going to have to interview you after you have your head checked out."

"Yes, sir," I say, closing my eyes as I think of Calli and Ben Clark ensconced somewhere above me, waiting for their mother to return to them. How could I explain to them what happened, what I did, if their mother does not come back?

Deputy Sheriff Louis

Fitzgerald and I crash through the brush, trying to move silently but failing miserably. It is black as tar. The quarter moon and the stars are swallowed up by the night and do little to light our way.

"Jesus," Fitzgerald curses, "we'll never find them in here."

"We will. Griff doesn't know his way around in here, but Toni does. She'll make sure that they stay on a path."

"God, I hope so," he mutters.

I lead Fitzgerald through the brush slowly, cautiously. I do not want to stumble upon Griff and Toni and cause him to panic. Shortly we come to a thinning of the trees where the forest intersects with the path and we both look out onto the trail squinting into the darkness. Nothing. We creep as quietly as we can up the path. Occasionally Fitzgerald or I step on a twig and the snap of wood causes us to stop and tensely look around. I am ashamed to realize that Fitzgerald is in better shape than I am and I have to work hard in order to keep in front of him. After several minutes of hiking I am only aware of my own breathing and Fitzgerald stops me by yanking on my sleeve.

"Listen," he orders. Gradually the voices become clear to me, one male, one female—one angry and one full of anguish. It is them. I nod to Fitzgerald to let him know that I hear it, too, and we proceed slowly, silently. We need to observe Toni and Griff without their knowledge, get a good handle on their position and verify that Griff has a weapon.

I move down the path in small increments, making sure that Fitzgerald is always in my sight, stopping every few steps to listen. It isn't long before I hear Griff screeching, "Shut up, shut up!" and hear Toni's frantic cries. I inch down the path, forcing myself forward in deliberate, slow movements, not wanting to give up my presence prematurely. The sliver of moon illuminates Griff pinning Toni to a tree, his mouth against her ear. If I hadn't seen a gun in Griff's hand, I would have thought it was simply two people in an embrace, that and the fact that Toni's sorrowful weeping assaults my ears. Farther on down the trail I spy Fitzgerald edging forward, gun drawn. I, too, pull my gun from its holster and step behind a tree.

Fitzgerald yells, "Police! Put the gun down." They don't appear to hear him.

"Oh, God! It was you, it was you," Toni howls.

"No, no, I didn't do it!" Griff whines. "I didn't hurt that girl!" He presses his hand against Toni's throat, and I crouch and take aim. He is too close to her.

"No," Toni wails, her words difficult to understand. "Calli, Calli. It's because of you she doesn't talk."

"Drop the gun, Griff," I shout. Griff pauses for a minute as if acknowledging our presence.

"What are you talking about? Shut up!" Griff tells her, con-fusion in his voice.

"I thought it was because of what she saw, when I lost the baby, I thought it was my fault. But it was you. You whis-pered something to her. What did you say? What did you say?" Toni's words muddle together and the ferocity of them make Griff step back. Again I take aim.

"Shut up, Toni! You don't know what you're talking about." Griff is trying to keep his voice low. I can see his body shake with rage. Or DT. He begins to weep himself. He leans forward so that his forehead rests on Toni's and then presses the barrel of the gun to his temple.

"Drop your weapon!" Fitzgerald booms. He is slowly edging farther away from me. If Griff chose to shoot, he would only be able to hit one of us.

Again I take aim, but he is too close to Toni and I can't risk the shot. In an instant, Griff moves slightly away from Toni, holding his gun toward her face, my chance. I reposition the grip on my weapon and I hear a shout and then the discharge, a loud pop that does not come from my gun. I am too late. I see both Griff and Toni collapse to the ground, both not moving.

Within seconds Fitzgerald is standing over Griff and Toni. I can't go any closer, I feel ill and disgraced.

"Come help me, hurry up!" Fitzgerald calls to me as he tries to roll Griff off Toni. I see her arms push at Griff, trying to force him off her. She crawls out from beneath him, covering her face with her hands.

I stand above her, not equipped to comfort her, not there, not then. I call for backup and an ambulance, even though it is plain that Griff is dead. Fitzgerald is the one to kneel down beside her and whisper reassuring words to her. I don't believe that she even knows I am here. She clutches onto Fitzgerald and will not let him go. Even as he leads her down the trail, she leans heavily on him while I stay behind to wait for the coroner and the forensic team.

Hours later I receive word that the gun that Griff was holding was not loaded. I console myself by telling myself that I was not the one to shoot him. Given the chance, though, I would have. Gladly.

CALLI

Her brother's words wash over her, the story he is telling her. She tries to ignore the many eyes staring at her expectantly. She thinks back to that moment on top of the bluff, to when she saw him and then saw Petra.

She was bent down to pick up the necklace, Petra's necklace. She sensed his presence before she saw him, could feel the weight of his gaze upon her. Fear, cold and black, sidled into her chest. Still bent over, she slowly raised her eyes and saw his mucky, thick-soled hiking boots that led into mud-splattered olive trousers; and this was where Calli's gaze stilled. He was standing above her on a broad flat rock the color of sand. She saw, hanging limply, a hand, small and pale, lightly grazing the drab of his pants, level with his knee. Calli straightened, the necklace gripped in her fist, to see her friend bundled in his arms. Petra's eyes were closed as if sleeping, an angry two-inch gash resting above her left eyebrow. A collage of purple-smudged bruises traveled along her cheek to her lips that were cracked and bloodied, down to her neck which lolled helplessly as he readjusted her in his arms. Her blue pajamas were filthy, caked with a deep-brown substance; her grungy, once-white tennis shoes were untied, the dirty laces hanging flaccid around her ankles.

"Help me," he pleaded. "She's hurt. I can't get her down the bluff on my own." He stared levelly into Calli's eyes, his wounded voice not matching the resolve she saw in his hard eyes. She knew him.

He was perched on the highest point on the bluff, where the trees cast long, sullen shadows, and every few moments a breeze swept across his sunburned forehead, lifting his hair briefly. A deep valley, a basin of lush greens and honey-yellows, lay in a blanket far behind him. Calli's eyes darted to Petra's fingers, which twitched briefly.

"She's too heavy. I have to put her down." He carefully moved to set Petra down, resting his hand behind her head as he laid her on the altarlike rock. Once again he stood, shaking his arms free from the residual weight of Petra.

"I'm glad you're here," he remarked. "I could never do this on my own." He looked at Calli, trying to read her expression. "If we hurry, we can get her down the bluff and to the hospital. She's hurt badly. She fell," he added as an afterthought.

The bluff on which he stood ended abruptly behind him and sloped into a steep, rough wall lined with slick green moss, and ended in a narrow, dry ravine.

"Please," he begged, "I think she's going to die if we don't get her out of here." His chin quivered and tears seemed to gather in the corners of his eyes.

Diffidently, she moved forward. Her gaze, though, never

wandering from his face. He reached down a hand to help pull her to the top of the crumbling limestone; powdery bits breaking away as she tried to find a foothold for her toes. His hand, smooth and cool, enveloped hers and she felt herself being lifted, the disconcerting feeling of being suspended in air fluttered in her stomach. His grip tightened and a moment of dread swept through her. A mistake, she thought, I should have run. She helplessly tried to free her hand in a futile tug of war.

She heard it before he did. The unmistakable beating of wings, slow and deliberate, followed by a drawn-out caw, almost like laughter. She felt the rush of air on her neck as it swooped over her. It was huge, the biggest bird Calli had ever seen, so black that it almost looked bluish, its wings spread so wide it looked nearly the same size as she was. The man faltered as the great black bird skimmed his shoulder, casting a dark shadow over the look of fear and revulsion that danced across his face as he released Calli's hand. She fell backward and struck the ground, finding herself dazed, looking up into a muted blue sky brushed in shades of pink found on the underbelly of clumps of Spring Beauty that bloomed in early spring. When she sat up and carefully looked around, she didn't see him.

She scurried up the rock where Petra was and peered over the side to the rift below. Then Calli crawled over to Petra and she stirred. Her eyes fluttered open and she looked at Calli.

"Mommy," Petra moaned.

Calli placed a dirty hand on Petra's forehead, nodded to her and patted her arm. She turned in every direction, looking for him. He was gone, but she had seen him before, she knew him, he had a funny name and a dog. He was out there, maybe watching her. She scuttled backward into the brush and hid.

Calli blinked her eyes and returned to the present.

"Lucky," Calli said simply to her brother, speaking for her friend who had always spoken for her. "It was Lucky."

BEN

Well, Calli, you did it. You finished the story and I know that wasn't any easy thing for you to do. I am surprised that it wasn't Dad, but that student of Mr. Gregory who ended up taking Petra into the woods and doing all those bad things to her. I wonder if Dad will ever forgive me for blaming him, but he looked so guilty and he did drag you out into the woods. I don't know how I am going to face him. I mean, I walloped him pretty good for a twelve-year-old. Mom isn't back yet with our stuff and I am just plain tired. But there is no sleeping for us tonight, what with the police coming in and asking you to tell the story over and over again. You do it, though. You retell that story over and over and they keep asking you over and over again if this Lucky guy did anything to you, but you say no, it was Petra, he hurt Petra.

Finally, Rose comes in and tells the police officers to beat it, that we both need a good night's sleep. We aren't sleeping, though, are we? We've decided to wait up for Mom, but she hasn't come to us, not yet anyway. You are so excited to show her that you can talk again, you just ramble on and on, I think just to hear your own voice, to listen to what it sounds like after so many years. It surprises me, too, the way you sound. Older of course, but I don't know, you sound smarter. No, that isn't it. Wiser, I guess. You sound wise. And I guess you are. I ask you if you think that Dad will ever forgive me for me thinking what I did about him and for hitting him. You say, "No," so softly I almost can't hear you, but I do. "No," you say, "but don't be sorry. He wasn't himself up there." You stop talking for a second and then change your mind. "He was himself up there, but still don't be sorry, you saved us."

I have to smile at that, you thinking that I saved you and Petra, and maybe I did. I guess I'll never know. It's nice, sitting here with you; we don't know what is coming next with Dad, but I figure it'll all turn out okay. "What do ya want to watch, Calli?" I ask you and you answer me, just like it should go.

DEPUTY SHERIFF LOUIS

I do not go home after the shooting. It is an empty place, what
with Christine and Tanner gone. In one crazy day I have lost
my wife and my son. I end up at my desk at the station,
writing my report, trying not to forget any of the key details.
I've seen a lot as a deputy sheriff; I have seen the aftermath
of suicides, meth lab explosions, I have seen women beaten
by their husbands who somehow decide to go back for more.
That makes me think of Toni, staying with Griff, who was
obviously a mess and didn't take good care of her, not the way
I would have, anyway. But there is something about seeing
someone you know inside and out on the edge of being
killed. Nothing prepared me for that, no amount of training
or years of experience readied me for seeing the barrel of a
gun pressed to the head of the girl I first saw careening down
a hill of snow on a sled when we were seven. Maybe it is a
gift, not being the one to shoot Griff. Now maybe I can go
in and help pick up the pieces of Toni's former life. Start where

we had left things so many years ago. Maybe this is my second chance with her. I hadn't been the one to kill her husband. But will Toni think of it that way? Would Calli and Ben?

Maybe I'm no better than Griff was. He gave up his family for alcohol and it looks like I gave up my own family, as well. But for me it was because of a woman I had grown up with, one I couldn't ever let go. So who is the bigger villain in the end? Is it Griff or is it me? I think that's a question I don't want to look at too closely, an answer I can live without finding.

Once when Toni and I were in the third grade we went walking in Willow Creek Woods. It was just the two of us, when all was innocent and a boy could still be friends with a girl and not be teased mercilessly by his peers. It was a brisk spring day, the light from the sun bright but lacking any warmth. Toni wore an old sweatshirt of her brother's and snow boots. We were walking across Lone Tree Bridge, carefully making our way across the thin tree trunk that had fallen across Willow Creek, holding hands, steadying each other so we wouldn't fall. There on that day, holding the hand of my best friend, I could not imagine a life without her, without Toni, and I still can't.

This morning I find myself calling Charles Wilson and apologizing on behalf of the sheriff's department for any inconvenience we have caused him.

"No problem," he says. "I'm just glad you found the girls." I hesitate before hanging up. "Did you ever find your dog, Mr. Wilson?" I ask.

"Oh, yes," he says. "He came home last night, tired and hungry. And embarrassed, I think, for the trouble he caused."

I apologize once again and wish him well. He's a good man, Mr. Wilson.

I go to the hospital, hoping to find Toni there with Ben and Calli. I come across her sitting in the waiting room, next to the information desk, looking at her hands. It strikes me that she looks much the same way as she did on the day she found out her mother had died.

"What am I going to tell them?" she asks me, not looking up at me when I stand next to her.

"I don't know," I tell her truthfully. I don't envy her that task.

She stands and wobbles for a moment uncertainly and I hold her elbow to steady her and follow her to the elevator doors. "Do you want me to come with you, Toni?" I ask.

"Yes," she says and reaches out for my hand.

ANTONIA

Louis helps me tell the children that Griff is dead. These are the hardest words that I have ever had to say, "Your father has died." It is strange, though, they don't ask how, they don't ask why. Ben and Calli just accept the fact, no tears, no anger, just acceptance. Not for the first time, I wonder what in the world have I done to these poor children. I think that perhaps they are just numb. It has been a confusing, painful two days on many counts. One more piece of horrific news probably weighs the same as all the other pieces of bad news that are being piled on them.

Do I cry over Griff's death? A good wife would say yes. But I am not a good wife. How many times did I wish that I would get the call that Griff was injured so badly on the pipeline that there was no chance for recovery, or that he was in a terrible auto accident and had died? Too many to count. Notice that these scenarios are all accidental deaths. I am too civilized to wish that someone would shoot my husband. But do I feel relief? Yes, I felt relief when his body slumped against mine, shot. I am relieved that it was not me who was shot, and I am relieved that I will not have to endure one more drunken tantrum from my husband, and that my children will not have to suffer through one again, either. I was not a good mother; a good mother would have packed her children up the first time her husband began throwing beer bottles at her; the first time he smacked her child a little too hard for spilling the orange juice; or the first time he made her child sit at the kitchen table for three hours because she did not, could not say, "May I please be excused." A good mother would not have tolerated any of these things. But as I said, I wasn't a good mother.

But I get a chance to start over, brand-new. To be a good mother, the kind of mother who protects her children, who will lay down her life for her children. Louis says that I already am that kind of mother, that I always was. But I don't think so, not really. Here's my chance. I want what I never got with my own mother, enough time. I just want enough time.

MARTIN

It takes eleven stitches to sew up the damage that Griff Clark did to my head when he hit me with the gun. As a result, I've got a concussion and have to spend the night in the hospital away from Petra and Fielda. This morning my head aches terribly, but I know that my daughter is in so much more pain and I am quickly preparing to leave, to make the trip to the hospital in Iowa City to be with my girls. Just as I finish tying my shoes, Antonia Clark comes into my hospital room. She sits on the edge of a chair while I wait for the doctor to sign my discharge papers.

"I should be coming to see you," I say apologetically. "How are Calli and Ben doing?" I ask.

"They're going to be fine," she tells me. "How is Petra?"

"She is out of surgery. She's still asleep, but it appears the surgeon was able to relieve some of the pressure on her brain from the injury."

We sit in silence for some time until I am finally able to choke out the words that need to be said. "I'm sorry, Antonia.

I am so sorry I came to your home with a gun. I truly believed that Griff had something to do with what happened to Petra. That is no excuse, I know, but I am sorry. It is because of me that he is dead."

"Martin, look at what Griff did to your head. Look what he did to Calli. Drunk, he took her from her home at four in the morning without shoes and dragged her through the woods so he could take her to who he thought was her real father. He ended up getting them lost, beat up his son and held a gun to my head. Griff wasn't all that great of a guy, Martin."

"No," I say cautiously. "But I'm sorry that he died. I'm sorry your family has to go through another bad thing."

"We'll be okay. We've got each other and that's what's important, right?"

I nod.

"Do you have a ride to Iowa City? You're not going to drive, are you? Your head must still be hurting."

"Louis said he would drive me to the hospital," I tell her.

"He told me they caught the man who did this," Antonia says.

"Yes. I believe he is somewhere in this hospital," I reply.

"You're not going to go after him, are you?"

"No. I learned my lesson the first time. And besides, it sounds like Lucky managed to hurt himself all on his own by falling down the bluff."

"I remember him. I met him at your house that one time, with his dog," Antonia says gently.

"Yes. I thought I knew him well," I respond. She reaches out and touches my arm.

"It's not your fault," she says kindly.

"That will be the question that I ask myself for a very long time. If a father cannot keep his child safe, who can?"

"You're a wonderful father, Martin. I've seen the way you are with Petra. Fielda chose you well. I wish I would have made such a wise choice myself."

"If you had chosen differently, you would not have the children you have," I remind her.

She smiles. "I do have great kids. We both do. Now go to Petra. When she wakes up, she'll want to see her father standing there. You two can compare stitches."

I laugh. I have not done that in such a long time. It feels good. It feels like things one day could go back to normal. I stand, shakily, my head still aching, and go off in search of my doctor. I am leaving. I need to get to my daughter and my wife.

EPILOGUE

Calli

Six Years Later

I often look back upon that day, so long ago, and wonder how it was we all survived. For each one of us it was a dark, sad day. Especially for my mother, I think, though she always says, "It was good in some ways. You found your voice that day, Calli. That made it a good day."

I have never thought of it as "finding" my voice because it wasn't really lost. It was more like a bottle with a cork pushed deeply into the opening. I picture it that way often, my voice like some sweet-smelling perfume, sitting in some expensive-looking bottle with a beautifully curved handle, tall and slender, made of glass as blue as the bodies of the dragonflies I see down in Willow Creek Woods. My voice was just waiting for the right moment to be let go from that bottle. No, it was never lost; I just needed permission to use it again.

365 The Weight of Silence

It took me such a long time to figure out that I was the only one who could grant that permission, no one else. I wish my mother would understand this. She still blames herself for everything, and isn't that a heavy weight to carry around?

This I know firsthand. I, for a long time, had thought it was my fault that my baby sister, Poppy, died when I was four. Silly, you think. How could a four-year-old be responsible for a baby's death? Now imagine this: that same four-year-old watching her mother and father arguing at the top of the stairs and that four-year-old seeing her pregnant mother tumble down the steps backward, reaching out for her with her outstretched hands. Now picture that four-year-old crying and crying, not being able to stop. Understandable. Now see the four-year-old's daddy trying to get her to quiet down, not with hugs or soft kisses, but other whispered words. "Shut up, Calli. If you don't be quiet the baby will die. Do you want that to happen? Do you want the baby to die? If you don't shut up your mother will die." Over and over and over, whispered in that four-year-old's ear. And the baby died, my little sister who had hair as red as poppies, whose skin was as soft as a flower's petals. I ate my words that day. Actually bit down, chewed them, swallowed them and felt them slide down my throat like glass until they were so broken and damaged that there was no possible way that the words could rearrange and repair themselves enough to be spoken. So I know what it feels like to feel responsible for something I really had no control over. That's how it is for my mother.

Petra never did return to school the year after this happened. She was in the hospital for a very long time. She had several surgeries and spent nearly two months in Iowa

City, then another month at our local hospital. My mother would take me to the hospital to see Petra once a week, when she was well enough to have visitors. It's funny, we didn't talk much during those visits even though I was able to talk then. We just didn't need to, to talk, that is. We could just be.

Petra and her family moved away about a year and a half after she was hurt. She was never quite the same after it all. She walked differently and school was a lot harder for her because of her head injury. I don't think anyone made fun of her; they didn't when I was around, anyway. I think that everyone, kids and adults, just felt so bad for her that no matter what, they couldn't let her be the same girl she was before. Kids our age didn't know what to say to her, and adults would get this sad, concerned look on their faces. All Petra really wanted was to be like everyone else.

I think, though, that it was the trial and all that went with it that really made the Gregory family want to leave. Her father felt the worst. He was the one who had welcomed Lucky into his home, hired him to do odd jobs around the house and who had got him a job at the Mourning Glory. The morning that Petra disappeared it was Lucky and his dog Sergeant who she saw through her bedroom window. She went after them to say hello and he grabbed her when they were well into the woods. I found out later that Lucky worked really hard trying to get Petra to trust and like him. He would give her little presents when he came over to their home or when Petra went to the Mourning Glory. He even told her that he went walking through the woods in her backyard all the time with Sergeant and that he would love if she came with them sometime. Lucky killed his dog, too. It seems

Sergeant actually tried to protect Petra when Lucky was hurting her. Sergeant bit Lucky and he ended up strangling the poor dog with his own leash.

The entire Gregory family had to testify and so did my whole family. It was a long, tiring, confusing ordeal, what with lawyers asking questions, reporters asking questions, and friends and neighbors asking questions. I think the prosecuting attorney was terrified that I would stop talking again; he would call our house every night during the trial to talk with me, just to make sure. Lucky was found guilty on all counts—kidnapping, attempted murder and sexual abuse. The only halfway funny thing about the whole ordeal was that old black crow who brushed by Lucky right when he was going to grab me, too, knocked him right over the bluff. He fell about fifty feet. Broke his leg and his collarbone. They didn't find him until late that next afternoon. As far as I know he is still in prison and will be forever. It was never proven that Lucky had anything to do with Jenna McIntire's death.

Petra and I still write letters back and forth to each other. She lives in another state; her father has retired from teaching. They live on a farm now, renting their land for the actual farming part, but they have a few animals, lambs, chickens, a pig, some dogs. Petra has invited me to visit a time or two but it's never quite worked out. She never wants to come back to Willow Creek, which I can understand.

My brother turned eighteen this year and has been working, saving up for college. He's leaving in the fall and my mother and I are already crying about it. He is big and tall and looks just like my dad, but softer, if you get what I mean. He wants to be a police officer and he will be very good at it, I think. I don't know what I will do without him when he goes away. I know many of my friends cannot wait for their brothers or sisters to leave, but it's different with Ben and me. It makes me just so sad to think of him leaving that I can't.

Louis is still a deputy sheriff, but my mom and Ben think he should run for sheriff next year, when the old sheriff finally retires. Louis comes over for dinner a lot and went to all of Ben's football games throughout high school. Ben and Louis are very close and I am sure this is why Ben is going to become a police officer. I wonder at times if my mother and Louis will end up together. I know he got divorced a while back and I think it's about time my mom had some fun for herself. I asked her the other day why she and Louis didn't just get married, it is so obvious that they love one another. Her face went all sad and she said it was complicated, so I let it go. At least for now. She still has these horrible nightmares, my mother does. I can hear her yelling from her bedroom and more than once I've seen her peeking into our rooms, checking on me, checking on Ben.

Louis's ten-year-old son, Tanner, comes to Willow Creek most weekends and on some holidays. His ex-wife ended up moving to Cedar Rapids, about an hour from here. Tanner is a funny little guy, quiet with serious eyes. Louis is crazy about the kid and gets all sad and depressed when he has to take him back to Cedar Rapids.

I still don't talk much, and that scares my mother. I can go for days and not say anything. I won't ignore anyone or refuse to answer, but I just go quiet. Sometimes my mom will get this very worried look on her face that lets me know she's afraid I've gone mute again. When I see that, I make a point to talk to her. It makes her feel better anyway. My mom got herself a job at the hospital as an aide, working on the skilled care floor. She works with old people, changing their sheets, helping them eat, giving them baths, helping the nurses. Not the most glamorous of jobs, she says. But she's always coming home telling us stories about who did what and who said what. She complains about the grouchy, persnickety ones, but actually, I think those are her favorites.

I have a picture of my dad that I keep in my treasure box. It's faded and curled around the edges, but it is my favorite picture of him ever. It was taken before I was born, before Ben was even born. My dad is sitting in his favorite chair and he has the biggest smile on his face. His face looks young and it's as pale as milk, except for the freckles that are on his nose. He looks healthy and his eyes are a bright green. They don't have that yellowish color to them that he had later. He is wearing a faded pair of jeans and a Willow Creek Wolverines football jersey. But best of all, the very best of all, is what he is holding in his hand. It isn't a beer bottle, but a can of pop and he's holding it out toward the camera like he is toasting whoever is snapping the picture. Cheers, he seems to be saying, cheers.

I don't hate my dad. I think I did for a while, but not anymore. I don't hate him, but I certainly don't miss him, either. After the funeral my mother took us into town and we bought as many gallons of yellow paint that we could put in our car. We painted the house, the three of us. Now it's a happy soft-yellow color. Warm and cozy. And anyway, that whole entire week was just incredibly hard for all of us. We needed something to look forward to, some hope, and having a yellow house was a start anyway. That's what Mom said. I told her that if my father hadn't been drinking that morning and dragged me out into the woods, I never would have come across Petra and she would have died. So in a way, he actually saved the day. She just looked at me for a long time, not sure of what to say. Finally she said, "Don't go making your father into a hero. He wasn't a hero. He was a lonely man with a bad disease."

We do go to my father's grave once a year, on his birthday. Ben grumbles about it, but Mom insists. She says we don't have to like the things he did but he was still a part of our family and wouldn't he be sad knowing that not one of his children came to visit him once in a while? Last year Ben laughed when Mom said this and answered her all sassy, "The only way Dad would be glad to see us was if we brought a six-pack with us." He did, too. Ben brought a six-pack of beer with him to the cemetery last year. Set it right next to his gravestone. Mom made him take it away, but Ben and I laughed over it later. It was kind of funny, in a sick sort of way.

As for me, I'm pretty much a regular kid. I go to school and do okay. I have friends and even run track and cross-country for my school. I like to run, I always have. I feel like I could run forever some days. And I like that I don't have to talk when I'm out for a run. No one expects you to chat while you're running five miles.

I don't go into the woods anymore very often, and definitely not alone. That makes me about as sad as anything. I loved the woods once. It was my special spot. But when I'm in there, surrounded by trees, I am always looking behind me to see if anything is creeping up on me. Silly, I guess. Mom asked Ben and me if we wanted to move, to go into town, away from the woods. We both said no. Our home was our home, and there are a lot more good memories there than bad. Mom smiled at this, and I was glad that we could make her feel better. The woods are still Mom's favorite place and she and Louis go walking there quite a bit. I asked her if she ever got scared while walking, afraid. She said no, that the forest was in her blood, that she couldn't be scared of something that had actually been so good to her. "It sent you back to me, didn't it?" she asked. I nodded. Maybe one day I would feel the same way about the woods, but not now, not for a long time.

I still see Dr. Kelsing, the psychiatrist that I met that night I went to the hospital; it's nice to have someone to talk to who wasn't in the middle of the whole mess. She lets me know that I'm not crazy. She says I was very brave and very strong to do what I did on that day. I don't know if that's true, but I'd like to think so.

I even kept on seeing my guidance counselor, Mr. Wilson, all the way through elementary school. I learned about a year ago that Mr. Wilson was actually brought in for questioning while Petra and I were missing. I bet that was totally embarrassing for him, but not once did he mention it to me. I would meet with him once a week and I'd still write in the beautiful journals that he gave me. On our last meeting together, during my last week of being a sixth grader at Willow Creek Elementary School, we sat at the round table and he asked what I would like to talk about on that day. I shrugged my shoulders and he stood. He was still incredibly tall even though I had grown several inches since first grade. He dug into his old gray file cabinet and pulled out five journals, all with black covers and all decorated with my artwork. I told him, then, about the dream I had when I fell asleep out in the woods the day my dad had taken me. The one where I was flying through the air and everyone was grabbing at me, trying to get me to come down. I told him that he was in my dream holding my journal in his hands, pointing at something. I told him I wondered what he was pointing at. He pulled the very first journal I had written in from the bottom of the pile and handed it to me.

"Let's look for it and see if we can find out what it was," he said. For the next half hour I looked through that journal, the one that said Calli's Talking Journal on the front and was decorated with a dragonfly. I flipped through pages, laughing about my terrible spelling and my stick figure pictures. But then I found it, the entry I was sure Mr. Wilson was pointing to in my dream. There were no words on the page, just a picture that I had drawn of my family. My mom was drawn really big right in the center of the page. She had on a dress and high heels, which was kind of funny because my mom never wore dresses or high heels. Her hair was drawn in a huge bouffant style and she had a smile on her face. My brother was standing right next to my mom, drawn just as big. His hair was colored fire engine—red and his freckles were red dots across his circle-shaped nose. He held a football in his hands. At first glance one might think that the picture of Ben was actually my father, but it wasn't. My father was in the picture drawn a little smaller and set back from the rest of us. He was smiling, just like everyone else in my picture, but in his hand was a can of what was clearly beer. The brand name of the beer was written in fancy blue letters, just like it is on the real can. But the drawings of those three weren't what caught my eye that day in Mr. Wilson's office. It wasn't even the drawing of me, dressed in pink, my hair pulled back in a ponytail. No, it was what I drew sitting on a table next to me in the picture. A beautiful blue perfume bottle with its lid set on the ground right next to it. And rising out of the bottle were these tiny musical notes, whole notes, quarter notes and half notes flying right up into the air around my stick figure head.

"This is the picture," I told Mr. Wilson, jabbing my finger at the page. "This is what you were showing me in my dream. My voice."

"Of course it was, Calli," he said. "Of course it was. You had it with you the entire time."

★ ★ ★ ★ ★

ACKNOWLEDGMENTS

I am deeply grateful to my family: Milton and Patricia Schmida, Greg Schmida and Kimbra Valenti, Jane and Kip Augspurger, Milt and Jackie Schmida, Molly and Steve Lugar and Patrick Schmida. Their unwavering confidence in me and their constant encouragement have meant the world to me. Thanks also to Lloyd, Lois, Cheryl, Mark, Carie, Steve, Tami, Dan and Robin.

A heartfelt thanks to Marianne Merola, my world-class agent, who saw a glimmer of possibility in *The Weight of Silence.* The gifts of her expertise, guidance, diligence and time are valued beyond words.

Thank you to my talented and patient editor, Miranda Indrigo, whose insights and suggestions are greatly appreciated. And to Mike Rehder, thank you for the beautiful cover art. Thanks also to Mary-Margaret Scrimger, Margaret O'Neill Marbury, Valerie Gray and countless others who generously supported this book and warmly welcomed me to the MIRA family.

Much gratitude goes to Ann Schober and Mary Fink, two very dear friends who cheered me on every step of the way.

A special acknowledgment goes to Don Harstad, a wonderful writer who has been an inspiration to me.

Finally, to Scott, Alex, Anna and Grace, thank you for believing in me. I couldn't have done it without you.

QUESTIONS FOR DISCUSSION

1. Antonia describes herself as a bad mother while Louis reassures her that she is, indeed, a good mother. What evidence from the book supports each of their beliefs? How does Louis's history with Antonia affect his own decisions as a husband and father?

2. Antonia and Louis's long history together is integral to *The Weight of Silence*. As a deputy sheriff, what, if any, ethical or moral boundaries did Louis cross in the search for Calli?

3. Ben and Calli grew up with an abusive, alcoholic father. Knowing that abuse is often passed on from generation to generation, what do you think are Ben's and Calli's chances of breaking the cycle of abuse in their future relationships? What instances from the book lead you to believe this?

4. How does the death of Antonia's mother play into the decisions Antonia made as a wife and mother? How do you think Antonia's life would be different if her mother had lived?

5. Martin Gregory, a proper, disciplined professor of economics, has always valued order, predictability and restraint in all areas of his life. How does his decision to seek retribution against the man he's sure violated his daughter fit into his belief system?

6. Antonia, Louis, Martin and Petra's perspectives are told in the first-person, present-tense point of view, while Calli's is told in the third person, past tense. Why do you think the author decided to write the story in this way?

7. What does the title *The Weight of Silence* mean to you? How does the title relate to each of the main characters' lives?

8. Before Calli and Petra's disappearance, the Willow Creek Woods was a haven for Calli, Ben and Toni. Calli, fearful of the forest after her ordeal, asked her mother if she ever got scared when walking in the woods. Toni replied, "It sent you back to me, didn't it?" What did Toni mean by this?

9. Martin Gregory had worked so hard to leave behind his farming roots by becoming a college professor, but after Petra's abduction and serious injuries, Martin subsequently moved with his family from Willow Creek to a farm. Why did Martin and Fielda decide to do this?

10. Toni describes Calli and Petra as "kindred spirits." What makes their friendship so special? Do you think Calli and Petra's friendship will last into their adulthood? Why or why not? Who do you consider to be your kindred spirit? Why?